THE PREPARATION
OF THE VICTIM

When Adriana started up the stairway, Olda turned, striding toward the front entrance. The five people meditating roused themselves when he called their names. Charlene and Michele joined them, one on either side of the old man, linking their arms through his.

Morrison studied him. "You spoke with Adriana?"

"Yes."

"Are you satisfied that it is as I told you?"

Olda nodded. "She vacillates between understanding and rejecting. To avoid the risk of the latter happening, we must act as soon as possible. Tonight. Deirdre has taken her to her room. I had a sedative added to her second glass of wine. She should sleep all of this afternoon. While she does, the rest of us can prepare." He turned to Lahpavi. "See to it that the first drugs are put in her evening meal."

Lahpavi nodded his understanding. "I have been ready for this ever since I was told of the plan seven months ago. Everything is in readiness."

"Good. The chapel must be prepared before nightfall. Then . . ." His voice trailed off, his lips parting in a malevolent smile.

Also by John Tigges:

THE GARDEN OF THE INCUBUS
THE LEGEND OF JEAN MARIE CARDINAL

UNTO THE ALTAR

John Tigges

LEISURE BOOKS  **NEW YORK CITY**

For Julie and Tracy

A LEISURE BOOK

Published by

Dorchester Publishing Co., Inc.
6 East 39th Street
New York, NY 10016

Printed in the United States of America

PROLOGUE

. . . looking behind her, (she) was turned into a statue . . .

Genesis 19:26

. . . the ashes rise up . . . as the smoke of a furnace.

Genesis 19:28

October 1, 1984

AN UNSEASONAL OVERCAST blanked out the stars, shadowing even deeper the large Victorian mansion that lorded it over the valley in which it hid. Surrounded by unbroken hills, the tiny combe shielded it, along with attendant outbuildings, from time and the outside world. Other than from the air, or from within the vale itself, the house could not be seen, and because the island lay off the normal routes of ocean vessels, the manor and its secrets were as safe as though they were on a distant planet.

Deep within the bowels of the house, life stirred as the owner and master of the island went about his covert duties. The dancing light of four dusky candles played on the tall, gaunt man's face when he stood before the black marble altar in the center of the room. Shadows clung to the inky drapes lining the walls of the small chapel while little if any light reflected from the smooth, piceous floor. Moving to his left, he lighted one more candle. The sound of his footsteps, the scratching of the match, quickly dissipated in the gloom surrounding him while the stench of sulphur hung in the air, mingling with the heavy smell of burning wax.

Turning his back to the altar, he lowered himself to a prostrate position, working his way down the five steps until his head touched the cool floor. Stretching both arms out at right angles to his body, he moaned, "Oh, Lord and Master of the Dark, hear me! Come to me, your slave. Help me in my hour of desire. I wish to serve thee to the fullest. Help me, Master! Help me!" The sound of his voice evaporated in the quiet while fervent sobs shook his body following the impassioned plea.

After several minutes passed, he clambered to his thin legs and moved to the table resting on the dais. Striking another match, he lighted five pieces of charcoal, their sulphured edges instantly catching fire, sizzling as the flames spit, racing around them. When the pieces lying in the bottom of the thurible had bleached to a grayish white, he sprinkled the coals with incense from a golden boat-shaped vessel. The heady, redolent smoke furled upward, around his head, before sweeping toward the floor in a lazy spiral. He picked up the thurible, shaking it to induce the lazy spirals into faster motion. The subtle odor of must and mildew, common to the entire house but most noticeable in the lower levels, mixed with that of the incense.

Ecstatic that his offering was being accepted, the man stood erect, rigidly at attention, unmoving, his eyes tightly closed as he waited. If the smoke refused to rise, falling instead to the floor, the sign was good that the supplication to the ruler of the netherworld would be answered. But he wanted much. He wanted contact with the Prince of Darkness himself. Would that prayer—*could* that prayer be answered?

Off in the distance he heard something. A tiny, minute sound . . . Nothing. It was nothing. Nothing. Most likely his imagination. The sound inched its way into reality.

From the void where it was given life, the sonance grew, swelling to a rumble before it ballooned to a monstrous, crashing fulmination. The impacts crescendoed into one rolling, cacophonous roar of wind, sending the old man first to his knees, then face downward on the steps once more. Even as he desperately tried to anchor himself to one of the risers, the sudden gale contained in the black room buffeted him back and forth across the sharp edges of the steps. Oblivious to the pain, the tearing and bruising of his thin body, he wailed an intoxicated moan of thanksgiving.

As quickly as it had come, as violent as it had been, the wind suddenly stopped. Dead silence. There was no sound other than his own heavy breathing accompanying his wildly beating heart. Struggling to his feet, he approached the altar once more.

He felt strange. Satisfied but not quite fulfilled. When he stood next to the black slab of marble, he breathed deeply. One more step. One more action and the service would be complete. The light of the flaming candles reflected dully off a crockery chamber pot resting near the rear of the altar. Deliberately unzipping his pants, he withdrew his penis and reached for the container before him. He emptied his bladder, the stream of urine splashing noisily. Once his fly was closed, he picked up a golden cup, dipping it into the pot.

"O Emperor Satan, Chief of all spirits who rebelled," he intoned, "I beg thee to favor me in this ceremony which I am about to complete to thy honor. Grant thy presence so that I, thine humble slave, might serve thee in whatever manner thou might decree."

He approached the five candles, addressing each long enough to dribble the fluid in the cup over the flames, extinguishing them one by one.

"Come to me, Mighty Satan! Command me! I am thine!"

As the last candle flickered out in a searing hiss, his words died instantly, absorbed by the heavy material hanging along the walls. The silence matched the raven blackness, both exerting an equally constricting grip on him.

"I have summoned you from your domains—*fire, smoke, wind, water, darkness.* Come to me, I beg of thee." His lips barely moved as he finished the final supplication.

A new sound began as a whisper that seemed to rise from within his own head. The dark adumbration of the room pressing in about him made it impossible to determine from which direction the unrecognizable words came. Realizing he could not distinguish what was being said, he concentrated even harder, but the sounds merely teased him, taunted him, dared him to comprehend what was being uttered. Focusing on the voice as best he could, he tried desperately to understand, to digest, to grasp the meaning of the sounds. Dared he speak? Dared he ask the Master to speak louder?

"*I AM SATAN!*"

The words blasted through his head, into the room, ricocheting from curtain to altar and back, buffeting the man about like a feather, finally knocking him to the floor.

Groveling in the dark, he cried loudly, "Master! Command me!"

"*You have done well. I have a plan which you will execute for me. There is one I desire—one who will fulfill my plan, which was thwarted a long time ago. Through you, I intend to produce the one being who will ultimately rule the earth. You, Olda, will be my instrument. Through certain manipulations in the past, I have managed to free a slut from the services of her God. She has since married and has a young sow. I want the young slut. She will be deprived of her loved ones and that tragedy will more than pre-pare her for me. You will lie with her but I will impregnate her. Her child shall be the Antichrist who was denied me in the past. This time I shall not fail. There will be no resistance to my plan!"*

The man held his head as the voice rever-berated within his skull, sending shock waves throughout his lanky body. Where had the voice come from? Were the words inside or outside his brain? He could not determine their source. When the voice stopped, he suddenly realized he had been holding his breath and exhaled loudly.

Puzzled by the strange message, he ventured, "Why—why have you waited, Master?"

A howl pierced the gloom while the sound of gnashing teeth sawed into the man's ears for several minutes. Little by little, the anguished sounds died away.

"Because I tempted His Son in the desert, He only permits me to roam freely on rare occasions. There are those who can call on me and have dialogue and intercourse mentally with me every twenty-eight years. If someone curses a soul and wishes me to claim it, I must wait until the time is mine. He grants me a time when I am in control long enough to gain souls for my army, but only for a brief period—once every life span of His Son."

"Every thirty-three years?" the man asked softly.

"You remember your Biblical History well, slave!"

The room fell silent. Concentrating on the

words he had just heard, the man mulled them over in his mind for several minutes before dividing by thirty-three. When he realized his answer did not match the theory presented to him, he said timorously, "But—"

"You are very clever. You must remember I tempted Him before He died. Then there is the extra day and few hours each fours years, which you did not take into consideration. Do NOT question me! The time is NOW! Never question me again!"

"Tell me what—what I—I must do, Master!" the man whispered, his voice quavering.

"You will know what to do when the time comes. You have the same help I gave to your grandfather. Then there are those following you who believe in me. They will also help in this glorious venture. This time I shall NOT FAIL!"

"Her name, Master! Tell me her name!" the man begged.

"Watch the front of the altar!" the voice ordered loudly, dwindling quickly at the same time to a harsh whisper before it ceased to exist.

The man groped for the table in the stygian blackness but before he touched it, another sound, new and different invaded the chapel. A loud hissing, sizzling sound, not unlike the charcoal when it had been ignited, but much louder, filled his ears, penetrating to his brain. He fell back, his eyes widening in the dark when he saw a sparkling light moving along the edge of the altar burning the letters A-D-R-I-A-N-A B-R-E-V-E-N-G-E-R into the marble. After forming the last letter, the light disappeared and the sound faded into crushing silence.

After several minutes passed, he whispered, "Master?" His voice broke emotionally into a whimper as he realized he was alone.

Regaining his feet, he stumbled across the room, reaching for the altar. When his fingertips brushed it, he screamed at the freezing coldness snatching at his warm skin. Carefully searching for one of the candles without touching the icy marble, he grasped it when his hand barely grazed it. He fumbled for the matches, striking one when he found them. The little blaze flared, settling down while he touched it to the wick. The single flame writhed, feebly attempting to light the room.

Withdrawing a handkerchief, he mopped his sweaty brow. Hands trembling, he gripped the edge of the altar, unmindful of the discomfort the cold caused. He had done it. He had actually done it! He belonged to Satan just as his grandfather had—not just in words but in deeds as well. He had actually spoken with his Lord and Master! He was going to be the instrument of the Prince of Darkness!

Breathing evenly, his body's actions under control once more, he moved silently toward the door, holding the candle in front of him. Patient. He would have to be patient. He knew the Master would not fail him. Patience would be essential until he could begin. But when? How long must he wait?

A fragile smile crossed his thin lips. Despite his

14

sense of exhilaration, he felt weak, used, spent. A good night's rest and he would be ready to prepare for the Master's plan. Satan, his Lord, had said that when the time came, he would know what to do. How could that be? Would the help he promised tell him what to do? The Master had said the others who visited him on the island from time to time would also help.

When he reached the door, he turned, looking back into the dark maw of the chapel. Across the room, the letters spelling out the name of the chosen woman glowed frigidly, wavering from whitish blue to fiery red as the temperature continued warming.

He wondered who Adriana Brevenger might be. What did the Master have in store for her? When he recalled the words: *You will lie with her but I will impregnate her,* he smiled, a drop of saliva oozing through his pinched lips.

In time, he would know Adriana Brevenger well. Of that he was most certain.

Part One

THE GUILT OF ADRIANA BREVENGER

One

October 31, 1984

HOMECOMING WEEK AT Claremont College had
been scheduled later than usual, and while the
days were quite warm, the nights tended to be
chilly. Most of the trees gracing the campus had
been stripped of their colorful array by wind and
rain and now stood forlornly, awaiting winter's
onslaught. Homecoming Week also brought
freshman hazing, and although the board of
regents had tried to outlaw it many times in the
past, the alumni constantly responded to the
president's plea for tradition and continuity,
threatening to withdraw financial support if the
practice was ever abandoned. President Guerdon
McKinney's mental capabilities had been re-
garded more than once from a distance with a
jaundiced eye by different regents but nothing
had ever been done to remove him from office for
fear of the alumni's reaction. As a result, 1984
found Claremont College's senior class harassing
the incoming freshman class with stunts and pre-

posterous rules and threats of awful retaliation if any orders or commands were disobeyed. The night of Hallowe'en found most of the windows in Hudson Residence Hall unlighted except for those at the end of the hallways. The dorm rooms were apparently dark, but activity stirred within at least one. The tradition of telling ghost stories on Hallowe'en had begun sometime in the distant past, and because Homecoming was so late that year, it had been incorporated into the hazing activities.

The rules were simple. The freshmen had to tell a *true* ghost story or pay the consequences, consequences that remained unmentioned and referred to only as "the ultimate penalty," whatever that might have been.

A window on the top floor of Hudson Hall flickered dimly with light of an unstable nature. Inside, a single candle, its flame bobbing on the tiny wick, reflected its light off the wide-eyed faces sitting in a circle in the center of the dormitory room. Jammed with students lying on the beds, sitting cross-legged on the floor, and standing wherever space afforded itself, the room fell silent when a young man, the center of attention, continued speaking.

"The next morning, they found the man, his coal-black hair turned white by whatever it was he had seen in the old barn," he whispered, his voice trailing off into nothingness.

A collective sigh filled the air as everybody released their breaths.

"Wow," Peggy O'Connor said, breaking the silence. "Is that really a true story?"

"So help me," Will Sturgis, the story teller

said, holding up his right hand in a mock swearing gesture. "That's exactly the way my father told me. I don't think I've ever heard of an instance when my old man even so much as bent the truth."

"Who's next?" asked Ramsey Flint, the hostess for the ghost story session. "Come on. All the freshmen in this building have to scare us tonight."

No one spoke as eyes darted from side to side. They waited for several minutes. Then someone spoke up. "Everyone has—except Brevenger."

"I've got one," the girl said from the doorway leading to the hallway.

"Who's speaking?" Ramsey asked, peering into the gloom.

"Me. Your neighbor from down the hall. Adriana Brevenger."

"Come on in, Addy. You'll be the last one. Move over, you guys, so she can be in the middle of the room. Then everyone can hear her." Ramsey stood, motioning for her guests to make room.

Will Sturgis got to his feet and the girl framed in the doorway stepped farther into the room from the hallway. She gracefully moved through the crowd, careful not to touch anyone's hands, legs, or feet. When she reached the space Will had made for her, she sat down, crossing her long, shapely legs. Her coppery hair in the dim light seemed to give off tiny sparkles of red and gold.

"Remember," Ramsey said quietly, attempting to sound ominous, "the story must be true. If we ever find out that a storyteller laid one on us, we'll get even somehow."

Good-natured giggles and snickers flitted about the room before the new entertainer could speak.

Adriana stared into the candle flame, her lips in a slight pout. Should she actually tell this story? Maybe she should make up something other than the one she had planned to tell. Would it make a difference to anyone if she did tell the true story she knew? Sure, Ramsey insisted that the stories all be true, but wasn't that just so much lip service trying to frustrate the incoming freshmen a bit? Hazing was almost nonexistent on college campuses other than in those fraternities and sororities who maintained the practice. And so far, Adriana had found Claremont College's bit of antiquity to be fun—not dangerous as she had been led to believe by the seniors in her dorm. In fact, she had rather enjoyed going into the swankiest restaurant in town, with Ramsey and several other seniors, and pretending that she had just been robbed and had no money with which to buy food and could they please give her a handout of some sort —like pheasant under glass or something. There had been other zany stunts the freshmen had been made to perform and other than the Homecoming parade, bonfire, and pep rally the next night, the dance on Friday night, and the football game on Saturday, this story telling session was the last organized event in their dorm.

She flicked her eyes about the circle of faces ringing the extreme edges of the candle light. She'd tell the story, they'd listen and forget it by the next day. What difference would it make if she told it? She cleared her throat.

"It's true all right—and probably one of the most frightening things I've ever heard," Adriana said. The sincerity of her voice assured the crowd that they were about to hear a good one.

"What's the subject matter?" Ramsey asked.

"Demonic possession," she said simply.

"Aw, shit," a voice moaned from the back of the room, "here comes *The Exorcist* again."

Someone laughed but was instantly shushed and silence fell over the room.

"I've read it," Adriana said. "It'll pale by comparison. For those of you who don't know, my mother was a member of a Catholic convent for over ten years before she elected to leave. The story I'm about to tell you took place while she was still a postulant. In fact, it happened to her best friend.

"Nothing much out of the ordinary had happened that fall after she entered the order, until Thanksgiving day. When the nuns and postulants were about to eat, right after offering their prayer of grace, they found human excrement—*shit*—in the dishes when they took off the lids."

"Ah, gross!" a boy shouted, making a gagging sound.

"Sh-h-h-h," Ramsey warned. "Go ahead, Addy."

"A few days or weeks before, a strange voice had been heard in one of the classrooms. It said some awful things."

"Like what?" Peggy asked in a tiny voice.

25

Adriana hesitated. She remembered the words exactly as her mother had told her, but should she say them? Her mother had balked at even relating the incident, but her persistence had paid off. The bizarre tale had caused her nightmares for several days after. But, then, she had only been fourteen at the time and highly impressionable.

"Well, the way my mother told me," she continued, "the nun who was teaching the class had said something about the fact that nuns are more or less brides of Christ when this mysterious voice boomed out and said: *'Sows! God will never fuck you! But I will, if you let me!'* "

Peggy noisily sucked her breath in but no sound other than an isolated nervous giggle could be heard.

"Anyway, the head nun went to see the bishop about the change in the Thanksgiving food—"

"Diet, you mean," the boy who had interrupted before said and laughed raucously.

"Just a minute, Addy," Ramsey said, standing. "Look, whoever's mouthing off back there, just knock it off. Let Addy tell the story. Smartass comments just detract from the overall effect. Now be quiet, damnit!"

A titter of laughter crossed the room but evaporated instantly.

"Go ahead, Addy," Ramsey said, taking her seat once more.

"While the Mother Superior was gone, the water in the pipes at the convent began smelling just like urine."

The hush in the room overpowered the void when she stopped.

"Nothing much happened beyond that," she continued, "until my mom's friend became ghastly ill one night. She puked up yellow junk—"

"It was green in *The Exorcist*," the boy in back shouted.

"That's it! Out!" Ramsey shouted. "Get him out of here. Now."

A rustling in the shadows beyond the halo of yellow light was the only sound. Then a movement caught the attention of everyone as they watched to see who was being ejected. Miles Thorp, an unhappy frown creasing his pimply face, made his way to the door. "That's all a bunch of bullshit anyhow," he said over his shoulder and left the room. "Besides, *I've* got studying to do, you assholes!"

"Okay. With the comedian gone, we should have no more interruptions," Ramsey said. "Go ahead, Addy."

"Where was I? Oh, yeah. And her stomach puffed up like she was, well, pregnant. But she wasn't. The doctor could find nothing wrong with her and the next morning, she was fine. Pretty strange, huh? But you haven't heard anything yet. A new priest, who turned out to be an exorcist, showed up to take the place of the chaplain. Then nothing happened at all after he got there until Christmas. At midnight Mass, the girl began speaking Chinese at the communion rail. Oh, yeah, I almost forgot. The head of one of the

27

statues was chopped off and placed in the hands of another one. Well, the Mother Superior sent this girl, her name was Bobbe, to her room. Later that night, my mother awakened and found Bobbe lying in the middle of the bedroom, stark naked. She was dead. Or at least, everyone thought she was and the doctor even pronounced her dead. When the priest went to give her the last rites of the Church, she suddenly woke up and laughing like a crazy person ran out of the room.

"That day, Christmas, my mother and a bunch of others saw Bobbe floating in midair in front of a statue in the garden behind the convent. Mom talked to her before anyone else right afterward and Bobbe told her that she heard strange voices that told her to do all kinds of yucky, far-out things."

"Like what?" Ramsey asked.

"Mom never told me."

"Damn," Ramsey said.

"I guess," Adriana went on, "they determined that she was actually possessed and began exorcising her a day or two later. Awful moans and shrieks and screams could be heard all over the place. But somehow she managed to get away from them and started a fire in the garage at the convent. Fire engines came and so did all kinds of people to watch the fire. Everyone at the convent had to search for her because they didn't want this possessed girl running loose with all sorts of strangers there.

"Well, as soon as the fire was put out or just

about out, Bobbe appeared in the bell tower. She yelled all kinds of weird things at the people below before she set herself on fire. Then she jumped and was killed by the fall and flames. Are you ready? Here comes the really strange part—a man—a real handsome hunk, according to my mom—showed up where she had been standing in one of the archways of the tower and grinned at the people. Just grinned. Then, he disappeared."

A tangible quiet held the room.

"Disappeared? Into thin air?" Peggy asked finally in a hoarse whisper, her eyes wide.

"Into thin air," Adriana said solemnly. "In front of several hundred people, I might add."

"What happened next, Addy?" Ramsey asked.

"Nothing. Everything went back to normal."

"Gosh, and your mother stayed there for another *ten years*?" Peggy asked.

"If it would have been me, I'd have left that day," Ramsey offered nervously.

Adriana smiled. "She wasn't right at the convent for ten years. She began teaching in '55 and left the order in '65."

From the lobby three floors below, the electronic clock chimed the hour of midnight and the group began scrambling to their feet. Hasty goodnights were said but Ramsey remained behind.

When everyone had left except the two girls who shared the room and Adriana, Ramsey said, "Is your mom all right now?"

"Oh, sure. She was pretty upset by the whole

29

thing and she gets a little funny on December 27, the day Bobbe died, but otherwise she's perfectly all right."

"Are your folks coming to school this weekend for Homecoming?" Peggy asked.

"Uh-huh! In fact they should get here sometime tomorrow. Why?"

"I—I'd like to meet her," Peggy said, blushing.

"You won't say anything about my telling you guys the story, will you?" Adriana asked, suddenly concerned about her indiscretion where her mother's past might be concerned.

"Why?" Ramsey asked. "Is it a no-no?"

"Sort of. Maybe I shouldn't have told you about it."

"Well, if you introduce your parents to us, we'll keep quiet. Right, Peg?"

"Huh? Oh, sure, sure. No problem. You can trust us."

Adriana smiled, relieved at the assurance given by her new friends. How would it look to her parents if they found out that their only child was telling everyone she met about a horrible incident that happened in her mother's past, the very first time she went away from home?

She enjoyed Connie and Tim Brevenger as friends as well as parents and would not want to do anything to make them distrust her. Her mother had expressed more than a usual amount of concern when she had decided on attending School almost five hundred miles from their home. Claremont College was formerly an all girl's school but for the last fifteen years had been coeducational.

Not that Connie did not trust her daughter. On the contrary, she had told Adriana many times that she had found being a mother at the age of thirty-five to be an exhilarating experience. As much as Adriana loved her mother, she found her father to be one of the most interesting and exciting people she had ever known. His ready sense of humor and ability to understand the two women in his life had endeared him to both.

"I've got to get to bed. Seven-thirty rolls around all too quickly. Thanks for asking me tonight, Ramsey, Peggy."

"Hey, our pleasure. Thanks for sharing a gruesome story with us. It was really cool," Ramsey said, walking Adriana to the door. "Don't forget about the parade of jackasses tomorrow."

"How could I? Everyone keeps reminding us poor freshmen," Adriana said.

"G'night, Addy," Peggy called from across the room.

The door closed softly and Adriana made her way toward her room at the end of the hall. Vicki Lemont, her roommate, was working on a paper and had bypassed the party. Each floor had had its own session and although Vicki said she was going to study and write, Adriana was willing to bet the girl was with her boyfriend. Such was the privilege of being a sophomore.

Adriana sighed. The week had been a full one and, thankfully, the teachers had been kind in their assignments. She looked forward to the rest of the week. Tomorrow her parents would arrive and she'd be able to spend a lot of time with them.

When she reached the door to her own room, she thought of Ramsey for a moment. The tall blonde had gravitated to her and Adriana felt that a lasting friendship might be in the making. The older girl's sense of humor and quick wit had delighted her on almost every occasion they had been together. She felt as if she would be able to count on Ramsey for anything.

Seconds after she closed the door, a light rapping brought her around to stare at it. The digital alarm clock next to her bed showed a few minutes past midnight. Conjecturing on the identity of her midnight caller, she hurried to answer, mentally betting that Vicki had forgotten her key.

When she swung the door open, she saw Ramsey. "Ramsey? What's up?"

"Can I come in for a moment?"

Adriana stepped aside. "Of course. What are you doing here?"

Ramsey turned to face her. Two inches taller than the red-haired girl, Ramsey Flint looked worldly and experienced and just a bit earthy in the carefully orchestrated manner in which she wore her hair "wild." Her brazen front hid a soft, womanly interior that could be tough if the occasion called for it. Adriana had seen the real person that Ramsey tended to keep under wraps

—kind, considerate, caring—and often wondered why she came on so strong.

"Are you all right?" Ramsey asked.

"What? Of course, I'm fine. Why, for heaven's sake?"

"I got thinking about what you had said. You know, your mother not wanting you to tell the story you just told us. You're not frightened, are you?"

"Of course not. I'm—" She stopped. Could *Ramsey* be the one who was actually frightened? Could the story have upset her to the point of wanting reassurance that "everything was all right and the boogey man wouldn't get her when she went to bed?" Adriana was just about to voice the query when she stopped in midbreath. Studying Ramsey for a mere second told her that such was not the case. The wide-set eyes sparkled from beneath the curly, tousled hair that hung over her forehead, showing compassion and concern for the girl they confronted.

"Don't be afraid to 'fess up, Addy," she said, in a mock scolding voice.

"Everything is just great, Ramsey. Really."

"I don't want you to kid me. After all, I *am* responsible for you this week. It wouldn't do anyone any good if it turned out that part of the tradition of ghost storytelling had been banned along with hazing because one or the other got out of hand."

Adriana felt relieved that she hadn't said anything about Ramsey's ability to handle a frightening story. It would have been embarrassing for both of them. If nothing else, it proved to Adriana that her feelings of a budding friendship that would last beyond this year had not been unfounded.

"When your parents get here tomorrow," Ramsey said, breaking into her thoughts, "I really want to meet them. So does Peg."

"And I'd like to meet yours. Are they coming?"

Ramsey's face and neck flushed. Turning away, she said softly, "No. I've never told you before but my parents are divorced. Mother is someplace in Europe, hobnobbing with the jet set or some other bunch of jerks and Daddy—well, Daddy is just too busy making scads of money to be bothered by something as mundane as Homecoming."

Adriana stepped closer. "I—I'm sorry, Ramsey. Really, I am. I had no idea."

"Hey," the blonde said cheerfully, "no big deal. I get along pretty good without either one of them."

"But," Adriana protested, "where do you spend your summers and holidays?"

"Look, Adriana, it's getting pretty late. If you really want to hear my life story, I'll gladly tell you some time. But not at twelve thirty in the morning. We *do* have to get up, you know."

"Okay. But I really do want to get to know you better."

"Same here. I tell you what. After this weekend, I'll shake loose of Brett and we'll spend some time together. Deal?"

Adriana nodded. Why Ramsey would want to get rid of Brett Fuller, if only for an afternoon, she could not understand. Brett was the second year Little All-American linebacker on the football team and already sought after by the United States Football League. But if Ramsey wanted her for a friend, she wouldn't object.

"Just make certain that Brett understands that you're not getting rid of him permanently. He's some guy."

"That he is," Ramsey said, a wide smile spreading across her face. "Gotta go. Sleep tight."

"You, too."

And Ramsey was gone.

The car hurtled through the night, racing along the dark highway. Tim Brevenger glanced from one side to the other, to the rear view mirror, then back to the road ahead.

"Are you getting tired, Tim?" Connie asked, stretching. "I can drive for a while if you want."

"No. I'm fine, sweetheart." Tim stifled a yawn and looked at his wife. Her red hair, showing just a wisp of gray, fell away from her face, displaying her finely chiseled profile. "What time is it?"

"Almost three. Maybe we should stop. After all, what good will it do if we get there and we're both exhausted?"

"There should be an exit pretty soon. If we see signs advertising motels, maybe we should stop. I still think it was a good idea to leave as soon as your meeting was over last night."

"I do, too," Connie said, a tiny sarcastic laugh

hidden in the words. "However, I didn't know it would last until almost eleven thirty." She unbuckled her seat belt, wiggling in the seat until she was comfortable.

"Hey, no problem. We've still got a good leg up on the trip and even if we do stop now, we'll get to school way ahead of schedule."

They fell silent as the numbers on the dashboard clock changed the minutes to approach the hour of three. Unaware that his foot seemed heavier than usual, Tim pressed harder on the accelerator.

Connie, tired from her long meeting and unaccustomed late ride, dozed fitfully. Gradually, her eyes remained closed and she slept soundly.

Oblivious of the car's increasing speed, Tim stared at the road. The speedometer needle inched upward toward seventy. Seventy-five. Eighty. Eighty-five. Suddenly, Tim became mindful of the lighted intersection ahead. Snapping out of his dreamlike state, he quickly read the signs along the road. One predominant message threaded itself through the different advertisements—there were no motels for the next twenty-five miles. Too far. He was much too tired to go that distance. Up ahead and to his right, he could see an off ramp leading to a road that passed over the four-lane highway. Unaware of his excessive speed, he eased the car, now exceeding ninety miles an hour, toward the ramp. The twenty-five mile an hour speed posted at the exit zipped past the car in an orange-yellow blur. When the road curved to the right, Tim

Brevenger continued driving arrow-straight toward the concrete embankment carrying the two lane road to the over pass. Once the banked curve to the right passed under them, the car took to the air, hurtling one hundred thirty feet before it struck grill first into the concrete retaining wall.

Connie was flung forward at the instant of collision, headfirst at the windshield. The glass was punched into shards by the impact, decapitating her. Tim, aware too late of what was happening, clung to the steering wheel, his horror-filled eyes watching the glaring white cement racing up to meet the car. The impact drove the engine through the firewall, smashing into his body, crushing his heart and lungs as his wife's body jerked spasmodically at his side. The car teetered on end, barely keeping its balance. An instant after the crash, gasoline from the ruptured tank sprayed onto the automobile, dripping inside, working its way toward the engine. The first drop exploded, setting off the faster-than-thought chain reaction that boiled upward in a lemon-gold ball of fire. The car slowly toppled over onto its roof.

There were no screams, no sounds other than the crackling of flames—and a deep-throated chuckle drifting out of the night . . .

Adriana could see her chubby, dimpled hands catch the ball her father had thrown to her. Beaming proudly, she turned to her mother, then grunted and awkwardly threw the ball in her mother's direction who had to run to stop it from rolling down a hill. Laughing uncontrollably, she looked for her father—to share with him this funny spectacle of her mother chasing the ball. Where had he gone? She couldn't see him anyplace. Hadn't he just been standing there, a little distance away, under that tree? Could he be hiding from her? That was it! She ran toward the trunk, stopping abruptly before tiptoeing around the bole. He wasn't there.

She'd get her mother to help her find Daddy. Spinning about, expecting to see her beautiful red-haired mother returning with the ball, she blinked. Now her mother was gone as well. Where were they? She tried calling but could not manage a sound. She didn't like this game. They were supposed to be playing catch.

Finally, she managed a squeaky, "Mommy! Daddy!" but could say no more. Suddenly, without warning, the ball dropped in front of her, bouncing up and down, not making the usual sound at all but one of tapping, tapping, tapping as it slowed to a stop. Then she heard a hollow laugh and sat bolt upright in bed.

The tapping came again but this time from her door. Looking across the bedroom, she focused her eyes. Again the soft staccato rap sounded, along with a call.

"Adriana!" the voice hoarsely whispered. "Addy? Wake up. Someone's here to see you. Hurry!"

Throwing back the covers, she grabbed her robe, slipping into it before opening the door.

The dim light of the hallway outlined the bulky form of May Baurone, the house mother.

"What—what is it, May?" she asked, shielding her eyes from the light she had just turned on.

"There's a policeman here to see you."

"A—a—policeman?" Adriana's eyes opened wide, then squinted at the heavyset woman.

May nodded, her double chin quivering.

"What's he want?"

She shrugged.

"Can I come down like this?"

"I guess so. He apologized for coming at this hour."

"What time is it?" Adriana asked, trying to focus her sleep-filled eyes on the alarm clock across the room.

"Six-fifteen."

Adriana ran a hand through her hair. "It must be pretty important to have him come by so early."

She quietly closed the door behind her, padding down the hall after the lumbering woman. Making her way past May on the stairs, she hurried ahead to the waiting room at the front of the building.

Highway patrolman Sam Newsome awkwardly got up from the straight-backed chair, fidgeting with his hat when the young woman came into the foyer.

"Miss Adriana Brevenger?" he said softly.

"Yes. I'm she. What is it?"

"I'm afraid I have bad news, Miss."

TWO

January 1985

SHE COULD REMEMBER crying. Crying almost constantly, night and day. But for a long time now, no tears had come. She had wanted to weep again but found she could not. Bits and pieces of memory occasionally crowded into her mind, shoving aside the warm, friendly sense of weightlessness and floating. Whenever she felt as if she were drifting, nothing seemed to bother her—no disturbing thoughts of that man and woman lying in their sealed caskets—no hazy pictures in her mind's eye of the boxes being lowered into the ground . . .

There were, on rare instances, a word here and there that made no sense to her:

"One month—"

"It is good—"

"You'll be happy—"

"—chosen one—"

For the most part those thoughts did not agitate her the way the other memories did—the flickering, unclear recollections of the cemetery and two fresh graves always brought on a deep depression—a blackness that wrapped itself about her, shutting everything out that tried to penetrate her protective barriers of silence, passivity, and brooding.

The thing she liked most about her life was the nothingness—the vacuum in which she could hide. There, her state of nonexistence made her feel at ease. When there was nothing—simply nothing—she was pleased, almost happy.

Day by day, by degrees, she had become aware of her surroundings, of the plain room in which she slept, of the larger room where other people roamed aimlessly about, gazing into space, sitting at tables, playing silly games. At least, she thought of what the people did at those tables as being a game of some sort. She had become acquainted with the circle of faces that stared at her whenever the woman who wore white clothes all the time looked at her and said, "Addy?" Not many people called her Addy. Her parents called her that, and "Honey," "Darling," "Sweetheart," and "Munchkin." Her daddy had called her "Munchkin" but that had been a long time ago, when she was a little girl. A couple of her friends in that nice place with all the brick buildings called her Addy. One in particular stuck in her memory—she was tall, with a nice face and wild yellow hair. But what was her name?

Now this woman in the white dress insisted on

calling her Addy and Adriana could not recall having given her permission. Why, Adriana didn't even know what the woman's name was. Had she ever been told?

She looked around. She had been here before. Yes, she could remember that. It was a nice room. At first she had no idea where she might be or who the other people were that seemed like her and yet for some strange reason were nothing like her at all.

One face particularly fascinated her. The man seemed compassionate and understanding, but he wanted her to talk. She didn't want to talk about anything with anyone. Most of the time he sat near her, rambling on about a lot of things. Things that made no sense to her. Once in a while he mentioned her father and mother. But there was something wrong—something terribly wrong with that. She didn't have a father and mother, did she? Hadn't they gone away some place, someplace without her? Where? Where had they gone? Why hadn't they taken her with them?

Vague images of a warm, friendly place—in one of the brick buildings, she was sure—with a handsome man in uniform standing near the door, fidgeting with his hat—often crowded everything else out of her mind. She clearly remembered the man's shiny buttons and glossy leather belts, one around his waist and one swooping up and over a shoulder. He had said something. What? Something—something about her parents. But they were at home. How could he know anything about them? Why, they were planning to leave that very day, leave their cozy bungalow and drive all the way to Claremont College for the Homecoming activities. She'd be with them for a few days. But this man's words—he said something awful concerning them. Said they had been in an auto accident. Said she had to come with him. Said her parents might be hurt seriously. She was needed.

She squeezed her eyes shut tight against the scene and shook her head, trying to erase the awful thoughts.

"What is it, Adriana?" the man's voice asked, cutting through the thick membrane of pain.

She peeked through slitted lids. Who had spoken? The voice sounded familiar. Then she saw him, seated close to her. It was the man whose face intrigued her for some unknown reason. He seemed kind, gentle.

"Do you want to tell me what's bothering you, Adriana?" he asked.

Staring at him, she shook her head. Why should she talk to him? He didn't understand anything about her thoughts or what she had been through. How could anyone understand that kind of hurt? She wasn't even certain herself about what had happened.

Forcing herself to remember, she recalled the man with the hat guiding her through a set of doors that slid open by themselves and being approached by a man in white, dressed something like that woman who always called her Addy. The new man looked sad when he shook her hand and said—and said—What had he said? Something about they hadn't made it. Who hadn't made what?

"I'm sorry, Miss Brevenger," he had whispered so softly she could barely understand him, *"neither of your parents survived. It was an awful accident."*

Then that sad-faced man in white had made her do something that was completely unforgivable. He had led her into a room where two bodies lay covered with sheets. She gasped when he pulled the first one back, showing the charred face of what had been her father. Gulping, trying to hold back the wave of nausea sweeping through her, she watched him cover her father's face and throw back the sheet over the other. Her mother.

"Mommy!" she had screamed, throwing herself across the body. The force of her impulsive embrace sent her mother's unburned head careening from the table to the floor in a sickening muffled thud, where it rolled several feet. When it stopped, Connie Devler Brevenger's open eyes stared at her daughter.

The next thing she could remember, other than that whispering voice coming out of nowhere from time to time saying things that made no sense, was the room in which she slept. And the large room with people shuffling around. And the man with the nice face . . .

"Adriana?" the pleasant voice asked once more.

She focused her attention on the man. Why was he so persistent in wanting her to speak to him? She was happy in her silence, happy in her own little world. Couldn't he understand that? Maybe she should tell him. But if she did speak, he might want to know everything and she wouldn't tell him anything. He might become angry with her and chastise her even more than she was being punished now.

Maybe she could lead him away from the thing she didn't want to tell. It could be her secret. Hers and nobody else's. He appeared nice—friendly. In a way, she was reminded of her father whenever she looked at him. Yes, this stranger was handsome and had a pleasing face. She knew that. Knew it well. But before she spoke to him, she'd look at him one more time. Just to make certain.

First she fixed her eyes on the room in front of her. Pretty plain. No, that was the ceiling. She could tell when the paneled walls came into view. Had she been sitting with her head tilted back? The walls were of nice dark wood and there were pictures and framed pieces of paper with writing on them, hanging above and behind the large desk. Suddenly she grew aware of the chair in which she was seated. Leather. Smooth, cool leather. Warm where she sat and rested her arms but cool otherwise. And it had a nice smell to it, too. Cream colored wall to wall carpeting matched the ceiling, which she found interesting, looking at first one, then the other.

"Adriana?" Morrison Tyler said softly. "I think you're ready to talk to me. Aren't you?"

She diverted her gaze to the source of sound,

finding him smiling. Such a nice face. A kind face. She wanted to kiss it, but held herself in check. Later perhaps. But not now. Certainly, not now. She should get to know him better before she did anything like that.

"You've been coming here to my office for quite a while now. Don't you think it would be nice if you at least said, 'hello'?"

She shook her head.

"Well, finally," he said approvingly. "A response. That's fine. I knew you were only fooling me. I've known all along that you understood what I was saying."

She cleared her throat but said nothing.

"No more kidding around, young lady," Dr. Tyler said firmly. "Are you ready to talk to me?"

She lowered her eyes. "Yes."

February 1985

"You're made remarkable progress, Adriana," Morrison Tyler said, smiling at the young woman sitting opposite his desk.

"You have no idea, Doctor," she said, "what I was putting myself through." She brought a hand, long, tapering fingers formed into a fist to her mouth, stifling a cough, no longer afraid of having someone comment because she had moved or spoken. The last weeks she had slowly crawled out of the dark hole in which she had thrust herself. At first, she refused the help of those about her, trying to hide from the world, ignoring the offers of assistance from the nurses

49

and doctors—most especially Dr. Morrison Tyler.

"Don't forget that I was with you every step of the way, my dear."

She nodded. "I guess I did forget. You've been just super to me. I don't know how I can ever thank you."

"Well, you'd better hold up on that thanks for now. We've got a long way to go yet."

Startled, she stared at him. How could she still have a long time to spend at this hospital? Hadn't she talked all her feelings out with him? Hadn't she come to grips with her parents' untimely deaths?

The most difficult aspect for her to understand had been the attitude of her mother's brothers. Her uncles. When Connie had decided to leave the convent, they had been angry with her, refusing to see her, much less talk with her, finally denying she even existed. Long before Connie had died in the car accident, her family had buried her memory. Despite her mental state, Adriana had somehow managed to attend the double funeral. None of her mother's relatives had been present, although each had been properly notified. Her father had no living family members that he knew of, having spent his youth in an orphanage. Her aloneness in the world had initially bothered Adriana once she began speaking again. But over the last month, it seemed less important with each passing day. To compensate for her loss, she looked on her psychiatrist, Morrison Tyler, as her family.

"I don't quite understand, Doctor. I thought I was doing pretty well."

"You are, Adriana. You really are. But I feel that there is still something you haven't told me. Something you probably feel afraid to even mention. Perhaps it could be the real reason behind your withdrawal for almost two and a half months."

"The real reason?" she echoed.

"Yes. Perhaps you feel liable or responsible for your parents' death. Perhaps you feel you had done something to cause the accident. Until we uncover that fact, you might have recurring problems."

Looking away from his steady gaze, she thought for a moment. Of course she had concluded long ago that she *had* been responsible. If she hadn't breached her mother's confidence by telling that awful story about what had taken place at the convent so many years before, nothing would have happened. But she had and she was being punished. If she had kept quiet, her parents would not have left that night to drive to Claremont. Mother and Daddy would still be alive if only she had kept her mouth shut. Her eyes burned from the tears forming.

Doubling up her fists, she savagely pounded on the arms of the leather chair.

The doctor sat motionless, watching her display of self-reproach. When she stopped, he said, "That's the part I'm referring to, Adriana. Right now, you were beating the arms of the chair. I feel you would like to beat yourself like that—or find someone who would be willing to oblige you. What is it that you're holding back? Why do you believe you should be punished?''

Rubbing her hands together to ease their pain, she looked into his steady gray eyes. His angular face appeared young, contradicting the graying brown hair that abruptly changed to white at the temples and sideburns. A square jaw supported his wide mouth that seemed ready to smile at an instant's notice.

She recalled her desire to kiss that face and mouth the first day she had spoken to him. For some reason, that craving had not changed. In fact, it had grown, swelling to the dimension of a constant, persistent thought when she was not occupied in some other way. At night, when she could not fall asleep and hadn't taken the sleeping pill the floor nurse provided, fantasies of Morrison Tyler entering her room to seduce her brought pleasures she had never realized in actual life. In her own way, she pictured him nude, hovering over her, saying, "*I must have you, Addy. I want your body as well as your mind. I want all of you. You're so beautiful. So sensuous.*" Then he'd reach out, stroking her breasts before he trailed a finger down her body toward her legs. Sensations of tingling enjoyment, floating, reeling, brought her breath in short gasps ending in a burst of color as she climaxed, only to realize that she had been masturbating.

Despite the fact that Morrison Tyler was old enough to be her father, she planned different ways to seduce him. If she could succeed at that, her life would take on a new dimension, a new meaning, one she had never dreamed possible. And she would no longer feel so alone.

"I don't believe I should be punished." She hesitated before adding, "Do I? I don't know of any reason." She looked away for fear the doctor would be able to read the lie on her face.

"There's absolutely nothing we haven't discussed that might be bothering you?" he persisted.

"Nothing, Doctor. There's nothing," she continued, looking at the door away from him.

"It's not nice to keep secrets from your analyst, Adriana," he reprimanded kindly. They had reached the point of familiarity where good-natured joking and teasing could be tolerated.

She smiled but sobered immediately. Perhaps he wouldn't love her when she told him of her feelings where he was concerned, especially if she had held back the part about her indiscretion. If he found out without her telling him, he might become furious and have nothing to do with her anymore. Still, she had to have something to hold onto, something that would remain hers, even if it were nothing but guilt for the deaths of her parents.

Wiping her eyes with a small handkerchief, she said, "If I tell you, I won't have anything left. It'll be all gone." She sobbed quietly.

"Isn't that the way you want it? Don't you want to be rid of everything connected with your parents' deaths?"

She nodded, the sobs becoming crying heaves.

"It was wrong. So wrong. So wrong to have told!"

"What was wrong, Adriana? Will you tell me? Come on. Rid yourself of this—this thing—whatever it is. If you do, we'll be even closer to getting you out of here."

"I—I—I'll te—tell you, Doctor," she managed.

"What does it concern?"

"About—about—some—something—that happened—a-a-a—long time ago. When, my mother —was—was—in—in the convent." The sobs grew as the memory of the story she had told in the candlelit room hammered at her unmercifully.

"What happened, Adriana?"

"A—a—girl—a girl was—was—possessed—by —by—the devil and I told my friends about— about it!" She dropped her head to the arm of the chair, weeping with abandon.

Morrison Tyler leaned foward, holding his breath as he waited for her to continue.

March 1985

"Are you pretty well settled in your new apartment, Adriana?" Morrison asked, raising his drink in a mock toasting gesture.

"It's absolutely beautiful. When we finish dinner, I'd feel honored if you'd come and see it," she said, her eyes sparkling not unlike the gold bracelet she wore. She picked up her glass, mimicking him.

"I'm the one who should feel privileged," he said.

When he flashed his broad grin, one he had not displayed all the while Adriana had been at the rest home, she closely studied him without being obvious. She had learned not to come on too strongly with Morrison. If she wanted to look at him *sub rosa*, she had to watch for his recognition or be prepared, in the event he caught her, to have a quick and ready answer to give him. He raised the glass to his lips and the smile vanished.

She loved that smile almost as much as she loved him, although she had yet to give voice to her feelings. How many times had she told herself to take one step at a time? And where had she heard that? From Morrison, of course. She doted on every word, every action, every idea he presented. And why not? She had been rescued from a black pit by this knight in shining armor. And tonight seemed as if it had been conjured up in the thoughts of the most romantic of novelists. It could not have been more perfect.

She recalled arriving at her new residence from the attorney's office where the final papers had been signed and the bulk of her parents' estate had been turned over to her. Even though she would be only nineteen at the end of April, her parents had had the foresight to establish a trust fund for her in the event of their deaths before she reached her majority. She had just entered her apartment when the telephone rang.

She stumbled over her words when she realized it was Morrison, asking her out to dinner. Without hesitating, she accepted and felt like a fairy princess when he picked her up in front of the apartment complex.

"You know," he said, shattering her reverie, "you will probably have to see me only once or twice more at my office."

She stared at him. *No!* That couldn't be! Since leaving the rest home, she had missed the routine and almost daily visits with the psychiatrist. At first, when told she was to be discharged, she had panicked, quickly settling down when she realized that her appointments with Morrison would continue on a twice-monthly basis at his downtown office. Now he was saying she would not have to come in anymore. What would she do? How would she survive?

"I'm not ready, am I, Morrison?" she asked in a tiny voice.

"You're ready right now. Since you told me about the party last Hallowe'en, your recovery has been complete. I'm not joshing you. You're more normal than anyone in the room," he said, making a sweep with his arm.

She lowered her eyes to the table top. Not once had she ever mentioned her feelings for him. What would he say if she broached the subject now? What did she have to lose? If she didn't say anything, he'd never know and she'd probably never have another opportunity like this. If he rejected her, at least she'd know where she stood. For that bit of practicality she could thank

Morrison. He had convinced her that keeping things to oneself was primarily harmful if the information remained at the surface of the mind, where it would create a barrier of sorts, keeping out an influx of positive stimuli.

"Morrison," he said softly, looking up at him. "I—I love you." She froze when that familiar smile spread across his face. Did he find it funny? Had she ruined everything by uttering her feelings? Then she realized it was an understanding expression, not one of humor or ridicule. "Morrison?"

"I—I'm not surprised, Adriana," he said, reaching out to take her hand. "It's not uncommon for a patient to feel strong emotional feelings for his or her therapist—especially when the patient has been helped dramatically, as you have been. Many times—no, I won't lie to you— most of the time, the patient will interpret these feelings as love. I want you to believe me when I say that I know you have been looking on me as a substitute parent, a surrogate father, if you will, ever since you began speaking in January."

She opened her mouth to protest but he stopped her with an upheld hand and continued. "Let me have my say first, Adriana. You may not want to agree with that. I only hope that you will listen when I say that in almost every instance, love was not present in these situations. I was hoping that it wouldn't happen with you since I like you very much as a person—as a dear friend, but nothing more."

Adriana turned away, the room slithering

about through the tears filling her eyes.

"Your refusal to speak, Adriana, as I have said in the past, was an involuntary choice on your part to escape the feeling of responsibility for your parents' deaths. If you didn't talk, you couldn't tell anyone what it was you felt you had done. And if that were the case, there would be no further talk or punishment concerning the issue. You know all of this. We've talked about it for hours. Let me assure you that when you exposed what took place last Hallowe'en, your cure was assured. Right now, you have no obstacles in your path. For all practical purposes, you're cured. Don't create—"

"You're making fun of me," she said, turning away.

"I would never do that, Adriana."

"Then how do you know that I don't love you? How can you be so positive about it?"

"Look at me, Adriana," he said, reaching across the table to turn her face to him. "Let's address the facts as they actually are. After I present my case, you can have your turn. Fair enough?"

A long silence fell between them while she thought about everything and nothing. She'd let him talk. Then *she'd* talk. She'd convince him. She nodded.

"I'm forty-seven years old. You're eighteen— all right, almost nineteen. I'm divorced and have two children older than you. You have your whole life ahead of you. How many years do I have left? Twenty? Twenty-five? Maybe thirty, if I'm lucky.

"I know that there is something in your future that will completely dwarf your feelings for me. There simply is. It would be awful if a broken-down divorced forty-seven-year-old proved to be the future of a beautiful nineteen-year-old woman!"

She could feel the sting of tears but stared at him. "So what if you are that much older? There have been a lot of successful marriages with greater age differences."

Morrison chuckled. "Now it's marriage you want?" he asked. "If—and I believe I am absolutely correct on this—if you are unknowingly looking on me as your father, wouldn't a physical relationship between us almost amount to incest?"

"Incest? Are you serious?" she blurted, before realizing he was joking. "I'm sorry, Morrison. I really am. But I've been through hell and you know it."

"Of course I know it. I truly sympathize with your loss. I also understand your feelings where your mother's brothers are concerned. It's an awful feeling—a frightening feeling to think that one is all alone in the world."

"Then why can't we be together? Why can't I be right?" She lowered her head, tears dripping onto her napkin.

"I wish I could answer that in a simple way, but I can't. Are we still friends?"

She nodded. "I don't have that many that I feel I can cast them aside just because things don't go my way."

"Good girl. If you're ready, I'd like to see your apartment, if the invitation is still valid." He smiled reassuringly and patted her hand.

"Of course it is," she said, standing.

April 22, 1985

Adriana tore open the envelope, withdrawing the letter.

> *April 19, 1985*
>
> *Dear Addy,*
>
> *I received your letter on the tenth and am a bit late in answering it. Sorry about that. How are your meetings with the "shrink" going? I'm sure you realize that you are making progress and will probably be back here at Claremont in the fall, ready to hit the books. The reason I mention your progress is that your improvement is quite noticeable in your letters. You sound very happy and together—just the way you were when we first met last fall.*
>
> *My thesis is completed and I'll be graduating soon, so from here on it's all downhill. Daddy has promised me a trip to Europe this summer. Hey, how about going with me? A change of scenery would do both of us a world of good. Think about it and I'll get in touch with you when I have some pertinent poop on the cost and stuff.*
>
> *I'm taking the liberty of sending you a small pic of me—actually it's my graduation portrait. If you find it offensive, throw it away. Besides, I don't hold a candle to you. It's true!*
>
> *Ohmygosh! It's almost seven o'clock and Brett*

said he'd pick me up at seven-thirty. I've gotta get going. It's Friday night and he said we're going out. All he wants to do is hump my bod since football season finished.

Do write, Addy. And think of that trip. Okay?

Love,
Ramsey

Adriana threw the letter on the table and picked up the picture to look more closely at it. Ramsey was beautiful. It was nice of her to be so complimentary in her letter, but anyone with even poor eyesight could tell the stunning blonde was in a class by herself. Adriana's thoughts strayed back to the letter for a moment. Europe? It sounded great. Fantastic! If Morrison felt she was ready by then, she'd give it every consideration since money would be no problem.

Morrison. She smiled. What a great man! He had helped her fully understand her feelings for him—helping her unravel her emotions to scrutinize them—discovering that she loved him as a friend and nothing more.

"We've got to be friends, Adriana," he had said. "I've grown quite fond of you in the last months and look upon you as a daughter of sorts. You and I being anything more to each other is out of the question, and I believe you realize that now. Don't you?"

"I was really mixed up, wasn't I?"

"Not that much. I could have taken advantage of the situation but I believe you're being saved

61

for something—no make that someone—mighty terrific. Your place in life will be—"

"Oh, Morrison, please! You make me sound like God's gift to men. I'm not, you know."

"Well, maybe I'm prejudiced. Maybe I know something you don't."

Adriana smiled again. Morrison could make her feel so important at times that she wondered if his intentions were strictly platonic after all. But Ramsey was a different situation. They were contemporaries. About three years difference in age, similar interests, and now the idea of going to Europe together seemed absolutely irresistible. They could tour the Continent, see everything, and take all summer or all year or all their lives if they wanted.

Ramsey had been one of the first people Adriana thought of when her recovery seemed imminent. A great deal of rapport had been created between them those first couple of months at school last fall before Adriana became ill. One of the nurses, during a group therapy session, had suggested that Adriana write to some friends since she had no visitors call on her. It would be good therapy to write her feelings down on paper, telling about her progress to someone. For several days she had wrestled with the idea of contacting people in her hometown but that seemed impractical at best. She had been gone from there for almost seven months and most of her high school friends were in colleges all over the country. No one at home even knew she was in a psychiatric hospital. Contacting her uncles was definitely out.

At first, when the thought of Ramsey popped into her mind, she wasn't certain if the blonde would even remember her, much less want to correspond. Recalling the feelings of a flowering deep friendship, she began thinking of Ramsey as a pen pal and not just an acquaintance she had had and lost. The first letter brought a prompt reply and they had been corresponding ever since.

Propping the envelope with the letter inside against the note pad next to the telephone, she promised herself to write that evening after she got home from her appointment with Morrison.

"Well, Addy," Morrison said from behind his huge desk, "today's the big day. Your last session with me. How do you feel—about everything?"

"I'm happy to say, Morrison, that you've cured me and I'm ready to take on the world."

"*I* didn't cure you, Adriana. You did that yourself. I just helped you when you needed it. I only hope that you can continue to be relaxed about everything. I'm positive that when school starts this fall, you'll be ready for anything."

"How about a trip to Europe?" she asked.

"Are you asking me to go with you?"

She giggled. "No. But a friend of mine with whom I've been corresponding has suggested it for this summer. Can I go?"

He shrugged. "Why ask me? Once you leave the

office today, you're on your own. If you want to go to the moon, go."

"That's great. I'd hoped you'd say that."

"Why do you want to go to Europe?"

"Why not? I've never been. I have no one to answer to for my actions. Besides, it would be relaxing."

"Won't you ever be able to relax here—at home?"

"I've learned to relax by emulating you, Morrison."

He chuckled. "Some time I should show you how I really relax."

"How?" she asked, sensing something unique about to be told her. "How do you unwind?"

"I don't think a young girl like you would find it too exciting. Especially if she's thinking about going to the Continent."

"What is it? Come on, Morrison. No riddles. Tell me right now or I'll shut up like a clam and not talk anymore. Then you'll have to take me on as a new patient," she teased.

"I really shouldn't have mentioned it," he said, his voice dropping to an apologetic level.

"Please, Morrison? It's not like you to start something and not finish."

He looked up, startled. "That's very alert of you to notice, Adriana. I had no idea you were studying me so closely."

"Well? Are you going to tell me or are you going to be responsible for making me feel paranoid?" She loved throwing out the terms she had picked up during her stay in the hospital.

Maybe when she returned to school she would consider changing her major to psychology or pre-med so she could become a psychiatrist like Morrison.

"Paranoid? How—"

"Just tell me, for heaven's sake! My worst fault is my unwavering curiosity." She sat forward in her chair, waiting.

"All right, you win," he said laughing. "There is a very private, very exclusive resort off the west coast of Florida where I go on occasion."

"So what's so wonderful about that?" she asked, disappointed that it apparently was something so mundane. She didn't know what she had expected, but somehow Morrison didn't seem the type to belong to such elite or privileged company.

"The thing that is so wonderful is the fact that it's like stepping back into the nineteenth century. The mansion has no electricity, no running water, no telephone. Nothing. Nothing to offer but peace and quiet. Good food and good companionship. Great atmosphere and great conversation with some of the most fascinating people one could ever hope to meet."

Adriana's eyes widened. Now it sounded marvelous. How many times had she noted since her discharge from the hospital the maddening pace of life around her? Before her confinement, she had taken such for granted. Once removed from her role in the everyday world, thrown into her own private hell, she had taken particular notice when she returned to reality and found life and society to be disturbing and frantic.

"You said it was exclusive, Morrison. Just how exclusive?"

He looked into her brown eyes before he spoke. "The only way you can be included is to be invited by a member in good standing."

She beamed. "Are you in good standing? Would you invite me?" She held her breath, waiting for his answer.

"Could you really stand such a primitive place, Adriana?"

"I've got nothing to do until the end of May—when Ramsey graduates. Then it's off to Europe for me. But in the meantime, I think I'd like to take a trip back into the last century—that is, if you weren't putting me on."

Morrison shook his head, smiling broadly, but said nothing.

"It sounds marvelous, Morrison. Please? Take me? I'd love to go. I want to go! I'll even pay my own way."

"No, no. It's not a question of money, Adriana. Nor is it getting you accepted. Neither are a problem. It's just that I wouldn't want to take you there and then have you suddenly want to go home. The arrangements for your return to the mainland are made far in advance and there's no way you can get back until the launch returns. If you decided it wasn't right for you—"

"A week. We'll go just for a week. Is that possible? Can you get away?"

He frowned for a moment and opened his appointment book. "I guess I can. All right. For one week," he said, moving around the desk, and holding out his arms. She accepted his embrace, returning it warmly.

April 22, 1985

Dear Ramsey,

Your idea of a trip to Europe sounds absolutely fantastic. I'm going to plan on it. I think we'll have a blast all the way. Imagine—you and me living the good life abroad!

Today was my last appointment with Morrison Tyler. But you'll never guess what happened! He told me about an exclusive resort he belongs to, and he is going to take me there for a week. It sounds divine. Absolutely antique. He guaranteed it. The main building is an old mansion and there's no running water, telephone, electricity, tv, newspapers, or anything that remotely resembles the world as we know it. It'll be a great way to prepare for being genteel and gracious in Europe. I'm really looking forward to going there and will give you a complete updated report when I get back. We're leaving tomorrow and I'm as excited as I was when I first came to Claremont a thousand years ago. At least it seems that long ago!

I'll give you a call when I get back a week from tomorrow. If I can't reach you, you call me that night. It'll be great to hear your voice again. Then we can start planning our trip. Gotta fly. Gotta pack. Gotta go! Bye!

Love,
Adriana

Part Two

REVILLION MANOR

THREE

Tuesday, April 23, 1985

ADJUSTING HER SUNGLASSES, Adriana stared out over the Gulf of Mexico. Huge cumulus clouds piled high on the western horizon, while overhead a Florida-blue sky spread unbroken. The waves off Sanibel Island uniformly moved the waters toward the shore until it lapped at the pilings of the dock on which she and Morrison Tyler stood.

"Do those clouds indicate rain, Morrison?" she asked, nodding toward the horizon.

"I doubt it. It's not really the season. If it were August—" he let his voice trail off for a moment. "I wonder where the cruiser could be. He said he'd pick us up at four thirty and it's almost five." He shook his watch, quickly placing it to his ear.

"You don't think he's forgotten, do you?" she asked, a tinge of disappointment in her voice.

73

"I doubt very—there it is. Finally." He pointed down the coast toward the south.

"May I ask you a silly question?" she asked hesitantly, turning to watch the craft plowing through the water toward them.

Morrison smiled broadly. "I can't think of you asking one. What is it?"

"I know this is going to sound dumb, but—" she paused for a split second. She had no idea where she had heard of, or read of such a situation. But she felt certain she had someplace. There was no way she could have dreamed up such a ludicrous idea. "Is it possible for a woman to give birth to a baby one month after conception?" She faced him, thankful for the dark glasses she wore. He couldn't see the timidity lurking there.

Morrison's eyes widened. He gasped for a moment, then began laughing. "Whatever made you ask such a question, my dear?"

His laughter bothered her. It sounded almost forced but then she hadn't really heard Morrison laugh that much. Was he embarrassed by the question? Why should he be? After all, she felt positive that he had listened to some pretty strange ideas in his role as a psychiatric therapist. "I think I've heard of it happening or I may have read about it. Well?"

"I honestly can say I've never read about it in any of my medical journals and I don't believe I remember anything like that being discussed in medical school."

She watched the bow of the cruiser settle in the

74

water as the boat approached the dock. It slowly drifted in until it gently nudged the weathered wood.

"Then you're saying it's not possible?" She stepped in front of her luggage as if she wanted a satisfactory answer before she would consider picking her bags up and boarding the vessel.

"I didn't say that, Adriana. Just that I've never read about it in any medical book or heard of it happening. I suppose when one thinks about the fantastic advances that have been made in the practice of medicine, almost anything could be possible within the given laws of nature. After all, just a few years ago test tube conception was only a wild, untested theory. Today it happens with some modicum of regularity."

She pursed her full lips while Morrison acknowledged the man waving from the cruiser, *The Sea Nympth*. Why did that thought keep hammering at her? For the last two months, ever since she had rid her mind of the storytelling session last Hallowe'en, it had hovered more persistently in her consciousness than at any time before. When she hadn't spoken, it occasionally wedged its way into her thoughts between the memories of her parents and all those other things. At no time had the opportunity come up during her sessions with Morrison to explore the subject. Now that she had asked him, she felt foolish, even though he had not said it was impossible.

"Come on, Adriana," he said, "let's not keep him waiting for us. It'll almost be dark by the time we get there."

She picked up her suitcase and overnight bag to follow him once he had lifted his own small valise. When they were on board and the captain had mounted the fly bridge, she sat back, resting against the stern while Morrison stowed their luggage below in the cabin.

The captain had seemed brusque with her and coolly indifferent to Morrison by not returning her salutation or answering his question about business. All he had done was give a hard nod of his head and mutter something about this being his third trip today. She hoped he had gone someplace else the first two times—someplace other than the island to which they were heading. She hoped there wouldn't be many people there. She wanted peace and quiet. A tender communion between herself and the antique past. She hoped they wouldn't get lost on the open expanse of the Gulf. Smiling broadly, she recalled what Morrison had said about wishing and hoping. "As long as your desires are within reason there's always the possibility they might be realized." She knew hers were realistic.

The sound of the motor rose several decibels once they had cleared the dock and headed for open water. The captain took what Adriana assumed to be a straight westerly course, directly away from the shore.

After some time had passed, Morrison came out of the cabin onto the deck, carrying two half-filled glasses. He sat next to her, offering one of the libations, and smiled.

"Let's drink a toast to Revillion Manor," he suggested.

She beamed. She loved the name of their destination. It was so musical, so elegant sounding. Her only fear was that she might not like it as much as she had anticipated. But that seemed highly unlikely since Morrison had told her much about it during the flight to Florida. The only real worry clouding her mind hinged on the owner of the resort, Olda Revillion, accepting her. Even the man's name sent a tiny sensation of thrill throughout her body. It sounded very old world, very continental.

The continent. For an instant, Ramsey's face blotted out every other thought, every concern. Adriana pictured the two of them, traipsing across Europe as far as they could. They'd visit England and maybe Ireland.

"What are you thinking about?" Morrison said, the toast temporarily forgotten.

She blinked her eyes. Europe and Ramsey were gone. She concentrated for a moment. "Oh. Olda Revillion. Whether or not he'll like me."

"Just be yourself when you get there, Adriana. He'll fall in love with you in an instant. I'll guarantee that."

She laughed inwardly when she thought of her taciturn state of several months before. Would Mr. Revillion have liked her then? Would anyone, other than Morrison, have liked her then?

Settling back for the remainder of the over two-hour ride, she turned to face the doctor who held his glass up again. "I'm sorry, Morrison. You wanted to drink a toast."

"To Revillion Manor," he said simply. "May your stay there be as fruitful as possible for you."

"To Revillion Manor," she repeated, raising the glass to her lips when he did the same. The liquid tasted sweet, smoothly coursing down her throat. When she brought the glass away from her mouth, she saw Morrison staring into the distance. What had he meant about her stay at the island being as fruitful as possible for her?

She barely noticed when *The Sea Nymph* altered course, taking a southwesterly heading.

By seven the sun had all but completed its plunge into the Gulf's western extreme, and the running lights of the cruiser seemed inadequate on the unbroken plain of water once dusk surrendered. Darkness quickly enveloped the tiny vessel and a note of concern sounded in Adriana's voice when she asked, "Will he be able to find the island if it's dark?"

"Don't worry yourself, my dear," Morrison said. "He knows what he's doing."

To Adriana, the words sounded reassuring, but in the half light she would have sworn the older man was frowning. No, scowling was a better description, she decided. What could be bothering him? Perhaps he *was* worried about their finding the island in the dark. She scanned the direction in which the cruiser headed but could see nothing. In her imagination, she had pictured a huge, rambling Victorian mansion, relocated on the beach, away from its pastoral setting. Since she learned they would arrive after dark, vast numbers of lights had flickered on in her mind's image, waiting to welcome her. But then, they went out immediately when she thought of the fact that the mansion had no electricity.

Suddenly, the motor idled down, and the skipper called down to Morrison. "We're here, Doctor."

She squinted, trying to make out the island which appeared to be nothing more than a dark mass looming out of the blackness ahead. No lights. No indication that humanity existed or could exist anyplace except on *The Sea Nymph*. How could he tell where the island was? Was it the correct island? A doubting fear tugged at her until Morrison turned around to face her.

"Are you excited?"

"I will be if this turns out to be the right place—the one you've told me about," she said.

"Let me assure you. This is the correct island."

"But there's no sign of life. No lights. Nothing."

Morrison laughed. "The manor is inland, over a hill. Someone will come down to the dock and meet us. In fact, there," he pointed at a small light bobbing up and down on shore. "See? Someone's coming now to welcome us."

She sighed, watching the lantern come to a stop. She could barely make out tanned legs in the dim aura of the flickering light. A soft bump stopped the cruiser when it struck a tire bumper hanging from the dock.

Morrison heaved their luggage onto the wooden platform and jumped out. Turning quickly, he offered his hand to Adriana. When she stood next to him, the engine roared and *The Sea Nymph* turned, disappearing into the gloom at the head of its whitening wake. In minutes a peaceful calm swiftly drowned out the sound of the cruiser's departing motor.

"Remember, Adriana," Morrison said good naturedly, "I don't want you getting any ideas about you and me while we are here. I wouldn't—"

"Don't worry. I've got my priorities pretty much in line. Since you rank right up there at the head of the list, I guess you could say that I've got you right where I want you." She snickered. "Don't take that the wrong way. What I meant was—"

"I know what you mean. I just—"

"Morrison!" A woman's voice filtered out of the night as the bearer of the lantern approached.

Adriana turned at the same time Morrison did, and gasped. In the dim half light, she could barely make out the features of the woman but she decided that she had never seen a more lovely person. Long flowing blond hair cascaded across both shoulders, falling across well-proportioned breasts that were held in check by a tight T-shirt. Tiny white pants did little to conceal any part of her long, well-tanned legs.

The woman walked directly up to Morrison, set the lantern down and threw both arms around his neck. She kissed him passionately on the mouth, making almost audible slurping and sucking sounds.

Her face turning red, Adriana looked away into the darkness. No wonder he didn't want to get involved with her. Why should he when he had such a creature waiting for him elsewhere?

When they stopped, Morrison said shakily, "Deirdre, this is Adriana Brevenger. Adriana, this lovely woman is Deirdre."

The blonde turned, moving lithly toward her. She threw her arms around the girl, embracing her. "Adriana, I'm so very happy to meet you. I've heard so much about you."

"You have?" Adriana asked, taken aback by the statement. "From whom, may I ask?" Her skin felt cool, almost clammy, where the woman had touched her.

"Why, from Olda, of course. He's told us much."

Adriana looked at Morrison. Her quizzical expression eloquently asked the unspoken question.

"I've told him all about you, my dear," he said.

Of course, that was it. How simple. If Olda Revillion knew all about her, he could more easily make a quicker decision about her membership in the club or society or however it was called. Naturally she felt she had an equal right to refuse belonging in the event she didn't like the place or the people or the cost of participating proved to be too much. Why had she felt a sudden pang of terror when Deirdre said that she knew all about her? For some reason she could not understand, now that she thought about it, she had interpreted it as being ominous that this beautiful young lady would even take the time to learn about her.

"Shall we go?" Deirdre asked. "Everyone is waiting to meet Adriana and to see you again, Morrison, darling." She picked up the lantern in one hand and Adriana's large bag in the other, seemingly without effort.

Adriana winced. She had struggled with that wardrobe suitcase after she had packed it, wondering how many people it would take to handle it enroute to the island. And this woman picked it up without batting an eye. In the half light, she had probably missed all the bulging muscles the blonde undoubtedly possessed.

Morrison took command of the remaining luggage and followed Deirdre with Adriana bringing up the rear. They followed a macadam pathway, not over three feet wide, through dense vegetation that crowded in on both sides.

"Perhaps you'd better walk ahead of me," Morrison said after several minutes, turning to his traveling companion. "I wouldn't want you to fall just after arriving at the island." He stepped aside and allowed Adriana to take his position in the file.

Something bothered Adriana. But what? The quiet of the place? Could the actions of the blonde be making her jealous? She mulled that one over in her head for a moment. No. She definitely was not jealous of the fact Deirdre kissed Morrison in a way she herself had fantasized doing less than three months before. Then could it be the woman? Adriana doubted that. There was no reason for envy or jealousy toward Deirdre. How could there be? She had barely seen her in the semi-darkness and knew nothing about her as a person. In fact, Deirdre had welcomed her in a most sincere way. Well, then. Could it be the quiet of the island that she noticed, albeit obliquely? Other than their footsteps on the hard path, she could not detect another sound. She listened carefully. She could hear nothing. No insects buzzing. No birds singing. Would they be out and about after dark? She didn't know. But there should be some night birds or something making noise. Listening carefully, she shuddered when all she could hear was their footsteps.

The walk turned upward as they climbed a hill. The vegetation did not thin out, and when they reached the top, they began their descent immediately. The night air cooled perceptibly as they continued downhill. Adriana shivered and rubbed her arms.

"It won't be long, Adriana," Deirdre said over her shoulder. "In fact, we should be able to see the lights pretty soon."

"Lights?" Adriana asked, reimagining her make-believe mansion with its electricity and twinkling windows.

"They're only kerosene lamps, but we have a lot of them and they do a more than adequate job."

Adriana felt as if she should answer but decided it would make her sound as though she hadn't paid the slightest bit of attention to anything Morrison had told her about the place. Of course, he had explained about the oil lights and everything else that made Revillion Manor into a virtual time machine.

Then she could see them. Warm, flickering pips of light in the distance, beckoning through the darkness to her. It seemed as though there were dozens of windows, each emitting a soft glow. The vegetation that had protruded over the pathway at times thinned until they were passing through what appeared to be a meadow. Off in the distance she heard a bleat, then an answering one.

"What was that?" she asked, stepping more quickly to be closer to the woman who was leading.

"The sheep," Deirdre said matter-of-factly.

"Sheep?" she asked, hoping for an explanation. Morrison had not mentioned sheep. But then, how could he tell her everything?

"We raise sheep and goats for meat and milk."

Adriana shrugged. "Oh."

The house grew in proportion as they neared it until, when they stood directly in front, Adriana felt totally dwarfed by the huge building. The large front door opened and a slender old man stepped onto the portico. His hair reflected silvery white in the golden glow behind him but his lively step showed no sign of infirmity, as might have been expected by someone first meeting him.

The door opened again and two women, both blonde, both tall and lovely stepped out. Adriana drew her breath in. They seemed to be almost perfect carbon copies of Deirdre. Triplets? Sisters? She had no idea.

"Olda," Deirdre said, "this is the young lady you've been telling us about. Olda, meet Adriana Brevenger. Adriana," she turned to face her, "this is your host, Olda Revillion."

He turned halfway, the lights exposing his features for the first time. A thin nose dominated his angular face until his eyes reflected the glint of light coming from the house. At first, Adriana thought they danced in a merry way but then saw that the happiness or warmth that she felt she had detected was not there at all. Something was lacking in those eyes. She could not quite put her finger on it but then decided that she'd wait until they were inside where she would be able to see better. Still, the eyes prevailed, holding her attention as they addressed her.

"My dear," he said, his voice choking just a bit. He took her hand in his, bending at the waist, and kissed it. Straightening, he said, "Welcome to Revillion Manor. You don't know how long I've waited to meet you."

"How long?" Adriana parroted and looked at Morrison who seemed to ignore her question.

"Ever since Dr. Tyler told us of you, I've wanted to meet you, my dear," Olda said in a way of explanation.

She relaxed. Why was she so on guard where her host and the people around her were concerned? Simmer down, she told herself. Take it easy. One had to know a person first to dislike or distrust them. She looked at the older man. His face appeared lined in an incredible, intricate manner. It seemed to her at first that his entire countenance was nothing but a mass of tiny, almost invisible lines. But then, again, she decided to wait until they entered the house to pass judgment on her ability to observe in poor light.

"I've very happy to be here, Mr. Revillion," she offered in a soft voice.

"Please, Adriana. We do not stand on formality here. It is much more relaxed if we call each other by our first names. Please, call me Olda."

"But—" she protested and stopped. She had learned in her talks with Morrison to look on herself as an adult now and not as a child any longer. If she were to succeed in a world of grownups, she would have to take part as one. He ultimately convinced her that if she thought of herself as an adult, she would be more than adequate to care for the money and property she had inherited at the deaths of her mother and father. From that day on, when he had persuaded her to believe that, she had called him by his first name. Now she would call this gracious man, Olda, as he requested and not feel the least bit uncomfortable.

He waved her objection aside and said to the two blondes behind him. "Charlene. Michele. This is Adriana Brevenger. Greet her."

They stepped around him, approaching her

with open arms. "Welcome, Adriana," they chorused. One stepped in front of the other and embraced the new arrival, kissing her on the cheek.

Adriana felt herself weaken, a lightheadedness balancing the queasy sensation in her stomach. The woman was running her tongue over Adriana's cheek. As gracefully as possible, she wriggled free but found herself confronted by the other.

"Don't frighten Adriana, Charlene," the second woman reproved, embracing in much the same manner but without the tongued kiss on the cheek. "We're happy to have you here, Adriana," Michele said.

"Thank you—both of you," she managed. "In fact, all of you have been so warm and friendly, I just hope I can match your expectations so that I can become a member."

"I don't think we'll have any problem there," Olda said, gesturing toward the porch and door. "Let's all go inside. It's getting chilly out here."

He took Adriana's arm, escorting her up the steps behind Michele and Charlene who carried all the luggage. Deirdre and Morrison walked up to the porch, arm in arm.

When Adriana entered, her expectations were fully realized and then quickly exceeded. A huge chandelier, its several hundred candles aflame, cast multicolored specks of light from prismed teardrops, about the room. A broad staircase vied for dominance of the foyer with the intricate light fixtures, ascending halfway to the second floor before splitting to each side. A round stained-glass window, blackened with night, served as a backdrop for the stairway landing. She looked at the zigzagging pattern of lead that held the different pieces of colored glass in place, anticipating light streaming through it the next day, to show the various hues and its design. Looking more closely, she tried to determine the picture, deciding it looked quite like an angel.

"Why don't you help Adriana register, Michele," Olda said, breaking into her thoughts. "Charlene, child, take her luggage to her room. Deirdre, you may welcome Morrison in a proper fashion in a short while. First, he and I must talk. Come, Morrison."

He indicated that the doctor should accompany him and moved to the left of the entryway, opposite a large grandfather clock, into what appeared to be a dining room.

Morrison fell in behind the tall man, following him across the room where they would be eating in a while, and entered Olda's office. Neither spoke until the door was closed.

"Any problems?" Olda asked, moving catlike to a small buffet standing to the side of the built-in bookcases. He picked up a flask, pouring two small wine glasses full of amber liquid.

"None. Well—" Morrison let his voice die.

Olda turned. "Tell me."

"It was nothing. Really. She asked about a one month pregnancy. That's all."

"Is it possible for her to remember that?"

"I wouldn't see why not. After all, I planted the

thoughts in her mind for two months before she ever started speaking. If I had used hypnosis, I could have suggested that she not speak of such things. But, since she bordered at times near perfect schizophrenia and vacillated between it and a cataleptic state, I could not countermand the orders to accept, by telling her to 'forget this when you awaken.' She would simply have obeyed and forgotten. No, I'm positive that the brainwashing effect will be exactly as we planned. Has Lahpavi arrived yet?"

"This afternoon. He is most excited," Olda said, raising his glass.

"How do you feel? Have you taken everything you were told?"

"Of course. I'm not one to disobey. Especially when so much of our own personal futures depends on what happens here in the next four to five weeks."

Morrison bowed his head.

"You know," Olda continued, "since I began taking the different spices, herbs, and concoctions Lahpavi sent, I've felt like an eighteen year old. I look at one of the girls and I get an erection almost immediately. It's incredible."

Morrison brought his glass to his lips. Everything would be perfect. Hopefully, once the object was accomplished, Adriana would join them.

"How is Adriana now?" Olda asked. "Do you have control?"

"Right now, she believes that she is mentally as strong and healthy as anyone."

"Is she?"

"I suppose she could go through life without any repercussions of any sort and lead a quite normal life. But I have control in the way I brainwashed her. Brainwash. I hate that word. I prepared her mentally to accept certain commands. She will be in a state of flux for quite a while once we begin and she will not know exactly what she should do. She will vacillate much between opposite poles of most issues she thinks about."

"Will she be willing to join us—once we are through?"

Morrison half emptied his glass and shrugged. "If everyone does their job and I can maintain enough control over her once she has delivered, I believe we can convince her. If that doesn't work, there are other ways."

"There had better be other ways. If this fails, I will hold you responsible."

Morrison glared at the old man. "I hardly find that fair. After all, I'm not the only one dealing in unknowns. There's Lahpavi. And there's you."

"Yes, there's Lahpavi and me. But you are the only one who must deal with the girl. If she isn't ready for this or something goes wrong, it won't just be me you'll have to answer to. Or the others. There is *one* I'm sure you will not want to atone to." Olda laughed evilly under his words.

Morrison downed the contents of his glass in a single gulp and stared at Olda.

The old man stood, placing his glass on the

buffet behind him and moved toward the door. "Come, let's see if she has gone upstairs yet."

Adriana watched Morrison follow the old man out of the entryway. Turning to look in the opposite direction, she saw, out of the corner of her eye, Charlene moving up the staircase, effortlessly carrying her bags and Morrison's. In front of her, large double doors opened into a drawing room. Seated about the parlor were three men and a woman. Staring at them, Adriana tried to understand what it was they were doing. Each sat bolt upright, their fingers interlaced in front of them, their thumbs pointing straight up. The four people stared into space as though daydreaming.

"Will you sign this, please?" Michele asked, offering a pen to Adriana as she indicated a small card on the desk.

Adriana quickly filled in the blanks and returned it.

"That's fine," Michele said. "We can go to your room now and you can prepare for dinner."

Maybe that was Adriana's problem. She suddenly grew aware of her stomach growling for lack of food. In the excitement of arriving, she had completely forgotten that the last food they had eaten had been on the plane—and that, only a brunch of sorts. An inedible soggy sandwich of indifferent luncheon meat, a fruit cup that had gone dry sometime before, and cut up raw vegetables. She had eaten the vegetables and some of the fruit, accepting the cup of orange sherbet the flight attendant handed her and downed it with gusto. After deplaning, they rented a car and drove through Fort Myers to Sanibel Island. By the time Morrison had disposed of the automobile and they had walked to the pier to meet the cruiser, it had been late afternoon. Other than the sweet drink they had drunk on *The Sea Nymph*, she had consumed nothing of substance since shortly before noon. She was famished.

"What time do we eat?" she asked, trying to contain her enthusiasm for a good meal.

"About nine or a little after," Michele said. "You'll have plenty of time. By the way, we'll be dressing for dinner. We always do here at Revillion Manor. You do have a formal evening dress, don't you, Adriana?"

"Yes, of course. Morrison told me I should come prepared for just such an occasion." The idea simply overwhelmed her. A formal dinner. By candlelight. Or, and she had noticed several sitting about the room, kerosene lamps. Either would be apropos to a relaxing evening. She sighed quietly to herself. If she became a member, she'd have to bring Ramsey here. Ramsey Flint would love it.

"That's fine." Michele moved toward the staircase, motioning for Adriana to follow her.

"Just a minute, Michele," she said, touching the woman on the arm to stop her. Quickly withdrawing her hand, Adriana noticed the same icy feel of Michele's skin but recalled how she had been chilled when they were walking down the hill toward the manor. "What are they doing?" She motioned toward the drawing room and its four occupants who still sat in the same position holding their hands in front of them, thumbs upward.

"Oh, that?" Michele asked, just a hint of of lilting laugh punctuating her question. "It's a form of meditation we do around here. It helps clear the mind of all kinds of fuzzies."

Adriana nodded, understanding what the girl had said. She recalled Morrison telling her on the plane of some of the mental exercises developed by Olda Revillion. "In fact," Morrison had said, "I'm planning to introduce some of the methods at a meeting next August in Vienna."

That particular exercise appeared not too difficult to master. Adriana turned, following Michele up the stairs but stopped at the landing to look over the foyer. She wanted to see it from that angle.

She stopped, startled. The people from the drawing room had moved into the entryway and stood with Deirdre. Morrison and Olda entered from the opposite side from where they had disappeared minutes before, moving toward the knot of people. Each interlaced their fingers, thumbs extended upward and stared at her.

A cold chill swept through Adriana's body and she pivoted, to continue up to her room. As she ascended the stairs, she could feel the seven sets of eyes following her every move.

FOUR

That Evening

SHAKEN, ADRIANA FOLLOWED Michele up the staircase to the right. When they stood on the second floor, the blonde turned to walk down a dark hall, motioning for her to follow. The corridor, dimly lighted by oil lamps bracketed to the wall every fifteen or twenty feet, quickly swallowed the women in its shadows.

Adriana moved slowly, unfamiliar with the hallway, her eyes darting from side to side. She could make out oil paintings hanging on both walls, and moved slower in an attempt to make out the subject matter of each. Dark with age, the indiscernible pictures blurred into hazy gallimaufries. She stopped by one, examining it, trying to comprehend its scene. The only distinct line seemed to be the horizon. What first appeared to be ruins of an ancient temple with white veiled nuns approaching it, instantly became, upon closer examination, sticklike trees without tops and the white blobs took on the shape of grazing sheep. One image in the foreground held her attention. A shrouded figure stood ominously guarding the trees or pillars and she tilted her head to one side. A shepherd?

"Adriana?" Michele called.

She jumped at the sound of her name.

"Are you coming?" The woman began retracing her steps but stopped when Adriana moved in her direction.

"Yes, I'm coming. I became engrossed in one of the paintings, trying to figure out what it represented."

"Don't bother," Michele said, laughing lightly. "Most of them have faded beyond recognition and look like just about anything the viewer wishes to imagine."

"Are they valuable?" Adriana asked, assuming they weren't since the paintings obviously had not been cared for over the years.

"I don't see how they could be. Most of them were painted by Olda's family many years ago and probably weren't very good in the first place."

Adriana hurried, keeping pace with her.

"Do you like art, Adriana?"

She turned to Michele. The manner in which Michele said her name sounded positively threatening. Could this woman be looking on her as a possible competitor? But a competitor for what? Other men? She hadn't seen any, other than the three in the parlor, and they had not appeared to be near her age or even appealing for that matter. Besides, there seemed to be more men than women at the manor so there shouldn't be any conflict in that respect. When she could see Michele's face in the dim light of one of the lamps as they passed it, she found her smiling kindly.

"Some, although I don't go much for modern art. I like a picture to be something one can recognize right away. Something—"

"It was a tragedy about your parents," Michele said suddenly.

Adriana felt stripped to the skin. How did Michele know? Had Olda told her? Had Morrison told Olda? Where were the professional ethics by which psychiatrists were supposed to abide? How many others knew of her loss—her breakdown—her recovery?

Michele reached out, touching her arm. Adriana felt her skin crawl. The woman's hand felt icy cold and a shiver ran down her spine. She stopped walking when Michele stepped in front of her.

"We were advised of it so that we could help you, Adriana. Without a family or close relatives or friends, we here at Revillion Manor would like to be thought of as your family."

"I—I—I don't know what to say, Michele," she stammered, realizing her suspicions were foolish and unfounded.

"Just think of us as family. If you have any problems or would like to talk about the new direction your life has taken or will take, feel free to contact me or any of the others. All right?"

Adriana managed a slight nod of her head but could not speak because of the thickening in her throat. Struggling to resist her urge to cry, she reached out and squeezed the woman's hand.

"We're here," Michele said, opening the door nearest them. "Wait till I light a lamp." She disappeared into the black room.

Adriana peered in when a match flared, quickly settling into a steady glow once the lamp had been lit. The soft light created shadows on ornate flowered wallpaper.

"As you probably remember Morrison telling you, we don't have electricity here," Michele said, picking up the large suitcase that had been deposited in the room a few minutes earlier by Charlene. Placing it on the brass bed, she fumbled with the catches.

"How quaint! How absolutely quaint," Adriana squealed, clapping her hands. "I love it. I've seen pictures of restored mansions and have been to museums depicting nineteenth century America. Big old-fashioned bedrooms sometimes with fireplaces, and furniture a lot like this. Oh, I just love it."

"I'm glad you do, Adriana. Most of the first-time visitors react just about the same way you have. Do you mind if I help you unpack?"

"I'd appreciate it, Michele."

The women quickly emptied the wardrobe suitcase, hanging the dresses, slacks, shorts, and blouses in the walk-in closet. The cozy smell of long evaporated moth balls overpowered the ever present damp smell, embracing them each time they entered.

"What a lovely gown," Michele said, holding up the last item she withdrew. The white, floor-length dress shimmered in the golden lamplight. "You have exquisite taste. But do you only have one?"

"I gathered from what Morrison said that one would be sufficient for the length of time I'd be staying."

Michele wrinkled her brow, creating unnatural furrows in her otherwise flawless complexion. "We're just about the same size. In the event you would like a change in dinner gowns, you can go through mine. I have dozens."

"That would be super, Michele. Thank you. In fact, thank you for everything," she said, making a sweeping motion with her arm.

"All part of the service, Adriana," she said, moving toward the door. "You have about an hour or so before we dine. Take your time and then come down when you're ready. Everyone is anxious to meet you."

The door closed quietly with a resounding click and Adriana sat down on the edge of the bed. She smiled ruefully as the last six months zipped through her mind. Half a year before she had been a freshman in college studying for her degree in biology. Then came that awful night when her parents died, her plunge into the inky blackness of silence, and Morrison Tyler's steady help in pulling her back to reality.

She gazed about the room. This was reality? She felt as if she had been transported back in time, but wasn't that what Morrison had said was so great about Revillion Manor? Many times, while recuperating, she had thought of the mad pace she would have to resume once she was discharged from the hospital, only to replace such disturbing ideas with a desire for a more calm and peaceful type of existence. Now, here she was—right back in the nineteenth century and loving every bit of it.

Standing, she took the last item, her small bag of cosmetics, from the suitcase, placing it on the bureau top before arranging her panties and bras in the small top drawers of the large maple dresser. At the bottom of her bag, she found the crucifix her mother had worn as Sister Innocence. Connie had given it to her when Adriana had asked for the symbol shortly before her twelfth birthday and had had it inscribed: *To Adriana, my "little Sister." Love Mom*. Now, she stared at it. God had been so unfair, so unkind to her, taking her parents in that cruel way. Why? Why? She didn't fight the tears streaming down her face. Instead, she allowed them to cleanse her emotions. How many times had she asked herself why? She threw the cross into the drawer and closed it.

When the tears stopped, she dabbed at her cheeks with a tissue. She felt better for crying. Morrison had convinced her that to allow feelings full rein would not be a sign of weakness as she had contended when they first discussed it. If she could manage to keep her mind busy and off her bad memories while with people, she would eliminate the problem of suddenly bursting into tears. However, when she was alone, it made no difference.

She knew she had to hurry. Get cleaned up. Dress for dinner. The last idea seemed such a turn-on to her. She reflected on other things that appealed to her—down to earth happy people, wild flowers, walks in the country during summer, a good book to read indoors during a thunderstorm or blizzard. Her likes were simple and the thought of dressing formally for dinner seemed to suit her just as the rest of them had.

But where could she clean up? She looked about the room. The only door, other than the one leading to the hall, was the closet. She had no bath of her own. Was there one someplace else in the house? Her puzzled gaze fell on the small commode standing next to the bureau. An ornate earthenware pitcher and bowl practically filled the top of the small piece of furniture. Peering at it, she found the pitcher full of water and quickly poured some into the basin before undressing. She found a bar of scented soap on a dish and washcloths and towels hanging across the rack built onto the back of the commode. The skin on her small breasts and stomach prickled under the cool water and her nipples hardened.

After sponging off her body, she dried herself, looking into the mirror at her reflection. Her smile was instantly returned and she gloated over her good fortune at having Morrison for her analyst and at his suggesting he bring her here. How lucky could she be? Especially when she considered the trauma of six months before.

She slipped into panties, opting to go braless because of the style of the gown she would wear to dinner. Applying liner to her eyes, she leaned closer to the mirror to insure a good job. A touch of color to her lips after brushing a slight pink to her cheeks completed her makeup. She stepped back to inspect her handiwork. The strong point of her face, she felt, was her mouth. Full lips turned down just a bit at the corners gave her an expression of pouting when she didn't smile. She had been told it was sexy by several of the boys she had gone to high school with but had not believed them at the time. When Ramsey Flint had said the same thing shortly after they met last fall at school, Adriana began to believe it.

Stepping to the closet, she brought out the white gown. She held it up before her body, admiring it in the mirror. After stepping into a half slip, she dropped the dress over her head, letting it fall around her body. She fixed the single strap in place and smoothed the bodice, delighting in the effect of her brown aureoles shadowing through the snowy material. Satisfied that she would turn a few heads, she vigorously brushed her hair. Marveling at the highlights in her coppery tresses reflecting from the single flame, she continued brushing until she had achieved a certain wild, unkempt, yet carefully engineered look.

Turning, she peered over her shoulder into the mirror, admiring the Grecian-like toga. The flowing panel fell gracefully down her backside, its hem curving around to angle up the front. Facing the mirror once more, she moved the single strap decorated with bugle beads, pearls, and rhinestones closer to the edge of her shoulder. She admired her image. She was beautiful.

Glancing at her watch, she decided to go downstairs even though she would be fifteen minutes early. Why sit up here by herself? Especially since, according to Michele, everyone was waiting to meet her. When she reached the door, she stopped. She had no key to her room. Michele had obviously forgotten to give it to her. Hopefully no one would enter her room until she returned with it.

She stepped into the hall and stopped, her nose catching the stale odor of the house again. Which direction should she go? From which way had she and Michele come? Tentatively turning to the left, she hesitated before spinning about to go the opposite way. Even if it were wrong, she would see a little more of the fabulous house.

Moving cautiously in the half dark, she soon found herself at the end of the hall. The mustiness seemed to be all over but she would probably not notice it in a day or two. Having passed several doors, presumably to other bedrooms, she knew she had taken the wrong way and was about to retrace her steps when she sensed more than saw that the corridor continued at right angles to her left. She reached out and drew her hand back at once. The walls were draped in heavy black. Moving closer, she fingered the material and decided in the darkness that the cloth was velvet. At the end of the lined hallway, she could see a single lamp, its light being absorbed by the raven drapes, vainly trying to illuminate the passage. Drawn to the speck of light, she glided toward it. When she reached it, she found the end of the hall covered with the same velvety material.

"Now, why on earth would anyone do something like this?" she said in a hoarse whisper. Were there no windows along here? Or doors? Why a hall with a dead end? Fumbling with the drapes covering the small wall, she found a door knob. Gingerly turning it, she found the metal handle impossible to budge. She drew back the heavy velvet and gasped, barely managing to stifle the scream she felt rising.

Staring at her with wooden eyes, the head of an animal seemed to lunge at her. She fell back. Was she seeing things? What *had* she seen? An animal? A goat? A goat's head? Carved out of wood? For what purpose? Reaching out, she pulled back the drapes once more.

The dim light played along the highly polished contours of the head carved into what appeared to be a door. She dropped her eyes to the knob again and tried it—still without effect. Barely able to make out the outline of the sculpture, she reached out, running her fingers over the face. It was a man's face. Higher on the head, her fingertips touched something that felt like horns. She dropped her hands, stepping back. The drape fell back in place. *The devil?*

Turning, she half ran, half walked back to the corridor on which her room opened. For reasons she could not ascertain, she did not feel unduly upset by the strange carving. But she should. Why would anyone in their right mind want something like that in their home? Perhaps that was the reason for the heavy drapes. To cover it up and keep it from the sight of guests.

When she reached her room, she opened the door to make certain everything was all right and, assured that it was, continued down the corridor.

Passing the oil painting she had stopped to study earlier, she knew she was headed in the right direction and in seconds stood on the landing that overlooked the foyer. The darkened stained-glass window loomed over her but she ignored it, knowing she could admire it in all its colorful glory the next day. Instead she looked down at the entrance—the chandelier and grandfather clock holding her attention.

Olda, dressed in tails, stepped out of the parlor to the left and looked up. "Adriana, you are a vision of loveliness. Have you found everything to your satisfaction?"

"Yes," she said, returning his look of admiration with one of wide-eyed wonderment, before adding hesitantly, "and no," when she thought of the carved head she had discovered.

"Well," he said, extending his hand to her as he waited at the foot of the steps, "we can't have that, can we? What seems to be the problem?"

"I don't want you to think I'm foolish, Mr. Revillion, but—"

"Remember, Olda, my dear," he said, smiling benevolently.

"Very well, Olda. When I left my room, I went the wrong way and found myself in a hall lined with black drapes. At the end, I found the most grotesque head—"

"Carved on the door?" Olda finished for her, chuckling under his breath. "My dear, I was hoping that you wouldn't find it by yourself. That either the girls or I would have the opportunity to explain it and other, how should I say, peculiar appointments around Revillion Manor? You see, this lovely home was my grandfather's and well, to say the least, he might appear to have been eccentric to the ordinary person when seeing the house for the first time. That particular door was carved for his private study, or as he called it, I'm told, his *sanctum sanctorum*. The hallway leading to it was done in black, just the way you found it."

"Why in heaven's name don't you change it? It's awful. Why would he want a carving of the devil—"

Olda threw his head back and laughed. "Do you think it is the devil, himself, my dear?"

"Why—why, yes. Isn't it?"

108

"I wouldn't know, never having met him face to face. I have no idea as to who or what it is supposed to represent. It could be Pan or some ancient God."

"I naturally thought—"

"I think you jumped to a hasty conclusion and worried yourself for nothing."

"Why don't you remove it?" Adriana asked, shuddering when she recalled the sensation she had experienced when she had touched the carven head.

"That I cannot do!" Olda's mood changed instantly. "Perhaps I will tell you sometime why I can't. Is there anything else troubling you?"

His normally serene countenance had changed and the stern visage he displayed almost frightened her. Either way, the older man was quite handsome, but she quickly decided that she felt more at ease when he appeared affable.

"Yes, there is one thing," she said softly, timidly, afraid of another adverse reaction from her host.

"What is that?" His attitude had changed again and he was the cultured person she had met earlier when she had first arrived.

"Michele neglected to give me a key to my room. May I have it now?"

Olda smiled. "If I had a key to your room I would happily give it to you. However, there is only one key in the entire house and that happens to be to the door to the study. I'm sorry I can't accommodate you, but all of us are in the same situation. I suppose you could say that we are on the honor system. However, let me assure you, you and your property will be safe."

Sleep in a house full of strangers without any protection at all? Could she do that? Of course, she wouldn't be the only one and she found a small degree of comfort in the thought. "I guess if everyone else is in the same predicament, I shouldn't be the one to complain."

"I promise you will not be bothered in your room needlessly, my dear. Come, let me escort you to the drawing room. Everyone is waiting to meet you."

Adriana took his proffered arm and felt swept back in time once more as she and Olda glided into the room he had quitted a moment before. The men present stood as they entered, the buzz of conversation dwindling to nothing. Olda guided her to the nearest couple.

The sound of subdued voices buzzed again when Olda said, "Adriana, this is Everhart Parrot of New York. Of course you remember Charlene from this afternoon."

Adriana nodded, thankful that he had identified the woman, since she was not positive if she would have the correct name for the right person. The resemblance of the woman standing opposite her to the other two truly mystified her. Were the three sisters? Or better yet, actually triplets as she had first thought? Another of the beautiful blondes moved into Adriana's view directly over Charlene's shoulder and she could compare them. The wide set eyes were a deep blue, almost violet, and fixed unblinkingly on whomever they addressed. There was a certain openness or sincerity, a distinct honesty in the manner in which the women looked at one. Adriana didn't find this unnerving but she imagined it could drive a man right up the wall if he felt the least bit insecure about himself.

Thin, finely chiseled noses with tiny tips seemed to point the way to the ample lips snuggled beneath. The mouths were the mouths of which poems were written and Adriana found herself wondering if the scarlet flesh of those lips would be as soft and yielding as it appeared. To further madden the new acquaintance, the three women wore their hair in much the same way— loose, flowing, and just below shoulder length.

Their bodies, like their faces, seemed to have been duplicated in the same mold. Although she could not see their legs now, Adriana knew they were muscular because of the tiny shorts she had seen them wearing when she and Morrison first arrived. The vermillion floor-length dresses they wore now did little to conceal their breasts or the contour of their hips. For just a second, Adriana wondered if she paled by comparison, recalling how pleased she had been with her own appearance upstairs. Michele's offer to lend her a gown made her wonder if the gesture had been genuine. Adriana knew her own breasts were much smaller than any of the three women's and she wasn't quite as tall and her hips were not nearly so flared as theirs. Maybe Michele was just being generous and would have helped Adriana fit the gown to her body. She mentally shrugged.

Charlene subtly dipped her head while Everhart bowed deeply from the waist.

Any other time, any other place, Adriana would have had to restrain a giggle. But here—here it seemed the only way to have a man acknowledge an introduction to a woman. A glow swept through her when she thought of herself as a woman. For some reason she couldn't comprehend, she extended her hand and he kissed it. A sense of lightheadedness swept through her when he stood erect. She hadn't noticed how attractive he was until that very second, when their eyes met. A touch of gray at the temples accentuated the blackness of his hair and brows. His eyes, equally black and piercing, studied her for several moments before he spoke.

"It is a great pleasure for me to meet one so beautiful," he said, his voice smooth, deep.

"Everhart," Olda explained, "is a well-known photographer both in this country and abroad. He'll probably want you to pose for him before too much time elapses. Is that right, Everhart?"

"It would be a great honor to have you model for me, Adriana."

"I'm flattered, Mr.—er—I mean, Everhart."

"I would like to take this opportunity, my dear," he said, "to extend my condolences on your loss."

Naked. She felt exposed, helpless, without defenses, her recovery teetering in jeopardy. Did

112

everyone here know? As Michele had said, this could be her family if she wanted. So far she had seen nothing to make her uneasy where the people themselves were concerned. When she looked at Everhart, her attention was quickly drawn to Charlene, who merely nodded in agreement with her escort.

"Than—thank you," she managed.

Before anyone could speak, Michele approached them and whispered in Olda's ear.

"Please excuse me, everyone. I'm needed in the kitchen." He turned, walking away with the blonde's arm hooked through his.

"Come, I will continue introducing you, Adriana," Everhart said, taking her arm to steer her toward the nearest couple.

Adriana marveled at the men, all formally attired in tuxedoes, looking as comfortable and at ease as someone lounging about in jeans and T-shirts. The women appeared as beautiful as models who had stepped from shadow boxes. The couple they approached stood with their backs to them and both turned when Everhart spoke.

Adriana caught her breath. It couldn't be. There, standing directly in front of her was Angelique Pantis, the movie star. She found herself perfunctorily greeting the gorgeous woman, who at the age of at least fifty-four appeared to be more like twenty-two or twenty-three. Long, flowing black hair, carefully coiffed into an upsweep, framed her milky white complected face. A touch of color on the cheeks complemented the full lips which seemed to have

113

no color other than that which nature had endowed. How could a person have such blood-red lips naturally?

Angelique's low cut gown did nothing to maintain the woman's modesty, displaying breasts that stood upright, firm without the help of a bra. Adriana wondered if she had ever had anything done to them to have them appear so youthful. Again she felt mediocre when she mentally compared herself with the woman standing opposite her. But how could she help herself feel any other way? The woman's skin appeared to be like that of a child's—soft, yielding, but with an elasticity that held it tightly in place.

Angelique extended a hand to Adriana. When the girl held it in hers, she shot a quick look at it. She had read someplace that the one part of the human body difficult to maintain a look of youth-fulness was the hand. But this hand she held could have belonged to herself or to Ramsey Flint or any other young woman. The skin felt as taut on the back as the skin appeared on her arms and shoulders and face.

Adriana had seen Angelique in many motion pictures and had read several interviews in which the movie queen had refused to talk about her beauty secrets. It seemed that her almost mystical ability for retaining her youthful appearance remained the topic of conversation among most women whenever the subject of aging came up. How she maintained her youthful looks had remained her carefully guarded secret, having turned down multimillion dollar contracts from publishers looking for a competetive piece to the other famous movie stars' workout book. For over ten years she had resisted, saying no one would ever find out her methods.

Adriana merely nodded, acquiescing when Angelique offered her condolences. The man standing with her remained silent until Everhart introduced him.

"Adriana, I'd like you to meet Doctor Rizahghyny Lahpavi."

She offered her hand and the heavyset man grasped it in his, bending to kiss it. When he stood straight, she felt a strange dampness on her hand and looked at the man's lips. They glistened with spittle and she shuddered in revulsion. What had he done? Licked her hand?

"How do you do, my dear," he said, the words heavily accented.

"Doctor?" she said, bowing her head in greeting. *Doctor of what?* she wondered. If he were a medical man, he'd have to clean up his act where hygiene was concerned. Again, she trembled ever so slightly from the thought of the man's saliva on her skin.

"I'm sure you know who Angelique is," Everhart said matter-of-factly, "and the good doctor here is an obstetrician, visiting our country from his home in the East."

"You have my sympathy, my dear," the doctor said.

Once more, Adriana found herself accepting in a mechanical way. Why fight it? If they knew, they knew. So what?

"Come, Adriana, and I will introduce you to the rest of the people," the photographer said.

They crossed the large room where they met Jefferson and Ivy St. Clair, who were visiting with Morrison. The married couple, both on the plump side, greeted her warmly, offering their warmest wishes for overcoming her loss, which by now didn't seem to bother Adriana in the least. Ivy St. Clair was barely five feet tall and weighed at least two hundred pounds. Her expensive gown fit her in a way that said it had been made expressly for her. Large jewels flashed gaudily from her pudgy fingers.

Her balding husband, Jefferson, appeared much shorter because of his expanded girth. From a distance, Adriana would have said he could not be more than five feet four or five. But standing next to her, he managed to top Adriana's own five feet six by at least two inches. His bulbous nose held her attention for a second too long, and she looked away to find Morrison staring into space.

If the condolences no longer upset her, Morrison suddenly did. He seemed unhappy, beleaguered with problems of some sort, almost unsure of himself. And that was definitely not in Morrison Tyler's makeup. After he had said hello, he ignored her, treating her in an aloof manner. Could something she might have said or done be bothering him? She tried to recall

116

anything she might have done wrongly but dismissed the concern when she turned on Everhart's command to meet her dinner escort.

She felt her jaw drop. The handsome giant confronting her stood at least six feet four. Dusty blond hair half covered his ears, spilling upward until it formed a wave in the center of his forehead. Thick eyebrows curved over gray eyes that stared at her fixedly, gently. She found herself staring at his nose, which she thought seemed too small for his face but when she considered his upper lip, graced with a moustache which tapered to the corners of his mouth, she decided it was just right. His teeth gleamed through smiling lips while the firm, robust chin bobbed up and down as he spoke.

"I'm very happy to meet you, Adriana. I hope you like it here at Revillion Manor."

"I—I'm sure I will, Mr. Messenger," she managed, thinking his voice seemed too highly pitched for the rest of him.

"Remember the house rules. First names are in order."

"Very well, er—ah, Bergen. That's a strange first name, isn't it? How did you come by it? Was it your mother's maiden name?" she asked, suddenly feeling foolish for having done so.

"No. It's just a name. My name. I will say this, I like yours. I've never met anyone with it before."

"It's not that uncommon. Perhaps you've been staying here at the Manor too long," she said, flirting impishly, conquettishly. She found herself attracted to him. How could she help it?

117

There was something about him that seemed vulnerable. Certainly not his size or appearance. Then it struck her. It was his size and appearance coupled with the voice. It seemed like a young boy's voice that someone had mistakenly inserted into this beautiful specimen of manhood. She wanted to take him in her arms, whisper in his ear, *"Don't worry. No one will laugh at your tiny voice—not while I'm around."*

"No, that's not it," he said, breaking into her thoughts. "In fact, I get around quite a bit. I look forward to visiting here to recharge my battery, so to speak. When I leave here, I feel there's nothing that can stop me in my line of work."

"Which is?"

He grinned, flashing his teeth in an infectious manner that sent a chill running down Adriana's spine.

"I'm an expediter for a worldwide organization. I do a lot of traveling and meet all kinds of people," he said casually.

A heavyset woman, wearing thick glasses, seemed to appear out of nowhere, carrying a tray filled with goblets. She hesitated near Adriana and Bergen before she said, "Sir?"

Bergen took a glass in each hand, offering one to Adriana. "Thank you, Roseanne," he said. "A toast to you and me, Adriana. May we be friends for a long time and close friends for an even longer time."

She looked up into his ash gray eyes, the strong face looking down at her making her feel at ease. The well-defined features seemed to be a sculptor's interpretation of the perfect masculine face. She returned his smile with one of her own. She raised her glass to her lips, letting the heady liquid flow smoothly down her throat.

When she stopped, she became aware of the silence. Looking about, she found everyone including Olda and Michele, who had returned to the room unnoticed, staring at her. Simultaneously, they burst into applause and cried, "Welcome to Revillion Manor, Adriana."

She looked from face to face until she stopped at Bergen's. "What was that all about?"

"Just a custom here at the Manor. You're officially welcomed now. A fantastic meal will complete it."

Adriana relaxed. Home. She actually felt as though she belonged here and these people, strangers until just a short time ago, were her new family.

The conversation began again and in minutes, Roseanne, the maid, appeared in the doorway to announce dinner. Bergen offered his arm, and they walked slowly to the dining room.

Adriana felt swept back in time. She walked on a cloud in a dream. This couldn't be happening—not to her. It was too good—too nice—too sweet—to be happening to her. Not after the experiences she had been through. Her parents' deaths. She suddenly could see Connie and Tim sitting on the front porch of their home. She blinked and they were gone. The months of silence, hearing only that strange voice uttering the nonsensical things—*one month—it is good—chosen one*. Why

—how could she think of those meaningless things when she should be happy?

She forced herself to look up at Bergen. He was attractive, handsome. And he was hers for the evening. She couldn't explain her shortness of breath whenever she looked at him, not unless his features actually took her breath away. Admitting that she could feel an infatuation growing for the man, she decided to let it run its course—if she were going to be enamored, especially on this island, in this house, with this man, she may as well let it be a full blown romantic interlude.

Tearing her eyes from him she looked straight ahead. What had she seen there in those slate-colored eyes? Concern? Concern for her? She hoped that was it. A feeling for her—one similar to her own for him? That would be almost too much to ask. But considering her last half year, things might be ready to do a complete reversal for her. If it started with Bergen Messenger, she couldn't be happier.

When they entered the dining room, Adriana sucked in her breath. The table, set for twelve, stretched half the length of the large room. Fine china, golden utensils, and sparkling crystal goblets filled the linened board. Candleabra placed every few feet adequately lighted the opulent room. Overhead, heavy beams supported an all wood ceiling.

Bergen held her chair and once she was seated moved around the table to take the place opposite her. The other couples filed in, taking their seats and when they were all present, Roseanne made her appearance, carrying a tureen of soup.

Dr. Lahpavi sat next to Adriana on her right while Olda, at the head of the table and opposite Michele at the far end, was to her left. The dark complected man turned to her and said, "Since your release from Morrison's clinic, has your physical health been adequate?"

Adriana turned to face him, almost stunned by the question. What would his reaction be if she replied in the negative? Perhaps an impromptu physical right here during dinner? She smiled at the lunacy of her thoughts. The man was merely interested in her well-being, she convinced herself, and probably could not make too much conversation outside of his own profession.

"Physically, I've been fine, Doctor. I'm sorry, Rizah—Riz—" she stumbled over his first name.

" 'Doctor' will do nicely, Adriana," he said, staring at her, a certain lack of humor in his eyes as if he had forgotten how to laugh or be happy.

For some reason an uncomfortable feeling swept over her when he flashed his teeth, his smile as mirthless as his eyes. She studied him when he turned his attention back to his bowl of soup. His prominent aquiline nose dominated his oval face while his eyes stared at anything he directed them at from beneath the black bushy eyebrows. His sparse hair was more white than black, contrasting with his olive-toned skin.

"Your health has always been good?" he asked, dabbing at his thick lips with the linen napkin.

"Why—why, yes, it has," Adriana managed, after swallowing the spoonful of soup she had just ingested. She looked across the wide expanse separating her from Bergen and found him engaged in conversation with Angelique. Well, why wouldn't he pay attention to her? She was beautiful with that blue-black hair and startling complexion. Her wide, full lips balanced the rest of her face—the soft sensual brown eyes, the dainty nose, the slightly shallow cheeks. Adriana dropped her eyes to the woman's bare shoulders. The gold lamé dress didn't show above the line of the table, giving Adriana the impression that the actress was attending dinner in the nude. No hope of attracting Bergen's attention while he sat next to the movie star. She turned to her host. How could she be feeling jealousy because Bergen and Angelique were sitting together? She mentally scolded herself.

"How long have you lived here, Olda?" She hoped a lengthy answer would take a lot of time away from her having to contend with the man to her right and, at the same time, keep her mind occupied and off Bergen.

"The house and island have been in my family for almost one hundred years. When my parents died, I became master of Revillion Manor. All of that was quite a while ago."

"I suppose you go to the mainland whenever you want?" she asked, finding her gaze riveted on her escort across the table.

"Why should I? I have everything I need right here. We have an adequate supply of meat in the

122

sheep flock, a large vegetable garden, many fruit trees growing domestically as well as many wild ones. Other than a few drug items and kerosene for the lamps, we have little need of the outside world."

Adriana paused. If she couldn't go to a movie or a football game or watch television once in a while, she knew she'd be a basket case in no time. What did he mean by "we have little need of the outside world?"

Roseanne appeared again to remove the soup bowls and tureen, returning directly with the main course of rack of lamb. When everyone had been served, a quiet fell over the room while they consumed the meal.

When she was almost finished, she turned to her host again and said, "What happens after dinner, Olda?"

"I'm certain you're very tired from your journey, my dear. We'll probably not get into any deep philosophical discussion tonight. It'll be best to wait until you are better acquainted with everyone here before we argue about right and wrong. Perhaps Michele, Charlene, and Deidre will favor us with some music instead." He looked the length of the table at his dinner companions, who nodded diffidently to his suggestion.

The maid quietly moved about the table, refilling wine goblets and after the last glass had been filled, Olda stood, holding his. "A toast, my friends. To the opposites. To the dark."

Everyone scrambled to their feet, raising their

glasses, echoing the strange pledge. Adriana slowly raised the goblet to her lips, quietly repeating the phrases to herself, wondering what they could mean but not questioning the words beyond a casual thought. She emptied her glass and waited for Bergen to come around the table to escort her back to the drawing room.

Once they were seated around the parlor, bits and snatches of talk filtered to Adriana but she ignored them, instead complimenting herself for having carried off the meal without any mishap. It would have been awful to spill soup or some of the mint sauce on her white dress. But nothing had happened.

A ripple of applause washed through the room when the three blond women entered. Charlene carried a violin, Deirdre a cello, and Michele crossed the room to a large harpsichord that had somehow escaped Adriana's attention earlier. A hush fell when the opening chords of a Haydn Trio filled the parlor. Adriana watched, amazed, as the attractive women played, displaying a highly developed technique on each of their instruments.

How could this be happening? How could any of it be real? Any minute she thought she would wake up to find she had been dreaming the whole thing. Bergen, sitting next to her, reached over, lightly touching her hand. That was real. She almost withdrew her own at the cool touch of his fingertips. Turning to him, she smiled. Did everyone here suffer from poor circulation? Why did everyone seem to have cold hands? Reflecting for a moment, she decided that wasn't really true. Angelique's hands had been warm as had the St. Clair couple's. She remembered expecting Dr. Lahpavi's hands to be cold *and* greasy when they met, but his too had been warm and dry. And the photographer, Everhart, had had a nice touch to his hands. She shook her head slightly, shaking the negative thought from her mind. She was imagining it. Still, Bergen's hand had not been very warm.

When the music stopped, Adriana felt truly alive for the first time since she had awakened that awful morning last November. An involuntary shudder tore through her body and she forced herself to sit still.

"Are you all right, Adriana?" Bergen asked, concern evident on his face.

"Just a chill. I'm fine," she whispered, hoping that the Iranian doctor had not heard her complaint. The last thing she wanted was any type of intimate contact with him.

"Girls," Bergen said, raising his voice and sitting up. He looked in the direction of the musicians. "Why don't you play 'Prayer' for us?"

Adriana snapped back, trying to recall what Bergen had said. Finally, she leaned closer to him. "What did you request?"

" 'Prayer.' Michele composed it. I think you'll like it."

She said nothing, leaning back to enjoy the music. It began as an eerie melody from the cello that was soon repeated by the violin in a contrapuntal style until the harpsichord entered. The

125

polyphonic chords began hinting at a dissonance until the two stringed instruments completely drowned out the keyboard. Close second chords glissandoed the full length of the fingerboards, resembling a harsh siren.

Then another voice could be heard along with the two string instruments and the occasional pounding murmur of the harpsichord. More highly pitched than the violin, the new sound rose and fell with the sliding screech of the bows grating across the strings.

Adriana sat forward, straining to identify the new sound. The wind? Perhaps, but certainly not in time with the music. A cat or one of the sheep? She doubted if a sheep could do much more than bleat and a cat would have difficulty in mimicking the sound that suddenly disturbed her.

"What is that? Bergen?" she whispered, turning to him.

Stifling a gasp, she quickly glanced about the room. Everyone sat in the same upright position as the one in which she found Bergen. Each person had their fingers interlaced, their thumbs pointing straight up. All of them appeared to be in a trance of some kind. Adriana could feel her skin crawl, the hair at the nape of her neck moving of its own accord.

When the music stopped, the strange sound could be heard no longer. The others began stirring. Then they applauded.

Completely bewildered, Adriana sat back before she turned to Bergen. "Are you all right?"

"I'm fine," he said, his eyes twinkling. "Isn't that simply a beautiful piece of music?"

At first she didn't know if he might be joking or was being serious. She decided that once the three instruments had begun playing and the haunting melody had disappeared, never to be repeated, that the music was no more than an exercise in noise. Still, what did she know about music? "I—I guess so. I'm not up on very much modern music. Personally, I liked their first selection much better."

"You'll learn to like it after you've heard it a few times."

She fervently hoped the rendition would not be a daily event or that the three girls practiced much during her stay. "What was that other sound I heard while they were playing, Bergen? Did you hear it?"

"I—I didn't hear anything out of the ordinary, Adriana. Perhaps you mistook the sound of the violin for whatever you think you heard. Charlene is a master of the instrument."

From his attitude and manner in answering her questions, Adriana thought she was being told not to ask any more about the music. Although she wasn't familiar with the violin, she felt positive it had been something other than the instrument. She peered up at him and he smiled but said nothing. For some peculiar reason she suddenly felt reassured. Perhaps it had been the violin after all.

Everhart, who had slipped out of the room

unseen by Adriana, returned carrying a camera. "Will some of you gather around Adriana so I may record her first day with us?"

The St. Clairs, Angelique, Rizahghyny, Morrison, and Olda moved toward the fireplace. Rizahghyny motioned for Adriana to join them and, when she hesitated, crossed the room taking her arm. Repulsed by his touch, she reluctantly allowed him to guide her to the group.

"Move to the center, Adriana," Everhart ordered, motioning for the others to move in closer.

Adriana sensed Olda standing directly behind her while the two doctors inched in from either side. She didn't mind Morrison touching her but a mild revulsion swept through her when Rizahghyny's coat sleeve brushed her bare arm. Why couldn't Bergen be standing next to her? Where was he? Off to the side she could see Charlene and Deirdre holding their instruments while out of the corner of her eye she could see Michele seated nearby on the bench at the harpsichord. Bergen moved behind Everhart who had raised the camera to his eye, toward the two musicians at the side of the room. Why wasn't he going to be in the picture? She smiled at the thought of him being in her picture. Did she want that? Now? Did she want to become involved with a man at this time? Would it be too soon? She studied Bergen. If she had to make a choice, it would be him.

"Hold it," Everhart said. The camera clicked, then whirred. "Thank you."

128

Poses were broken and Olda stepped around Adriana. "I think it might be a good idea for all of us to retire. I'm sure that Adriana and Morrison are both exhausted after having traveled so much today. Good night, everyone." He strode toward the foyer and hurried up the steps.

Subdued good nights were said and the couples who had been paired off for dinner made their way to the broad staircase. Bergen slipped his arm through Adriana's and they followed.

"I'm very happy you are here, Adriana. I know you'll enjoy your stay and that it will be the first of many."

She looked up to find his gray eyes almost white, digging into her inner mind, penetrating deeper and deeper until she felt her soul touched —violated. Embarrassed, she coughed. "All of you have made me feel so welcome, that I—" Her voice cracked and she lowered her head.

"Now, Adriana, no tears," he said softly. They continued toward her room in silence.

When they reached the door, they stopped.

"You get a good night's sleep." He grasped her hand in his and bowed, gently kissing it.

"Good—good night, Bergen. Thank you."

He turned, moving down the hall in the direction from which they had come, soon disappearing in the dim lamplight.

Adriana entered her room, quietly closing the door. Quickly undressing, she slipped into her nightgown and stood before the mirror, brushing her hair. The evening replayed in fast motion but stopped everytime Bergen's face hovered in her mind's view. He was handsome. Strikingly so. And considerate. He seemed to be exciting in a quiet, almost restrained way. At least he was younger than Morrison. She felt that a relationship with a man might be a good thing. She would be able to concentrate on something other than herself and her awful memories of the last six months. At least the last four had been progressively better. Better than the first two—of which she had no memory at all. What *had* happened during November and December? She didn't recall anything until the day in January when she had finally spoken to Morrison. She'd have to make it a point to ask him about those two months. Sometime. But not now.

She looked at the brass bed and moaned, anticipating the comfort she would find there. After turning down the bedcover, she went to the dresser to extinguish the lamp. Instead, she merely turned it down low until a murky half light danced about the bureau itself and nowhere else.

Opening the window a few inches, she lay down on the bed. The cool night air prompted her to pull up the sheet and a light blanket. Downstairs, the huge grandfather clock struck once after tolling the Whittington chimes. One o'clock. She tried remembering where the clock stood. Her eyes closed, only to open when the lace curtains ruffled in an errant breeze. They closed again and she slept soundly.

A click sounded in her ears and she sat up in bed, eyes wide open.

"What was that?" she mumbled. She had heard something but what? It had come from—the door? Yes, the door! As if someone had locked it. But that wasn't possible. Olda had said there were no keys to any of the doors except the one with the ugly carving. Had she been dreaming? The thought of sleeping in a house full of strangers without her door being secured had bothered her earlier. Now the sense of anxiety returned.

She eased off the bed and tiptoed across the room. Reaching out, her fingers closed on the brass knob, turning it.

The door was locked.

Downstairs the clock struck three times and she staggered back to the bed. Why worry about it now? she groggily reasoned. If someone had locked her in, they would more than likely free her in the morning. Her eyes flew wide open. That was stupid logic. She blinked when she realized a throbbing headache pounded at her temples. Too much wine and good food. Too much of the good life too soon, too fast. Perhaps she should pound on the door and attract someone's attention. She returned to the oak door and clenched her fist, ready to strike it when she heard a murmuring from far off, growing in volume as the voices approached the door. As they neared, it sounded as if they were chanting something over and over. When the muted voices seemed to be right outside the room, she froze, scarcely breathing. Then the sound faded as the voices moved down the hallway.

Her eyes widened when she could no longer hear the whispers. Had she imagined that? Was she suffering a relapse?

The strange words from her illness spoke in her mind.

"One month."

"It is good."

"You'll be happy."

"Chosen one."

Her brows knitted together as she puzzled over the words. Earlier she had thought of them and had dismissed them. She did the same now, concentrating instead on the voices she had heard in the hall. She stood perfectly still, trying to recall if she had distinguished any words or phrases. It had just been a mumble of sorts. Would she be safe here tonight? Perhaps she had imagined the voices. If the door were locked, at least she would feel safe within her room. She tried turning the handle once more. It refused to move. She returned to her bed and lay down. Her eyelids began drooping and eventually she slept deeply once more.

FIVE

Wednesday, April 24, 1985

WHEN ADRIANA ENTERED the dining room the next morning, she found Morrison sitting at the table, sipping a cup of coffee. Perfect. She would ask him some of the questions that had surfaced since their arrival last evening.

Concern about the incident outside her room and the sudden return of the strange phrases had convinced her that she might need more of Morrison's attention and time.

She remembered awakening, blinking her eyes to the bright sunshine pouring through her window. A light, salty breeze had ruffled her curtains, moaning around the corners as it caressed the house. Could the wind have been her chanters last night? The sound of clicking grated on her and she stared at the door. Was her door being unlocked? Leaping from her bed, she faced the doorway. Again the sound came but from behind her this time. She spun about, moving toward the open window. A shutter, loose on the hinges and not held securely by its hook, strained whenever the wind slipped between it and the house. The gentle zephyr withered, rose again and the louvered covering moved, the dry hinge protesting with a clicking sound. Was this the key she had heard in the door's lock? Still, the knob had refused to yield to her hand the previous night.

After dressing quickly, she started downstairs, thankful to find the lobby deserted.

She moved into the dining room and Morrison looked up.

"Well, good morning, my dear," he said, graciously rising.

"Good morning," she said, taking the chair he held for her.

"I assume you slept well. Most everyone does here."

Adriana sat back while he poured her coffee, studying him. He seemed the same Morrison she had loved and accepted as a friend, not ill at ease or upset as he had appeared last night. Shaking her head, she said, "I guess I did—for the most part."

"The most part? It sounds like you may have had a problem sleeping."

"I want to ask you something but I don't want you to think I'm imagining things."

"That sounds like you want a promise from me."

"Just be my friend, Morrison. Let me tell you

what happened. If you think I still need your help I won't argue, even though I admit I liked the idea of being free."

"It can't be that serious, can it, Adriana?"

Her name rolled off his tongue in a strange way, one that sent a shiver down her spine. He had always called her Adriana, but suddenly his inflection of the word seemed wrong.

She puckered up her mouth for a moment. "I don't know if it's serious or not."

"You'll have to tell me. I'm not much on mind reading." He smiled broadly.

Adriana relaxed, quickly telling him of the chanting she heard when she awoke after retiring, of the locked door, of her confusion, her headache.

"How's your head feel now?" he asked.

"I've just got a bit of a headache. Nothing to be concerned about."

"What time was all this supposed to have happened?"

She stared at him. "Don't patronize me, Morrison."

"I'm sorry. Do you know what time it was when you heard the sounds outside your door?"

Nodding, she said, "I heard the clock in the lobby strike three."

Morrison's forehead wrinkled into neat rows of furrows. "Was your door locked this morning?"

Now it was Adriana's turn to frown. "I'm here, aren't I? Of course it wasn't. But I swear that it was when I tried it."

"You did admit to being confused. Perhaps the new bed, a different room, the whole of Revillion Manor had affected you. It's quite possible."

"I did have a pretty bad headache when I awoke. I guess it was from the wine and the excitement."

"Besides," Morrison said, staring out the window across the room, "Olda told you, I believe, that there are no keys for any of the doors."

"There is for one."

"I forgot. But if there are no keys, how could anyone have locked your door?"

"Well," she said, "that's what it sounded like. I thought I heard it again this morning. But it was only the wind wiggling one of the shutters."

"There. You see? A perfectly logical explanation. You have nothing to be concerned about. Waking up right after going to sleep can work peculiar effects on one."

She smiled, noting the curious expression of relief crossing the psychiatrist's face. Passing it off as being thankful that he wouldn't have to work here on the island or worry about her, she raised her cup to her lips.

"Could I have dreamed the whole thing?" she asked.

"It's possible. The sound of the shutter could have triggered a whole series of thoughts that seemed especially real to you."

"The one thing I have learned from you is never to sell the human brain short of its potential capabilities."

138

"Enough shop talk, Adriana. What are you planning for yourself this morning?"

"I don't really have any plans. What is there to do?"

"If you're thinking of organized activities, there's nothing other than dinners and evenings such as the one we enjoyed last night. Remember the key words here are rest, relaxation."

"What do you suggest?"

"How about a walk around the valley? You really haven't seen anything of the island. Go exploring. How does that sound?"

"You'll come with me, won't you?"

"I wish I could. I have a meeting with Olda in a few minutes." He checked his wrist, smiling when he found it bare. "It was my idea that no one wear watches here. Time seems to crawl—when you are not constantly aware of its passing. The grandfather clock in the lobby runs erratically, I'm told."

Adriana looked at her own wristwatch, vowing to take it off when she returned to her room. "Is there anything I should look for or be aware of when I'm outside?"

"Aware of?"

"You know. Is there anyplace off limits or dangerous? I've never been on an island before."

"The entire place is as safe as your own room." He stood, dabbing at his lips with a napkin. Half folding it, he threw it on the table. "Enjoy your walk, Adriana. I'm sure you'll be happy here."

"I will. Thank you, Morrison—for everything."

He smiled before turning to leave the room.

When she was alone, Adriana finished her coffee and stood to leave. Roseanne waddled into the room, carrying a tray for the final breakfast dishes.

When she passed through the lobby, Adriana checked the clock with her watch. Both indicated it was nine thirty, and she slipped the small piece of jewelry off her wrist, placing it in her jeans' pocket. Who needed to know the time in paradise?

Crossing the wide front porch, she found Rizahghyny Lahpavi, the St. Clairs, and Angelique sitting along the wall to her left. They stared straight ahead, their hands folded in the same peculiar manner as everyone had done several times last night. All of them stared across the valley to the opposite hill, lost in a deep trance or meditation. In school she had talked about transcendentalism with several of the students but hadn't taken a stand on it one way or the other. For some reason she had always felt in control of her own being and thoughts. Her mother had been most responsible for many of her attitudes toward life.

A tear squeezed past her lashes when Connie's face suddenly focused in her imagination. Shaking her head, she walked across the wide path skirting the front of the house, taking a smaller one that led across the valley.

"Are you certain that the fact she heard us chanting last night will not cause us problems,

Morrison?" Olda sat forward, staring at the doctor seated opposite him across the desk. At first he had experienced a sense of panic rising within him. He could not fail—not now. Ever since he had come to the island, he had worked toward this goal. He could not tolerate failure or even a minor setback at this juncture.

"Based on our conversation and the fact that she believed everything I told her," Morrison said, "I'm convinced that I'm still in control of her mind. You see, even though she thinks for herself, she interprets very little of any new stimuli."

"I don't understand completely," Olda said, a puzzled look clouding his angular face.

"Most of the things I introduced to her subconscious during November and December have prepared her. The ideas discussed since then have merely integrated themselves into her overall thought pattern and seem quite natural to her. Whatever she hears or learns from this point on will be accepted without much resistance, almost readily." Morrison smiled confidently, pleased at his accomplishment.

"Even those things," Olda persisted, "that seem foreign and unnatural to her? Things that are completely opposite her parents' philosophies and teachings?"

Morrison nodded. "She might question her ability to judge properly or wonder why she doesn't feel opposed to certain ideas but she will not fight them—or, more importantly, us."

"I'll turn everything of that nature over to you, Morrison. What are the rest of us to do in the meantime?"

"Just carry on in a normal manner. If she asks you a question, answer her. Don't try to fabricate anything. That would be self-defeating. Tell her the truth. If that isn't done, if she doesn't assimilate the knowledge we offer, how will we ever convince her to join us?"

Olda nodded gravely. "Very well. I'll pass the word and have anyone with questions see you. As far as the physical aspects are concerned, Rizahghyny will prevail there."

Morrison stood to leave.

"Where are you going now?"

"I'm to meet Deirdre in a short while. I thought I'd go for a walk and meditate for a while before I do."

Olda chuckled. "You certainly enjoy fucking her, don't you?"

Morrison grinned. "I can't help it. She's utterly fantastic. I've never—"

Olda held his hand up. "Don't go into a tirade on her attributes. I know of them first hand from Michele, although I've abstained for the last six months in preparation."

Morrison turned, walking to the door. "What do you have planned for this morning?"

"I'm going to the library. I've studied the rite every day for the last half year. It must be done properly, correctly, otherwise we could fail. If that happens, none of us will want to accept the consequences."

142

"I'll see you later then," Morrison said, striding through the doorway and into the dining room.

When he reached the outside, he watched Adriana's tiny figure walking toward the hill opposite the house. He'd go another way since he didn't want to talk with anyone right now. Crossing in front of the porch he saw the St. Clairs, Angelique, and Lahpavi frozen in meditative prayer. With dedication such as that, they were sure to succeed.

He recalled the first time he had met Angelique ten years before. She was all but finished in Hollywood at the time and had been introduced to Olda through a mutual friend. Once the aging star realized that the world could be hers through her devotion to the Prince of Darkness, her career turned about when she regained her beauty during a trip abroad. Newspapers, tabloids, and fan magazines broadly hinted at some sort of mysterious surgery or other. However, her indoctrination into the realm of Satan's power had been her career's salvation.

The St. Clairs, literally willing to sell their souls for material wealth and surface success, had built a janitorial empire in New York City when their immediate superior suddenly died, bequeathing them his business and wealth. Everyone who belonged to Revillion's coterie had in some unorthodox manner achieved worldly goods and riches at the expense of their free wills, future salvation, and sense of ultimate well-being. Each had sacrificed their spark of individuality when they chose to follow Satan, accepting worldly rewards in exchange for servitude.

Morrison inhaled deeply, marveling at the tangy saltiness. He loved coming here and almost cursed the necessity of maintaining his practice. Still he had been given success in the practice of psychiatry after he made his agreement. As an additional reward, he had been introduced to Deirdre and her wondrous abilities. A wry expression crossed his face when he thought of his former wife and family, all of whom would have nothing to do with him. Not because they knew of Deirdre but because he had changed from the gentle, benevolent man he had been into a total stranger. He had not changed to his professional world, but in subtle ways had become another person where his family was concerned. When the divorce was final, he and his wife,— ex-wife—had had words outside the courtroom. A vicious scene ensued and his children, all in their teens, sided with their mother.

Embarrassing photos taken at the courthouse appeared in the newspapers and his children elected to look upon their father as having died. There were times when Morrison regretted the loss of their friendship and companionship, but whenever that happened, the mere thought of Deirdre and her tenderness, her body, her mouth, her love for him and him alone swept away the bittersweet memories. A week with the blonde satisfied him for a month or two and he never once repented his decision.

The only person currently on the island who puzzled Morrison was Rizahghyny Lahpavi. Olda had told him that the obstetrician had had communion with the Prince of Darkness just as he had when Satan had been summoned to the island the previous October. Morrison had pondered that aspect more than a little. Did that mean that Olda and Lahpavi were equals in this venture? For some reason he doubted it and the reason he did was simple. Olda was to father the child Adriana was to bear. Lahpavi was merely the attending physician for both the prospective mother and father. Olda had been given strange condiments for the last six months and by his own admission felt rejuvenated. As far as Morrison could determine, Olda was still the main personage next to Adriana.

A pang of guilt suddenly pervaded him. Adriana. Adriana who trusted him. Adriana who had been shocked to the roots of her sensibilities when her parents had been killed. Killed by whom? How far was their Black Leader willing to go? He shook his head. Satan would do whatever he had to in order to gain his ends. The murder of Connie and Tim Brevenger had been necessary and it had been done.

He could not afford the luxury of feeling a culpability where Adriana was concerned. He had done what was commanded of him. He would obey any command to maintain his wealth and Deirdre.

Shaking his head to rid himself of the thoughts of Adriana, he strode away from the house toward the nearby hill. Within an hour Deirdre would be lying with him.

On the far side of the valley, Adriana could see the flock of sheep in bold relief against the green backdrop. The smell of the Gulf swept over the hills into the dale on soft breezes. A peacefulness, a dense quietude pressed in on her. From the first mention of Revillion Manor when Morrison had told her of it, she had wanted to see it, to experience it, to be gently thrown back in time. Her anticipation had not been greater than the island's realization. She knew Morrison would forever be the target of her gratitude.

Morrison. A smile turned up the corners of her mouth when she thought of her infatuation for the older man. At first it had been difficult to admit that he was right when he evaluated her feelings as nothing more than an everyday occurrence in the life of a therapist. When she accepted that, their friendship had begun growing. All he held for her were her own best interests and their successful attainment. How typical of him to suggest a walk by herself and then assuring her that she would be happy.

What had he said? "I'm sure you'll be happy here." He had said that when they parted in the dining room. "You'll be happy here." No. That wasn't it. "You'll be happy." That was the phrase. Had that particular theme come about from her therapy? Had Morrison assured her that if she conquered her problems brought on

146

by the deaths of her parents, she would then be happy?

But it wasn't just that particular expression that had risen to the surface of her consciousness of late. There were the others: *"One month." "It is good." "Chosen one."* All of them went with "You'll be happy."

As she walked, she concentrated on her therapy sessions with Morrison. Try as she might, she could not recall him ever saying any of the phrases from the time she finally agreed to talk that day in his office until just now when they parted company in the dining room. Little by little, every meeting with him was relived over and over in her mind, until she felt that each one could be mentally reenacted in its entirety without missing much at all. Nowhere in the archives of her mind could she find the phrases. Where had she heard them? Positive she had heard them and not read them someplace, she ran through the sessions again, one by one. Still nothing.

Prior to her parents' death? Was that when she had heard them? Could she have been told to be happy? That, "You'll be happy for one month?" That, "It is good for you to be happy for one month?" How could she build in the phrase, *"chosen one"*? Did they even go together? Or were they merely bits and pieces of sentences she could no longer recall? More than likely she had heard something like them when she was growing up. But why were they suddenly being played and replayed like a hit record on the radio?

What about November and December of last year? When she apparently talked with no one? Had someone then said something like the phrases to her when she had no way of responding? She concentrated. November. December. Nothing. Something. A voice. *Yes.* She could hear a voice now and it was saying the phrases. But had that actually been during her two month blackout? Could it have been from a dream?

She shook her head, shivering when a gust of wind enveloped her. Her forehead, her face, her arms, her body were all sheathed in perspiration. What was wrong with her? Too much worry about something over which she had no control? Wasn't that what Morrison would say? Probably.

Never would he admit that it could be a premonition. She remembered a brief discussion they had had on the subject during one of her sessions. He had flatly refused even to entertain the thought. What had she said that triggered that particular discussion? Something about—of course. She had asked him what the phrases meant and he had become agitated. Her explanation had been that she was going to win something—she was being chosen for something—she would be happy because of her being chosen and it might happen in just one month. But he had said it was all foolishness and that she should forget it. And she had until just now. Still it didn't tell her where the phrases originated. Had it been simply a dream? A dream concocted by the mind of an emotionally upset young woman?

Leaning against the trunk of a palm tree, she shook her head. Weak. She actually felt completely exhausted by her thoughts of the last few minutes. Slumping to the ground, she rested her head and shoulders against the rough hole. She closed her eyes for a few moments.

When she thought she heard something, Adriana did not open her eyes. It felt good to have them closed. Shut out the world and its problems. But here on this island there were no enigmas or mysteries or puzzles to bother her. She opened both eyes, swallowing the shriek being born in her throat when she recognized Angelique Pantis standing over her, completely nude.

"I'm sorry," Angelique said. "I didn't want to startle you."

"I—I'm the one who should be sorry, Miss Pantis," she said, struggling to her feet.

"I was going to do a little sunbathing and relaxing and had already undressed when I saw you." She smiled, reaching a hand out to touch Adriana on the arm.

Withdrawing more by instinct than will power, Adriana forced a smile, averting her eyes from the perfect body standing in front of her.

"You're shy, aren't you?" the older woman said.

Adriana could feel her face flushing. "Not— not necessarily. I—I'm just a bit surprised to see one of the most beautiful women to ever appear on the movie screen, standing in front of me, naked as the day she was born."

Angelique laughed, the notes dancing in the quiet of the grove. "I am rather uninhibited when it comes to displaying my body, as you know, if you've ever seen any of my pictures."

Adriana smiled, reticently nodding her head.

"Would you prefer I dressed?" Angelique asked, obviously enjoying Adriana's sense of embarrassment.

"It's not important. I'm going to continue my walk and I don't want to disturb you."

"Really, you wouldn't be disturbing me. In fact, why not join me? There is something very beautiful about lying in the open, letting the sun shine upon one's body, enjoying the caress of soft breezes like the hands of a well-trained lover."

"No, thank you. I do want to see the rest of the island or as much as I can before lunch."

"Very well. If you have any questions, you can come back here and we can talk. I'd like to get to know you better."

Adriana turned to leave but stopped. "May I ask you something, Miss Pantis?"

"Please, call me Angelique."

"How often do you come here to the manor, ah, Angelique?"

"Whenever I can. I find it most refreshing and when I return to work, I find I am rejuvenated to the point of being able to wear everyone out on the set—and off, for that matter." She laughed throatily at the thinly veiled meaning.

"How long have you been coming here?"

"I guess it must be a little over ten years now. I don't know how familiar you are with my past but ten years ago I was all washed up. Since I became a member of Revillion's group, my career has gone into orbit. The success I've had is almost incredible. In fact, I believe the amount of work I do has kept me young—no, more rejuventated me to the point of feeling and looking like a woman in her twenties." She held her arms out at her sides and turned a full circle in front of Adriana. Angelique's breasts stood firmly upright, perfect nipples erect. Her body curved gracefully inward to a tiny waist, flaring out for hips that were not too large or too small. Her firm buttocks, smooth, devoid of cellulite depressions, but flawed with a small birthmark, french-curved around to meet her long shapely legs. Facing her audience of one, she dropped her arms.

Adriana caught herself exhaling. She had actually been holding her breath. It seemed more of a dream than reality that she had just been shown the "body divine," as Hollywood billed the ageless actress, in a one on one confrontation. She could not deny that Angelique Pantis, movie queen, was as beautiful a woman, fully clothed or naked, as she had ever seen.

Dropping her eyes away from the woman standing before her, Adriana said, "What about the others? Have they been coming here very long?"

"I have no idea. When I come here, they are

usually here as well. Perhaps our batteries need recharging about the same time and we just naturally are all here at the same time."

"Well, I think I'll continue my walk," Adriana said turning to leave.

"Adriana," Angelique said huskily.

She stopped, turning to face the woman again.

Angelique stepped toward her, intently fixing her eyes on Adriana's. "Enjoy your walk. You'll be happy here."

Adriana swallowed but said nothing. Did everyone want her to be happy here? Even this movie actress who chose her friends and lovers from among the wealthiest people in the world? Turning once more, she waved and walked away.

Why fight it? If everybody on the island wanted her to be happy, she'd show them. She'd be happy.

The floor of the dale continued curving upward as she approached the hill opposite the mansion. Halfway to the top, she stopped, turning to view the buildings in the distance. From here the house with its attendant outbuildings was even more beautiful since she could see it in its entirety against the opposite side of the valley. Overhead, a flight of pelicans crossed the sky from one side of the island to the other. Flopping back, she lay on the hillside, chewing on a blade of grass. Perfect. It was simply perfect.

A gentle breeze played out, slipping between the fronds and branches of the trees, singing as it made its way. The rustling of the leaves accompanied two stems rubbing against each other in a clicking duet. The sound she had identified in her room suddenly came back. Had it been the noise she had heard the previous night? Or had someone actually locked her door? And if they did, why? To keep her from seeing the chanters or whatever they were in the hallway soon after?

She sat up. "I was not dreaming," she said aloud. "My door was locked. I tried it. I heard chanting right outside my room." A chill coursed down her back and she hugged herself. Why would Morrison lie about it? Was he lying? Did he know about the chanters? What would people be doing chanting and parading through the halls after midnight? No, it was three o'clock. The clock had struck. It didn't run erratically the way Morrison said it did. Her watch and the grandfather clock had been on the same hour and minute when she checked the time before leaving the lobby earlier that morning.

Was Morrison trying to protect her? Protect her from what? He was the one who said she was more normal than most people. For some reason, she felt she must arrive at a conclusion in a very short time. What were her choices? She had imagined the whole thing and needed more help from Morrison, despite what he said about her mental health? On the other hand, if something strange were going on, she could convince Morrison to leave with her today. But Morrison was the one who brought her here—the one who had been here before—the one who said at first she wouldn't like it and then agreed without much argument to bring her here. The thought struck at her like a blow to the face. Could she trust Morrison?

Should she confront Olda? No. His attitude and manner seemed enough to warn her to do no more than pass the time of day with him. Perhaps she was being unfair. But until she could put everything in its place, who could she trust? One of the three girls? Michele, perhaps. Michele had been warm and helpful when she accompanied her to her room for the first time last night. What about Bergen? Where was he today? Maybe he would be the best one to search out and have answer her questions. She quickly found herself wondering why she hadn't thought of him earlier.

Shaking her head at the divergent and confusing elements racing through her mind, she interlaced her fingers, stretching. Her hands caught her attention and, without separating them, brought the palms toward her, extending her thumbs upward in the same manner as she had seen others doing since her arrival. What was the symbology? The trancelike state that seemed to accompany the gesture appeared more than disconcerting when she took everything into consideration. It might be a method of meditating but—

She stood, fishing in her pocket for her watch. Withdrawing it, she held it to one ear to make certain it still ran. The ticking, barely discernible, assured her it was and she marveled at the slow passage of time when she was not constantly aware of it. She still had at least an hour before the twelve thirty lunch time. Turning to continue her ascent to the top of the hill, she stopped. How had she missed it before stopping to lie down?

The small building, windowless on the two sides she could see, hugged the hilltop.

There are books inside. What would make her think something like that?

Making her way toward it, she decided the walls were made of rock plastered over with cement and thought it looked like a miniature school house. Going to the far side, she found a door, apparently the only opening, and reached for the knob. It turned easily and she recalled Olda's statement that there were no keys for any of the doors—save one.

Pushing the door open, she peered into the half light of the windowless room. A centered table and chair seemed to be surrounded by bookcases lining the walls. She smiled at her lucky thought. But why had she had it in the first place?

"Hello?" she called quietly. No answer. Easing forward, she stepped inside. Behind her, the fourth wall held rows of books as well. Her eyes slowly adjusted to the gloom, all the while puzzled as to why a library would be out of the main house and so far removed.

The first books she looked at were in languages she didn't recognize, some so faded they appeared nameless. On the second wall she found one, its title clear in the light. *Lucifer.* The book next to it carried the title *Pwcca.* As she moved around the room, she found books entitled *The Old Religion, Queen of the Witches, Malleus Maleficarum, Inno a Satana and Other Poems*.

Adriana hurried from book to book. All dealt with Satan, witchcraft, or the occult. She looked furtively around the room. Most of the books were old—very old. Some she examined were written in foreign languages, some in old English. Her head spun. What could be the purpose of a place like this? Weren't such things as these books sacrilegious in a way? Did the people who came here actually believe in such things? Or could it only be Olda Revillion who did?

On the table in the middle of the room, a huge book lay open, as if waiting for someone to read its contents or to continue reading. She ran a finger along the lines of old English: *To fummon demons, utterance of the nine divine and myftic names: Eheich, Iod, Tetragrammaton Elohim, El, Elohim Gibor, Eloah Va-Daath, Ed adonai Tzabaoth, Elohim Tzabaoth, Shaddai—*

Adriana stared at the yellowed pages. Why would someone want to summon a demon? Did the others know of this place? Did Olda? He had to. He owned the island and everything on it. Including this building and books. Could Morrison be involved in whatever Olda believed? It seemed obvious that the room was used from time to time, and Olda had to be keeping the room clean since she found no dust or dirt of any kind.

156

She looked about, unsure as to what she should do. Could she trust that Morrison was as ignorant of this library as she had been until a few minutes ago? If she decided that he couldn't be relied upon, how would she get away? There were no boats on the island that she knew of and the one that had brought them had left immediately. Maybe she could hide someplace until the boat came back. She could leave her room tonight and hide in the hills. It seemed to be the only workable alternative at her disposal.

Maybe she was relapsing. Losing her mind for real this time. She knew she shouldn't have read that incantation. Maybe a demon was taking possession of her soul this very instant. Did she even have a soul? She hated to admit it now, but she had grown lax in the practice of her religion after arriving at college. It seemed so much more comfortable to sleep most Sunday mornings than to get up and go to Mass. Her mother would have been unhappy had she known, but her mother was dead. Maybe that was why she had been killed—because of Adriana's lack of faith. No. She and Morrison had discussed that aspect many times and he had finally convinced her that that type of thinking was useless and without foundation.

The thought struck that she should get out of here. It obviously lay off the beaten track for a reason. Not everyone would be allowed inside, despite the absence of a locked door. If she made Olda and the others angry by being caught here, they'd throw her off the island. That in itself would be good. But what if everything here had a logical explanation? She would be throwing away her chance to be accepted as a member.

Glancing about the room to make certain she had not changed anything, she turned to dash from the room and ran headlong into the arms of Olda Revillion.

SIX

Wednesday, April 24, 1985

OLDA'S THIN ARMS held Adriana tightly. Their inordinate strength belied his apparent frailty. The suddenness of his appearance, the shock of being grabbed, the embarrassment of being discovered combined to work their curious effect on her. A scream, blocked by her constricted throat, struggled to be heard. She thrashed about trying to free herself but the old man was too strong.

"Please, Adriana. It's all right. Please, I'm not going to hurt you. Stop fighting. It's all right." He crooned the words, his voice soothing her agitated state.

Little by little she calmed. The thwarted scream was swallowed, forced back to the depths from where it had come. Her erratic breathing slowed until her breasts rose and fell in an easy rhythm. Still, her eyes flitted about, first to him, then around the room, to the table, back to Olda.

"Are you all right now, Adriana?"

She jerkily nodded, then said, "Ye—yes. I'm

fine. I'm sorry. I shouldn't have poked my nose in here.''

He released his hold on her and she stepped back away from him. Slowly moving around the table, she stopped when it separated them.

"If anyone has a right to 'poke their nose in here,' as you put it, it is you."

"Me?" A look of incredulity spread across her face. Why should she have a right to this place? To read these strange, awful books? "Why me, for heaven's sake?"

"Hardly heaven's sake, my dear," Olda chuckled.

"What is this place?" she asked, sweeping the room with one arm. "What kind of weird collection is this?" Adriana looked about the walls at the books wondering how she could feel so calm, so unruffled. For some peculiar reason, she had felt from the moment she walked in that this place would not be strange or foreign to her. A sense of *déjà vu* had allayed what should have been her initial reaction of disgust and rejection. But somehow, she had understood that these books belonged here—and that she did as well. She caught Olda studying her, and she looked away immediately. She would have to ponder her thoughts later when she was alone. Now she wanted some questions answered. Before she could speak, he stepped around the table, pulling the chair out for her to sit down.

"Please, Adriana," he said, indicating she should sit down. "I want to explain some things to you."

Once she was seated, he moved to the far side of the table, sitting on its edge. "First, let me explain a few of the terms of my grandfather's will. The ones that I must strictly obey. You'll recall I mentioned the fact that I couldn't change some things around here. This little library is one of them. Not that I would want to, even if I could."

"You—you like this place? These books?"

"I've grown to like them, yes. To understand them. To appreciate them."

"But they're of the devil—and—and witchcraft —and—and demons and all kinds of gross things," she managed.

"As my grandfather's only living heir, I must maintain his property in exactly the same condition it was the day he died. I inherited everything on this island and in his bank accounts. Over thirty-seven million dollars after the estate was settled."

Adriana winced. "Then why, for heaven's sake, do you take in paying guests?"

"Because I want to share my good life. You've already seen the refinements of our evenings, the relaxed atmosphere of the entire island. The outside world has lost these things. But let me assure you, I do not allow just anyone to come here."

She thought back to the first mention of the manor and its atmosphere that Morrison had made, nodding her head. If the general public knew of Revillion Manor and its tranquility, the place would be overrun by hundreds, even thousands of people and its uniqueness would be lost for all time. More than likely Olda knew what he ws doing in that respect.

Clearing her throat she said, "Did your grandfather believe in witches and demons and things—"

"—that go bump in the night?" he finished for her, smiling. "I imagine he did. I never met him that I can recall. I'm told that I was here with my parents when I was just a babe."

Fully relaxed, Adriana scrutinized her host. He seemed kindly, friendly, even grandfatherly in the way he spoke and looked at her. "Do you believe in these things?" she said in a tiny voice.

"I won't say that I disbelieve that Satan or Lucifer exists. Let me tell you about my background. You see, I was a Roman Catholic priest for nineteen years."

Adriana, shock screeching through her like an electric current, looked up, completely taken off guard.

"I see that you're surprised. In some ways, I am too when I think on it. My parents lived in upper New York and shortly after I was born, they elected to move here to the island to be with my father's father. On the way, there was a train accident and my parents were killed. For some reason, I wasn't even hurt. I was no sooner pulled from the wreckage than the railroad car in which we had been riding caught fire and all of their identification was burned. I was placed in an orphanage and as a ward of the state of Georgia, where the accident took place, was shuttled from one institution to another. Eventually, all record of how I had become a responsibility of the state and where I had first entered a home for children became so mixed up, no one could trace it."

"How did your grandfather find you, then?" Adriana asked, caught up in the plight of a small boy.

"I wore a locket with the name Revillion inscribed inside, and this proved to be the single clue that led to my discovery many years later. Because my grandfather did not read newspapers and had no other communication with the outside world other than an occasional trip to the mainland for supplies, he knew nothing of the accident or the deaths of his son and daughter-in-law until much after the fact. By the time he learned of the mishap, he was not aware that I still existed."

She marveled at the offhanded manner in which Olda told of the tragedy. Still, he had never known his parents as a boy or an adult and probably thought of them as just two people who had affected his life in some way.

"For some reason I have never been able to understand, I was sent to an orphanage in New York State when I was about three years old, and was raised in a home run by some order of nuns. It was there I became interested in the priesthood. A kindly Jesuit, who acted as chaplain for the home, convinced me his order was the one to join when I let it be known I wanted to become a priest.

"After my ordination I taught college courses

in theology, and one day an attorney, one who worked for my grandfather, came to my quarters and informed me that I was the sole heir of a large estate. You see, when my grandfather eventually learned that my parents had been killed on that train, he was named executor of their estates. It was only then that he discovered that I had been born. He started the search for me when he found out from the railroad company's records that no baby's body had been found at the site of the accident."

Adriana held up her hand indicating he should stop. "Why did it take so long? To find you, that is. Why couldn't he just have gone to the orphanage for your records?"

"This was quite some time after I left Georgia for New York. Remember I said my records became so mixed up, no one could learn anything from them. But eventually, my grandfather's lawyers solved the mystery and discovered me because of the locket. Revillion is not a common name. The search had been an obsession with him until the day he died. His will allowed unlimited expenses for locating his only living relative. Almost fifty years after my parents died and five years after he died, they found me."

"How ironic," Adriana said realizing the frustration of Olda discovering that he was totally alone. She could sympathize with that feeling. A pang of hurt for the old man's unrealized dream coursed through her.

"At first," Olda continued, "I was quite dubious but they finally convinced me that I was

166

who they said I was. They had straightened out the records and a picture they showed me of my father could very easily have been me. The resemblance was truly uncanny." He stood, holding out a hand toward his enraptured audience. "Come, we can talk while we walk back to the house."

Reluctantly taking it, she stood, walking around the table. She found herself drawn to this man who seemed to share a similar background to her own. "If what you say is true, Olda, and I have no reason to disbelieve it, why did you give up the priesthood?"

"I thought you might ask that," he said, making a gargling sound in his throat before clearing it. "Believe it or not, I had never been baptized. This oversight nullified all of the sacraments I had received, erasing my priestly vows—everything. Of course, I could have been baptized and everything would have been fine. Even the baptism of desire wherein I could have merely wished to have been thusly indoctrinated into the Church would have sufficed had I not had time to go through the ritual itself."

"I don't understand, Olda."

"I imagine they don't teach much about such things anymore. If I had been, let's say, in a car accident and was not a Catholic, I could *want* to be baptized and if no one was around to perform the rite, my desire would be sufficient in the eyes of—of your God."

"My God?" Adriana said, pulling her hand from his.

"Your God. I no longer embrace any faith other than that of my father and grandfather. You see, I was given the chance to remain in the priesthood but I decided the wealth would be more beneficial to me in this lifetime. Maybe I acted in haste but I haven't repented in leisure." He threw back his head, laughing heartily at his joke.

Adriana failed to see the humor of it. "The faith of your father and grandfather? What might that be?"

"Let me pose a philosophical question for you, my dear. What if the concept as generally accepted by mankind that God is good and wrong is evil were in error? What if the idea of God is evil and the accepted idea of evil as represented by Satan were the true path? How would you feel about your past life?"

Adriana stopped, looking aghast at him, her face immediately softening as if she understood what he meant. "You're serious, aren't you?"

"I've very serious. For ages, man has accepted that notion of good and evil almost without question. Oh, there have been sects that deviated from that theory and some have gone to the full extent, worshipping the devil and creating evil deeds as being positive functions."

"Do you believe this?"

He stopped, turning to face her before answering. "I live it, my dear."

Why didn't she feel threatened by this man, by his ideas, his philosophy? In the farthest recesses of her mind, similar thoughts suddenly surfaced as though she had studied the same thing or been told about the conception. "Don't you find it difficult to accept this, Olda, considering your past as a priest and being reared a Catholic?"

"Now that I understand, I have no problem. What about you? Morrison has told me that you were raised a Catholic. Do you find the ideas so far afield from your own upbringing?"

Adriana furrowed her brows. "I do and I don't," she managed. How could she even contemplate the thought? How many times had her mother and she talked about the convent life Connie had led? Always, Adriana had found the stories fascinating, the little vignettes fulfilling, whenever she had asked a question her mother felt could be answered by something out of her own past. Still, here she was giving consideration to the theory that the negatives rather than the positives of her own background are the cornerstones of belief and action. But was her life until now a postive one? Could her mother have been so wrong? After all, she had quit the convent for a life more "natural," as she had said, when her daughter asked the inevitable question.

"You don't find the whole idea upsetting, do you?" he asked taking her hand in his again to resume their walk across the valley.

"I—I'm not certain. I think perhaps I do."

Olda's brow furrowed but smoothed immediately when he found her studying him from the corner of her eye. "Does the idea of something new or contrary to what you believe truly unsettle you? Why, if man had been like that through history, we would still be living in trees or caves. I—"

"Please, Olda," she broke in, "don't confuse me anymore than I am right now. Are you trying to convert me to your way of life, religion, beliefs?"

"I'm afraid I have wronged you, Adriana. Naturally, if you should so choose, I would be delighted. The rest—"

"What about the rest? Do they believe as you?"

"Of course."

Good God, what had she gotten herself into? "Even Morrison?" she asked, feeling her spirit sag before the old man answered.

"Most especially, Morrison."

"Angelique Pantis? The St. Clairs? Every—?"

"All of them. However, do not feel threatened. Should you decide against us, no hard feelings will exist. You will be free to go."

Her head swirled. Suddenly she felt more alone than at any time since November when she had been told of her parents' deaths. "You're sure? You're not kidding me? I can just leave? You'd trust me?"

"Of course, my dear. We have nothing to hide, nothing to fear."

"Then, I think I'd like to leave right now."

Olda chuckled. "That I'm afraid is impossible."

Adriana felt her throat thicken. "Wh—why?"

"First I'd have to contact the captain of the cruiser who brought you here. Secondly, in case you haven't noticed, the clouds are building up. I'm afraid we're in for a spring storm."

She jerked her head upward, toward the blackening sky. How had she missed the rolling clouds hovering overhead? What would the house be like during a thunderstorm? Real cozy. Very homelike. Super friendly, especially with everyone in the house worshipping Satan instead of God. Maybe the storm would pass over. Maybe Olda was wrong about everyone on the island sharing his beliefs. Maybe she'd be able to find an ally among them. But who? Michele? Michele had been friendly and warm last evening when she and Morrison had arrived. Could she be a member as well as Morrison? She had been totally fooled by him. If Michele were, then her duplicates must be also. Lahpavi looked like he would belong to something as weird and offbeat as a devil worshipping cult.

But what about Bergen? Did she even want to know if he embraced the same strange beliefs? His face took shape before her mind's eye. She sucked in her breath—God, he was handsome. Even if he did think as Morrison and the others, would she find him unattractive because of it? For the time being, she decided not to ask—prolong the thought of him being the way she wanted, not the way he probably was. She needed time to think, to weigh the pros and cons of accepting people who were as different as any she had ever met. If she liked Bergen the first time she met him, it would seem logical to continue liking him thereafter, despite his religious beliefs.

She shook her head. She was mixed up. Looking at Olda, she asked, "What about Michele and the other two girls?"

"Ah, the girls. Quite different cases, those three."

"You mean they're not—not like you?" She hesitated, fearful of what his answer might be. She would feel better knowing that she might have a friend or friends present. Noting just a hint of a smile at the corners of the old man's mouth, she concluded that perhaps Olda was a friend as well.

"Those three are nothing like me. Or like those who come here to the island to worship Satan. And," he added with a laugh, "I don't mean in appearance, either."

She breathed an inaudible sigh. Thank God. She wasn't alone. Olda must have told her the truth. She would be able to leave with no fears about repercussions because of the information she had been told.

As they approached the house with its broad porch guarding it, she saw the St. Clairs, Morrison, and Everhart sitting, their hands held in front, thumbs upward, staring across the valley.

"Why?" she said simply, nodding toward the foursome who apparently did not notice their approach.

Olda smiled benevolently. "They're praying. Praying for you and your conversion."

Adriana shuddered. Awful. Simply awful to believe in such things. But the one aspect that bothered her the most was the absence of total

172

revulsion on her part. She somehow seemed to accept the thought of such a negative religion without question. As if, Olda had said, *"Hey, look, we're all Holy Rollers here and would like to have you join us in a jaunt across the floor."* She really didn't think harshly of him or his proposal. Why didn't she? Couldn't she? Could she still be harboring doubts where her own faith was concerned? Skepticism had surfaced shortly after first speaking to Morrison in his office. She had wanted to blame God for the deaths of her parents. Morrison had steadfastly—Wait, no he hadn't. In fact, now that she concentrated on that portion of her therapy, she suddenly found herself amazed at the fact that he had almost agreed with her. Had Morrison used suggestions and subliminal ideas to prepare her for Olda and his sales talk? She'd have to think on that more once she was safe in her room. Without the door locked.

Walking up the wide front steps, she turned to Olda and said, "What about Charlene, Michele, and Deirdre?"

"What about them?"

"If they don't belong to your religion, what are they doing here? Why are they sealing themselves off from the rest of the world by working here? They're so beautiful they could be top models or actresses or anything they wanted to be in the outside world."

"Well, they are a great help to me in operating Revillion Manor."

"They look like college girls."

"My, no. They're beyond college age. I like to think that the atmosphere at the manor has kept them young. I have no idea how old they might be. In fact, I could say, I inherited them along with everything else."

"You don't inherit people," Adriana scoffed.

"Of course not. But they were here when I arrived and all three had been working for my grandfather for some time."

Adriana stared at him. He appeared to be sincere but how could that be? The girls were simply not that old. Olda had said that he had been a priest for nineteen years. If he had been ordained when he was about twenty-five, he would have been forty-four years old or so when he took over Revillion Manor. He looked to be about sixty-five years old now, if her estimate were correct. At times because of his heavily lined countenance, he looked much older. But even so, that would mean he had been here for at least twenty-one years. The three young women could not be much over twenty-two or twenty-three years of age. She voiced her disbelief.

Olda shrugged. "I don't pretend to understand too much about women. I do know some of the actresses in Hollywood are well preserved into their fifties and sixties and some even beyond that. Take Angelique for example. Perhaps my girls have discovered a fountain of youth on the property and are keeping it to themselves."

Suddenly Bergen Messenger crowded back into her mind. Where was he? She would like to

174

speak with him, to make an ally of him, if possible.

Before she could speak, Olda said, "It is a shame that Bergen had to leave this morning."

Her heart sank. "He—he's gone?"

"Yes, he had to call on a client in Egypt or some such place. He'll be back."

But when? Adriana wondered. Could she trust the three blondes? After all, they worked for Olda. Bergen didn't. He came here of his own volition. If she had to rely on someone, she would prefer that it be Bergen.

Inside, Roseanne confronted them with a tray holding wine goblets. Olda took two, offering one to Adriana. Lifting the glass to her lips, she sipped the tart liquid, inhaling its fruity bouquet.

"May I propose a toast, my dear?" Olda asked.

She nodded, believing there could be no harm in complying.

"To what might have been." He raised the goblet to his lips and downed the wine.

Adriana took most of the small glass's contents and said, "It might be yet." After all, she had thought along the same lines herself while talking out her feelings and problems. But had she been led to talk like that? Encouraged to blame God? By Morrison? Of a sudden, she caught her thoughts. No! Most emphatically, no. It was wrong. There was no way it could ever be right. Worship the devil, indeed. She finished her wine.

No sooner had the glass been emptied than

Roseanne was prancing about behind Adriana with her tray. Olda took her empty one, placing both on the silver platter, exchanging them for full ones. He overcame Adriana's mild objection by thrusting one into her hand.

This time she sipped. Moving into the drawing room, she sat down in a lady's chair next to a marble-topped lamp table. "Don't think I'm bored," she said, yawning when Olda sat on the opposite side, "but I'm deliciously sleepy. All the fresh air and long walk this morning, and now the wine is getting to me."

"Why don't you take a nap. You can eat later when you awaken." He stood, gliding toward the foyer. "I'll call Deirdre to help you to your room."

Seconds later, when Deirdre entered, moving directly toward her, Adriana wished it had been one of the other two. She still recalled her surprise when Deirdre threw her arms around Morrison's neck, kissing him. When she stood, she felt dizzy. Deirde reached out, taking her arm.

"Olda asked me to help you to your room."

Adriana nodded. When they left the drawing room and entered the foyer she saw Olda standing nearby. "Forgive us, Olda," she mumbled. "I didn't mean to be nasty with you. Bear with me, I'll be all right."

He smiled but said nothing.

How could so little wine be affecting her this way? She felt drunk. No, not drunk but simply unsteady on her legs. She hadn't eaten anything. That could be it. Her vision seemed clear. She was merely tired. Tired, hungry, and two too many glasses of wine. Deliciously tired. Beautifully sleepy. A nice nap would fill the bill.

Deirdre held her arm in a steadying grip but released her when Adriana stopped to study a photograph hanging near the first step. Stumbling toward it, she focused her eyes to study the picture. The people in the photo were dressed in what she guessed was turn of the century clothing. The mansion had served as backdrop. A tall, older man stood in the middle of the front row with no one standing directly on either side of him. She moved closer. The first row had a man on the end and then there was enough room for at least two people before the row continued with the central figure. Another space big enough for one person and then a woman and—she gasped. How could Olda be in a picture like this? But there he stood. She turned to Deirdre. "Is that Olda?"

"No, that's Olda's father and this woman is his mother. This lovely gentleman in the center is Olda's grandfather," she said pointing first to the man on the right side of the front row, then to the woman at his side, and finally to the figure in the middle.

Adriana noted despite her foggy state of mind that the house appeared to be exactly the same as it did today when she and Olda crossed the valley.

"I'm sure Olda has told you that he must keep the property exactly the same as when his grandfather was living. He has, hasn't he?"

Adriana nodded. "When was this picture taken?"

"I don't remember the exact date but it was taken shortly before Olda's parents died."

Adriana nodded again, turning to follow the striking woman up the stairs. Something Deirdre had said didn't quite make sense. But what had it been that upset her? She watched the blonde turn to continue up the right side of the split staircase and froze.

The stained-glass window that had caught her attention the previous evening and had been dismissed, when she couldn't quite make out the picture depicted, now glared forth, spewing shafts of dark blues and greens and blood-reds over the foyer. What she had thought of as an angel the night before now loomed larger than life and clearly depicted a brooding, winged Lucifer, pondering upon his throne. Smaller demons of less import writhed in supplication at his feet as they worshipped him. Recalling her conversation with Olda in bits and pieces, she grinned foolishly and wondered where the master of Revillion Manor might be hiding in the picture. The bright amber eyes of Lucifer, staring at the steps, transfixed Adriana for a long minute. She seemed hypnotized by the bits of glass.

Snapping from the brief moment of nothingness, she continued up the steps. When they reached Adriana's room, Deirdre left without saying anything. Grateful to be alone, she lay on the bed trying to put her thoughts in order, the strange window on the landing all but forgotten. She closed her eyes in an attempt to concentrate better. What had been bothering her? Something Deirdre said had not been quite right. But she couldn't put her finger on the error.

Satan is good. God is evil.

It is good.

Come, join us. Had she heard that one before?

You'll be happy.

Chosen one.

One month.

The bits of thought exploded in her mind like flashbulbs. Her eyes opened wide before drooping, closing as a deep sleep quieted the troublesome thoughts.

When Adriana started up the stairway following Deirdre, Olda turned, striding toward the front entrance. The five people meditating roused themselves when he called their names. Charlene and Michele joined them, one on either side of the old man, linking their arms through his.

Morrison, his forehead sweaty, studied him. "You spoke with Adriana?"

"Yes."

"Are you satisfied that it is as I told you?"

Olda nodded. "She vacillates between understanding and rejecting. To avoid the risk of the latter happening, we must act as soon as possible. When is she most likely to conceive?"

Morrison looked away for a scant moment before returning his eyes to him. "I checked her records earlier this morning before I came to breakfast. According to them, her last menstrual period began exactly two weeks ago tomorrow, on the eleventh of April. She should be fertile between yesterday and the day after tomorrow."

"Excellent. Excellent," Olda said, rubbing his hands together. "We will act tonight. Deirdre has taken her to her room. I had a sedative added to her second glass of wine. She should sleep all of this afternoon. While she does, the rest of us can prepare." He turned to Lahpavi. "See to it that the first drugs are put in her evening meal."

Lahpavi nodded his understanding. "I have been ready for this ever since I was told of the plan seven months ago. Everything is in readiness."

"Good. The chapel must be prepared before nightfall. Then—" His voice trailed off, his lips parting in a malevolent smile.

The people sitting before him bowed their heads, interlacing their fingers at the same time, thumbs upright, and continued their meditation.

Adriana stared at the head lying on the floor at her feet. A scream fighting to be released clogged her throat until she thought she would suffocate. Her mother's eyes opened, staring at her. Unfriendly eyes, not at all like her mother's, darted from side to side. The lips, white in death, parted in a half smile.

"Addy? Adriana? *It is good!*" Her mother's head laughed. *"You'll be happy, my little chosen one."* The hollow voice stopped suddenly when

180

worms, white maggots began flowing from the orifices of the skull. Melding into one, they formed a long black snake, whose head undulated, changing shape constantly until it appeared like a goat's head—then more like a familiar visage she knew from someplace. Where had she seen such a face and head? One with curved horns crowning it? Again the face changed, becoming Morrison Tyler for a split second before writhing into Olda Revillion's countenance. His nose shifted, becoming more finely made, his narrow-set eyes moved away from each other until they beamed at her in a loving way from beneath arched brows. The whole head slipped away in form taking on a more rounded appearance, the white hair capping it darkening to a dusty blond until it dominated the mouthless face. Lips spread forth once more but not those of Olda Revillion. Instead, they were much softer, more kindly, and protected by a moustache. Relief swept away her sensations of fear and revulsion. Bergen Messenger smiled at her. "Adriana," the head at the end of the long black snake whispered.

"Bergen?" she mumbled aloud. "You're back? I'm—Bergen? Where are you?"

"Adriana?"

His voice changed. More high pitched than normal. More feminine. More sensual.

"Adriana?"

The snake spewing forth from her mother's head disappeared. Bergen's image withered, fading from sight. Only her mother's head lay at her feet. Again the mouth opened, emitting a roaring crash.

Adriana sat up. Her dark room surrounded her. Outside, wind scourged the house. Rolls of thunder echoed overhead. A blast of light blinded her momentarily. Reverberating explosions directly above the house shook the walls, the windows, the doors. She threw her hands over her eyes until the lightning died, leaving the room black once more.

Then she recalled seeing someone standing next to the bed, all blue white in the sudden brilliance of the lightning. "Who's there?" she asked breathlessly.

"It's me. Charlene. I hope I didn't frighten you."

"How—how long have you been standing there?"

"I only came in a few seconds ago. I called you but you were really sleeping soundly." Charlene's voice drifted away.

When a match flared at the dresser, Adriana relaxed. The warm friendly light of the kerosene lamp fanned out, swathing the room in gold. "I must have been dreaming. It—it was horrible." She shuddered when the imperfect pictures formed in her mind for a brief replay.

The wind, rising in its furious attack on the house, defiantly screamed galelike curses at the people safe within.

"How long has it been storming?" Adriana asked.

"About thirty minutes or so. It should let up

soon. Are you hungry? From what Olda said, you haven't had anything to eat all day."

Adriana thought for a moment. She hadn't eaten breakfast. After her walk and talk with Olda, she had had two small glasses of wine and then Deirdre had brought her to her room. She *hadn't* eaten all day.

"What time is it?" she asked, looking out the window, unable to determine if it were still daytime or early evening.

"Almost eight o'clock."

"I should be hungry enough to eat a door! But I'm not certain if I want to come downstairs for a formal dinner or not."

Charlene smiled, her full lips parting to reveal perfect teeth. "We've all eaten. Perhaps a light supper here in your room might be the thing for you. How does that sound?"

Adriana nodded. "Make it light and not too filling. I feel like I want to sleep the clock around even though I've slept for almost eight hours."

"How are you feeling? You don't feel ill or anything, do you?" The tall blonde moved to the side, her eyes revealing genuine concern for the girl lying on the bed.

"I'm just drowsy. I'll probably wake up about midnight and not be able to go back to sleep. I feel fine otherwise."

"I'll get something and be right back."

"If you see Olda, tell him I'm sorry. I'm certainly not behaving the way the other guests are, am I? Tell him I appreciate his patience with me today. I acted terribly."

"He thought nothing of it. Believe me, Olda is a most patient man. If you want to learn more about—about things here at the manor, he will be happy to inform you. All of us will, in fact. If you choose not to, we'll understand."

Without another word, she turned, leaving the room.

Adriana sat back on the bed. Charlene and her two look-alikes still remained a puzzle that tantalized her. How could they have been here when Olda assumed control of his grandfather's estate? That was just not possible. Then, too, something Deirdre had said bothered her just before she went to sleep. Something about a picture. The picture in the foyer. Something about Olda. No, not him his parents. Olda had said they were killed on the way to visit or move here. Deirdre said the picture was taken a short while before they died. One of them had their facts wrong or was lying.

Rising from the bed, she moved to the window. Flashes of lightning danced from cloud to cloud, building a charge to strike the earth again. For the moment, the wind had died down and the thunderclaps were not as threatening as they had seemed when she first awoke. Tomorrow she'd speak to Olda about leaving. Considering what Olda had said, she would have no problem there. They wouldn't hold her against her will.

A chill swept over her. All she had on was a nightgown. When had she changed? Maybe Deirdre had helped her? Who was she kidding? She didn't know anything about anyone here, except Morrison. And she wasn't that sure about him anymore. She had never once suspected that he held beliefs different from anyone else she had ever met. She'd simply have to disregard everything that had been said by everyone since she arrived.

The door swung open, bringing her about to face Charlene who balanced a tray on one hand, closing the door with the other.

"How are you feeling?" she asked, placing the tray on dresser.

"Better," Adriana said softly. "What did you bring me?" Her stomach growled at the thought of food. But was food what she needed right now?

"Some broth in a cup, several slices of bread and cheese," Charlene said lightly. "It's all light and will be much better for you than a heavy meal."

"Will you join me?"

"I'm afraid I've eaten. Besides there's just enough there for you."

Adriana picked up the tray, placing it on the small table nestled against the corridor wall.

"Enjoy," Charlene said leaving the room. The door closed with a loud click.

If she could only lock the door herself. Adriana sat down at the table, inhaling the aroma. It smelled like the meat they had had the previous evening. Mutton broth? A little wouldn't hurt her. They would hardly take the risk of poisoning someone. She sipped it, swishing it around her mouth. It had just a faint undertaste that she couldn't place. Almost a musty taste as if it had been stored in a damp place. In a way, the soup tasted like the house smelled. Still, she had never had mutton before, quickly deciding that it must naturally taste like this.

A smile played on her lips. Paranoid. She was becoming afraid of her own shadow. Olda held some peculiar beliefs. Some of the others did as well but not all of them. He had said the three girls were not believers. At least he had implied that. What had he said exactly? They were not like him—or the other believers.

Nibbling at the bread and sliced cheese, she took several more spoonfuls of broth before pushing the tray away. She was just too upset to eat.

Something about her partially eaten supper and the tray it rested on bothered her. No utensils of any kind. Clever. They thought of everything. A knife in the wrong hands could be a dangerous weapon. She might hurt someone and run away. But to where? The island was as effective a prison as any bars on windows or locks on doors. She couldn't escape. Or was her paranoia taking charge again?

Outside, the thunder began again, flashes of lightning stabbing the darkness with bloodless wounds.

Moving back to the bed, she sat down heavily. Her head spun. Her arms barely moved when she willed it and her legs felt as if they weighed tons. She should stay awake. Stay awake, defend herself. Her eyelids drooped. What was wrong with her? She might still be tired. Perhaps a little nap wouldn't hurt. If they were going to come, it wouldn't be this early. Of course. Sleep now. Wake up later. Be wide awake when they do come for her. Argue with them. Show them the error of their ways. Convince them. Convert them back to Christianity.

Eyes half closed, she chuckled at the thoughts zipping through her mind. No one was going to come and *get her*. Her whole body was tired. Her thoughts were crazy at best. Her mind was just as tired. Turning, she pulled her legs up on the bed and lay back. She stared at the ceiling. Downstairs, she could hear the clock strike nine. Then, after the quarter hours, ten. Eleven. Twelve.

Nothing happened. One o'clock came. She continued staring at the ceiling. Two o'clock.

Get up, walk around. She marveled at the fact that she had stayed awake so long. Maybe she could make it through the whole night. Get up. Her legs refused to move. Sit up. Prop herself up with her arms. Her arms wouldn't move.

Then she heard a click at her door as the knob turned. She tried to raise her head, to see if the door was opening or being locked again. Her head and neck rejected her brain's command to move.

Desperately trying to wriggle a finger, a toe— something—she sobbed.

The door opened quietly.

She rolled her eyes toward their bottom. Straining to look down the length of her body, she struggled to see who or what was coming into her room.

Part Three

THE MACULATE
CONCEPTION

SEVEN

Thursday April 25, 1985

IT WAS maddening. Frustration as Adriana had never known pummeled her thought processes. She couldn't move. Mentally commanding that something move—anything—she remained lying rigidly on the bed. In the flickering lamplight she stared at the door, tears forming in her eyes from fear of the unknown as much as the extra effort she exerted to see beyond the flat plane on which she lay.

The door swung slowly inward. The murky shadows beyond the feeble halo of light moved, taking on form until a robed figure stepped into the room.

Her mouth, frozen in a partially open position, would not respond to her commands. Scream. She wanted to scream for all the world to hear. Nothing happened. Her vocal chords, held tightly in the bonds of paralysis, would not function.

The only thing she could move were her eyes. They darted from side to side like those of a trapped wild animal. She could do nothing but watch as the shadowy figure at the foot of the bed was joined by three more dark shapes. Floating to the dresser, one blew out the lamp, plunging the room into an onyx blackness.

Her mind raced. She had to get away, but how? Who were the people dressed in what appeared to be monk's robes? She couldn't see their faces, which were hidden by cowls. What did they want? Again she tried to scream, emitting only a gurgling sound. How could she be paralyzed? What had caused it? The wine? Something in the wine? She had slept soundly after having it. The food? Could the food have been drugged? Even her voice was gone, but she seemed to be thinking clearly, analytically. She wanted to scream, *"God help me! Someone help me!"* Only a bubbling sound gargled in her throat and mouth.

The four figures moved to the bed before she could make out the darker shapes in the gloom. One stood at each corner. She willed, demanded that her body move, to cringe and back away from her enemies but nothing happened. She sensed strong hands gripping her legs and upper body. She tried vainly to resist but succeeded only in her mind. Physically she was powerless.

Outside, a new storm began building, sending jagged lightning forth to reveal hidden secrets lurking in the shadows surrounding Revillion Manor, even daring to penetrate the inner

194

reaches beyond the darkened windows of the huge house. Blue-white light spasmodically filled the bedroom for brief seconds before blackening it and Adriana's vision. Tympani rolls of thunder rose and fell, cresendoing above the island until the window casements rattled.

Adriana felt herself being lifted, lifted high until she realized she was being carried on the shoulders of those holding her. As she was being borne away from her bed and the window toward the murky ink of the hallway, she knew she would not be able to make out anything, much less her captors' hidden faces once they entered the dimly lit hall.

Reaching the corridor, she heard the breathing of more people. She was doomed. Her bearers turned to the right, moving slowly toward the black hall she had stumbled into the first night she arrived. The lamp at the end, its light retained by the raven drapes hanging along the walls, merely served as a beacon. When they reached the end, the door with the horrible carven face stood open and the procession passed through, descending a long flight of twisting, turning stairs.

Once they stood on level flooring again, Adriana could make out little of the place in which she found herself. Another single lamp did nothing to illuminate her surroundings.

Could she be dreaming? Dreaming again? She recalled the ugly nightmare she had been experiencing when Charlene had mercifully awakened her. Was all that she experienced now nothing more than a dream? Still, it seemed so realistic. Too realistic.

Detecting a faint smell of incense dawdling in the air, she blinked her eyes when she heard a lamb bleating somewhere in the room. This had to be a dream. She could hear the muffled rumbling of thunder outside but it sounded distant, far removed from where she had been brought. She sensed more people surrounded her in addition to those carrying her immobile body.

"Place her on the altar," one of the robed figures tersely commanded.

She knew that voice. It was Olda. Olda Revillion. The devil-man. She could feel herself being lowered until she lay on a cold surface. *Altar?* Were they going to sacrifice her to some heathen god or demon? She was going to be murdered by lunatics. But where they lunatics? Mad people?

Amazed by her ability to rationalize both sides of the issue, her mind froze when the phrase *chosen one* invaded her thoughts. Was this the meaning of that recurring idea? What were the other ones? *Be happy* or something. *One month?* One month of what? Torture? Imprisonment? *It is good?* What if it were good? But good for whom? What if she liked whatever they had in store for her? Suppose Olda were right in his perverse way of thinking. Good is evil—evil is good. Maybe she should be willing to see what being the chosen one involved. If it *were* good and she, the chosen one, would be happy, what else mattered? Would it last only one month—

this status that seemingly was about to be bestowed on her?

Cold hands touched hers, moving them until they extended at right angles to her body. A sound of tearing cloth puzzled her for a moment but she quickly realized her gown had been torn away when a new degree of coolness swept over her body.

A sudden flare of light blinded her. Someone was lighting candles. Out of the corners of her eyes she could see her own hands holding black tapers. Each figure was given a rushlight, its flame dancing, bobbing at the top, casting shadows over the holder's partially hidden features, exposing part of a nose here, a bit of lip there—but never the whole face.

One of the robed people moved closer and Adriana could see Michele's well-defined features in the soft light.

"Don't be frightened, Adriana," Michele whispered. "We will not hurt you. No harm will come to you. Relax and enjoy." She reached out, pulling the remnants of the torn gown away, exposing Adriana's body to the stares of the congregation.

A sob formed deep within Adriana's breast but would not sound. Her eyes widened, horrified to see Michele holding a knife, its blade at least eighteen inches long. The woman drew a circle in the air above the prostrate figure, slowly bringing the point of the weapon to the bare breasts, first touching one nipple, then the other. Carefully, she laid the knife on Adriana's abdomen, the point hovering over her navel. The figures surrounding the table backed away, moving downward, and she decided the altar on which she lay must stand on a raised platform of some sort.

What would happen next? Why didn't she feel some degree of shame or at least discomfort, lying nude on a table in front of people she hardly knew, assuming those in the robes were the same ones she had met two days before? Even Morrison, if he were one of them, was looking at her body, the body she had wanted to give him. An ironic chuckle fought to be heard but her vocal chords resisted. Had he saved her for something other than the sexual gratification she had offered?

Her thoughts stopped when a soft tinkling bell sounded someplace in the room. Voices began chanting. "Xilka. Xilka. Besa, Besa! Barahi Iaca Bachabe! Pala Aron Asinomas."

When the strange words finished ringing in her ears, a single voice, one she recognized as Olda's said, "I will go unto the altar of *my* Lord."

The balance of the group answered, "And unto *my* Lord, give the sins of my life."

Adriana's eyes flooded with tears. This couldn't be happening. Her mental protestations withered when Olda continued.

"I sin for smooth devils. Horned devils. Sullen devils. Playful devils. Shorn devils. Hairy devils. Foolish devils. For devils, devilesses, and young devils. All the offspring of devildom come from your devilish tricks, quicker than light. Be with us here for our mass tonight."

"May almighty Satan rule the earth," the group below intoned.

"Come, oh Pentamorph," Olda chanted, "be with us mighty Satan. Be with us, Beelzebub. Be with us, Asmodeus. Be with us, Mephistopheles. Be with us, Mulciber. You who dwell amid smoke and fire and wind and water and darkness, witness our sacrifice to you this night."

"So be it," the gathering answered. Adriana's eyes, tears flowing down both sides of her face, watched terrified. They were going to sacrifice her. Kill her. Slit her open like an animal about to be butchered. From someplace above her, she could barely hear the grandfather clock in the foyer of the house—someplace in another world —playing its chimes before striking the hour. She concentrated as best she could, listening to the melody. When it stopped, she waited for the hours to be tolled. One. Two. Three. Three o'clock. But wasn't the hour for all the things evil in the universe to come forth, midnight?

Olda, who faced the congregation, mounted the steps leading to the altar, walking backward.

Adriana, positioned in the form of a cross clutching two candles, held her breath when she realized someone was coming toward her. When Olda reached the top, he turned, looking down at her.

"Don't be frightened, Adriana. You will not be harmed. In fact, you may come to enjoy our ritual." Leaning down, he kissed her pubic hair.

Although she could see what he had done, she could not feel his lips touch her. Did he think she would enjoy something like this? The very fiber of her being, her background, her ancestry rebelled, repulsed by the thought of what she had witnessed. And yet she found a certain fascination with the prospect.

Olda turned, facing the people below him. "Satan be with you."

"And also with you," came the mocking answer.

For the first time, Adriana could see that Olda did not wear a robe like the others. Instead he wore a fiddleback chasuble. When he turned, she saw nothing else under the stiff garment, both sides standing open, exposing his thin, naked body.

Olda moved toward her head, to his left.

She blinked. What would happen next?

Opening a book beyond her, he mumbled, none of the words sounding intelligible to the girl lying on the black marble altar.

He slowed and in a louder voice said, "Satan shall rule us for ever and ever."

The group below answered, "So be it."

Out of the corners of her eye, Adriana could make out golden esoteric symbols decorating the black garment Olda wore. Centered among the weird designs on the front, a duplicate of the wooden carving on the door above stared at her with ruby eyes. When Olda turned to face his diabolistic congregation, a similar countenance kept vigilance over her.

"Satan be with you, my friends," he said again, turning back to the altar.

"And also with you, friend Olda."

"Master of Slanders! Dispenser of the blessing

of love! Steward of voluptuous sins and monstrous vices—Satan! It is you we worship and you to whom we offer up this sacrifice of blood."

"Hail, Master!"

The cries from below seemed choked emotionally and the floodgates containing her fears opened, the pent-up terror coursing through Adriana's body. *Sacrifice of Blood? They weren't going to harm her?* Just drain her body of her blood, that was all. Didn't that hurt? Just a little?

With what kind of madness had she gotten involved? Madness? Yes. But at the same time her own prurient nature began edging out her logical fear, blotting out her reason, her sanity, her inherent loathing. What would they do next? Mesmerized by the man standing next to her, she looked about, overhead, to her right, to her left, down her body where she saw Charlene standing near her feet. The blonde ran her tongue over parted lips, her eyes glazed in an entranced stare.

When Olda turned to face his beautiful acolyte, she moved toward him carrying a chain from which dangled a golden censer. Picking up a boat-shaped utensil, Olda withdrew several heaping spoonfuls of incense granules, which he sprinkled over red hot coals nestling in the bottom of the cuplike container held by Charlene. Bluish smoke curled around for several minutes, permeating the air with a sweet, heady fragrance. When the censer had been closed, Olda took it from his assistant, incensing the nude form lying on the altar. Where the plumes of smoke had risen at first, they spiraled downward now, swirling, caressing, enfolding her nakedness.

"Hail, Master!" the congregation intoned sporadically when they saw the incense fumes engulfing the altar.

When Olda finished, he descended the steps backward to the floor of the black room where he incensed each participant. Returning to the altar, he waved the smoke around Charlene and she did the same to him.

Adriana felt a strangeness plying her body, the first thing she had experienced since awakening on her own bed. Her insides seemed to be on fire. Her lower abdomen tingled as wave after erotic wave washed over her. She had experienced the feeling before—whenever she had masturbated. Often she had wondered if the same thing happened during intercourse.

Somehow she had managed to get through high school with her virginity intact, accepting her mother's advice not to become promiscuous for the sake of physical gratification alone.

"Be positive the man to whom you wish to give yourself is the type of person you would not be ashamed to bring home to meet your father and me," Connie had said when they discussed the subject.

For a millisecond of time, the thought of her dead parents careened through her mind, only to be lost in the sea of desire filling her consciousness and body.

The sensuality heightened, invading her totally as it moved downward to her legs, upward to her small, firm breasts, coloring the taut, upright nipples. She felt the frenzy building until she thought she would go mad.

Olda looked down, smiling at her. Placing one hand on her right breast, he picked up the long knife from her abdomen. He turned to Charlene. "It is time for the blood."

Adriana didn't care. Cut her, beat her, strip the flesh from her body. It would all feel good. It would all satisfy her desires for release from the sexual storm hammering at her.

Obliquely watching the girl at her feet turn and leave, Adriana reveled in her corybantic delirium. As an orgasm teased her, darting to the surface only to hide within her flanks again, she wanted to give vent to her emotions—to scream, to moan—but could not.

Of a sudden she grew aware of Olda's hand kneading her breast. She could feel it. So good. More. More. She wanted more.

A new cry rose from the blackness, a frightened sound that passed barely noticed by Adriana.

Charlene and Michele moved into view at her feet, holding a young lamb between them. The animal bleated, rolling its frightened eyes. Charlene rubbed the lamb's ears, quieting it while Michele lifted it by the hind legs.

Olda moved away from Adriana's side, bringing a whimper from her when he removed his hand from her breast. More. She wanted more than he had given her. Would his interest stop there? A cry built, disappearing in her frustration when it failed to sound.

"Lamb," Olda said loudly, addressing the inverted animal, "the priests of Adonai have made you a symbol of sterility raised to the rank of virtue. I sacrifice you to a much better god—to Satan. May the peace of Satan always be with all of us present."

As he slit the animal's throat and it bleated its death song, the cult answered, "So be it, our Lord and Master."

Charlene produced a pan to catch the lamb's blood as Olda looked downward, his fingers interlaced, thumbs pointing upward.

"Astaroth, Asmodeus," he said softly, "I beg you to accept the sacrifice of this lamb, which we now offer to you so that we may receive the things we ask."

Somewhere in the darkness, somewhere in the black pit of hell, the sound began. A siren softly making its presence known. The pitch rose slowly, much like it had done during the presentation of "Prayer" that first evening. This time, however, it sang alone, coming forth to join the worshippers in their efforts.

Unmindful of the new sonance penetrating the gloom, Adriana, fascinated, watched the droplets of blood plummeting into the container Charlene held. Her loins continued burning with desire, thoughts of propriety gone, forgotten.

Olda, smiling because of the inception of the song rising in the background, moved back toward her, the knife held in front of him like a sword. Reaching out, he again massaged her right breast.

Adriana closed her eyes, reeling in the fulfillment of her wished-for desire. But would the anticipated explosion come? Would she be released from the painful yet delicious furor lashing her body?

He stopped massaging long enough to make a tiny incision at the base of her breast. Squeezing it again, he caught the droplets of blood in a gold chalice when they coursed down her ribcage. Charlene, standing opposite Olda on Adriana's left side, held out a cruet filled with the warm blood of the lamb, which Olda poured into the chalice holding Adriana's blood. Handing both vessels back to Charlene, he again folded his hands in the peculiar manner.

Charlene poured a small amount of the claret liquid into eleven similar chalices. As each was administered, Adriana could barely hear the splash and fixed her attention on counting them. When she heard the eleventh and no more, she wondered how many people were present. Did each have a cup? Eleven cups, eleven people? Who could they be? A new wave of pleasure began building to overwhelm the old one which had subsided, but she forced herself to concentrate on identifying those present. She knew Olda and Michele and Charlene were there. She had seen them. Who else could be in the room? The St. Clairs? Angelique Pantis? Everhart Parrot? How many was that? Six? No, seven. More than likely, Deirdre was here, and if she were, then Morrison had to be as well. Nine. Lahpavi? The dark, sinister features formed in

205

her imagination, the black eyes glaring at her. Yes. He would be involved. That was ten. Had Bergen come back?

Bergen Messenger's handsome features replaced Rizahghyny Lahpavi's scowling countenance. She hoped Bergen would be included. She'd have no problem offering herself to him. The new waves continued building, heaping upon each other as the elusive orgasm persisted in driving her mad. Olda had said something about Bergen. Something—Why couldn't she think straight? Something about his being different from the others. Yes. That was it. No. He had said the three girls were different. Not Bergen. And they were here. Why wasn't Bergen? She wanted him. She wanted him to take her maidenhead. Tear it. Rip it to shreds. Then stuff her full with himself. Pound at her body. Fill her vagina to overflowing with his seed. Maybe he was here. Maybe he would be the part that was good. After all, if she were the chosen one, shouldn't she have some say in what went on?

The rush continued its way through her exhausted muscles. Even though she could not move, could not feel as much as she normally might, her body screamed its depletion.

If I have been chosen for this, she thought, *then Satan, I pray to you that Bergen Messenger be here in this group. That he will do to me that which I want done. Let him fuck me.*

The waves continued washing over her.

Olda moved back into her line of vision. The lamb had been placed next to her legs, head

206

toward her feet. He turned the carcass over, deftly slicing the genitals from the dead animal with the long knife. Charlene removed the lamb and Adriana watched, entranced, as he cut the organ into twelve equal parts, depositing one part in each of the twelve chalices lined up next to her body. Bowing, he kissed her pubic hair again before turning to face her.

"Don't be frightened, Adriana. The best is still to come. Are you enjoying your body's reaction?"

Even though she could not answer, he understood her, seeing the pleased delirium in her eyes.

He picked up a black host from the altar, holding it at arm's length toward the floor. "Master, help us!" he cried.

"Master, help us!" the circle repeated.

The siren sound grew louder as if in response to the plea.

Throwing the black host to the floor, he stomped on it, grinding it to powder before turning back to kiss Adriana's burning groin once more. He raised his chalice, intoning, "Astaroth, Asmodeus, I again beg you to accept the sacrifice of this lamb—to accept its blood and the blood of this virgin daughter of a nun so that we may receive the favors we ask. We do this in the name of Satan."

"Master, help us!" the people screamed.

"Come to the altar of the Slanderous One and drink of *his* nectar," Olda ordered.

Adriana heard shuffling feet as the others who had remained out of her sight mounted the steps backward. When they reached the top, each turned, kissing her throbbing vagina before accepting a chalice from Olda. An electricity of passion raced through her as each nuzzled her. After moving away, each person threw the hood of the robe they wore back, exposing their identity. The St. Clairs, Angelique Pantis, Everhart Parrot, Charlene, Michele, and Lahpavi all followed suit. Then Deirdre followed with Morrison, who smiled widely at her. How many had she seen? Eight? No, nine. Perhaps, Bergen were here after all. A sound, born deep within her chest, managed to gurgle to the surface. Her eyes rolled back and forth, anticipating the next person to kiss her. It had to be Bergen.

Charlene and Michele stood on either side of her, startling her with their sudden appearance. Michele held Adriana's head up while Charlene brought one of the cups to the paralyzed girl's lips. The coppery, salty taste of blood washed in her mouth before flowing down her throat. Adriana marveled at the fact she did not vomit the sanguineous offering back into the cup.

Michele lowered the girl's head to the altar. *She* had been the tenth. Bergen *had* to be the eleventh and last one. There simply could be no one else. A sense of anticipation filled her mind when she saw the last hooded figure backing up the steps toward the altar. When the form turned, bending to kiss Adriana's vulva, and straightened to take the chalice, the hood dropped back. It was Roseanne, the maid.

Adriana felt cheated, angry, infuriated that Bergen was not among the worshippers. How dare they tantalize her, tease her into a sexual madness she had never known before and then not provide the perfect mate for her? Where could he be? Had he actually left the way Olda had said?

Opening her eyes, she saw Olda—Charlene and Michele flanking him—standing at the end of the altar near her feet. The women deftly lifted the chasuble over his head, exposing the old man's nakedness. Her eyes traversed the length of his body to the line where the black marble blocked his lower body and legs. Once the black vestment had been laid aside, the women returned, holding him by his arms which he stretched toward them. They effortlessly lifted him onto the altar, where he knelt, lowering himself to all fours.

His eyes gleaming, mouth hanging agape, a thin stream of blood glistening on his intricately lined chin, Olda advanced animal-like toward her. She could barely see his penis because of his small pot belly hanging in front of it. When he crawled nearer, she saw the tip of it bobbing back and forth, peeking from its nest of gray hair. She didn't want Olda. She wanted Bergen.

Little by little, she yielded to the argument of burning passion raging in her loins. She didn't care who her partner might be. She had to be satisfied, fulfilled or she would lose her mind. Knowing she couldn't resist, even if she wanted, she found herself anticipating the old man's organ being thrust into her. She didn't care what he did to her. Satisfaction. She needed it, demanded it, knowing it would release the ache in her body.

When his thin legs straddled her, he knelt up-right, interlacing his fingers. "We have drunk the blood of your salvation, Mighty Satan."

"Hail, Satan!" the group screamed.

Adriana's eyes flinched at the nearness of the cry. She had been intent on watching Olda approach, not noticing the people who stood on either side of the altar, close enough to reach out and touch her if they desired.

"May all our lustful thoughts reach fruition and gain our Lord and Master's end here on earth!" Olda shouted.

"So be it!" the people responded, pulling their own robes off.

Adriana watched wide-eyed as they exposed their nudity. Jefferson and Ivy St. Clair, pudgy in their middle years, sagged in all the wrong places and she wondered about their sex life. Standing next to them, Morrison, his arms around Deirdre's bare shoulder, studied Adriana's nakedness. Despite his age, he appeared to be in fine shape and she admired the perfect body of the blonde standing next to him. No wonder he had rebuffed Adriana. Or had he only done so because he knew what was in store for her? The sight of Roseanne, displaying rolls of fat, sickened Adriana. Lahpavi stood almost directly behind Olda, out of her view, but she noted his swarthy skin and the graying hair covering his chest and arms. On the other side of the doctor and behind Olda's right side, Angelique Pantis, her firm breasts rising and falling rapidly,

210

nestled close to Everhart Parrot who fondled her. The other two blondes, virtual clones of Deirdre, stood side by side, tongues running over their lips, anticipating Olda's next order or movement.

She could see Olda lifting one leg and her own being moved aside to allow him access to her. The same was repeated with the other and he lowered himself onto her. He jabbed at her with his stubby erection, grunting in rhythm with the motion.

Adriana opened her eyes when she felt nothing. Disgust warped her face momentarily when she saw Olda having trouble breaking into her. Her own concentration gone, she suddenly became aware of the rising and falling song ricocheting through the blackness beyond the halo of light from the candles. She tried to focus on it, to pull it into her range of understanding. It seemed familiar. Where had she—? When the girls were playing! She had asked Bergen about it but he had seemed to avoid her question. Bergen? Bergen. Her attention went back to the throbbing in her groin. She wanted satisfaction. Needed it. Demanded it.

Someone spoke from behind Olda, and Adriana recognized Rizahghyny Lahpavi's smooth, oily voice.

"Let me help, Olda," he said above the sirenlike melody, stepping around Roseanne.

A tiny gasp refused to sound when Adriana saw a small scalpel in his hand. Olda backed off and the doctor made a quick move with the sharp blade. Adriana felt nothing other than the undulations of raw passion tearing at her.

Olda approached again and this time penetrated Adriana, ramming home his erection.

Blues, purples, yellows, oranges, vivid shades of red all burst simultaneously in her vision. Never had she known such exquisite sensations. She wanted to scream, to shout, to hum, to sing, to laugh, to moan but no sound would issue from her larnyx. The paralysis refused her the pleasure of sharing her releasing passion and sense of achievement. Blinded by delight, Adriana could no longer see anyone pressing in about the altar. Everyone had disappeared. She was alone. Alone with the sound of Satan. Diving to the depths of the universe itself. With Satan. The onslaught of maddening desires gave way to a tidal wave of hot molten lead flowing into her body. She reluctantly drew back to the chapel, growing aware of Olda's lessening movement and felt herself spiraling down, down back to the marble on which she lay.

Opening her eyes, she saw Olda withdrawing his limp member. It was over. The orgasm completed. Her virginity gone. The sacrifice finished. The song of Satan—no more. She sensed a pang of regret. She wanted more. Bergen could have done it longer.

Charlene and Michele helped the spent man off the altar, stepping aside to make room for Lahpavi to approach.

Adriana swallowed. She didn't want him. She didn't even like him. Why should she allow him to copulate with her?

Instead of crawling onto the table, Lahpavi again stepped around the corpulent body of the maid. Morrison and Deirdre moved aside. The doctor leaned over her lower body, holding out one hand to the far side. Michele placed a large syringe in it and he reached toward Adriana's groin.

Adriana watched, wide eyed. What were they doing? She tried to raise her head but nothing would respond. Her breath coming in short gasps, she watched as best she could. Lahpavi appeared to insert the syringe into her vulva and she suddenly felt a flooding of cool liquid pouring into her, mixing with the sperm of Olda Revillion. In seconds it was over and everyone stepped back.

Olda, his black chasuble back on, appeared at her side where the doctor had been standing. Holding his arms outward and pointing toward the floor, he intoned, "She is yours, Mighty Satan. This Ancient One lying on your altar is now yours. She will produce that which you most desire. It is fulfilled." He turned facing the group who had moved back to the floor level. "Satan be with you."

"And also with you."

"We are finished. Do what you will."

"Hail, Satan!"

No one seemed to notice the satisfied chuckle permeating the blackness, seemingly to punctuate their prayer.

Charlene and Michele removed the candles from Adriana's hands, and the four who had brought her stepped onto the raised dais again. While the rest of them donned their robes, the bearers covered their heads, then lifted Adriana to shoulder height.

Carrying her toward the steps, the balance of the group fell in behind, heads bent, chanting incoherently. When they reached the door to Adriana's room, they entered, and the bearers lowered her to the bed. Two of the women dressed her in a gown after the lamp was lighted. Lahpavi stepped forth into its glow, and Deirdre held a small black bag out to him.

Striding to the bedside, he motioned for the lamp to be brought closer. He opened the bag, withdrawing several small bottles and a hypodermic syringe. Once it was prepared, he wiped a spot on her arm with a cotton swab and quickly injected her.

He turned to face the people. "It is finished. By Saturday, Sunday at the latest, we will know."

A murmur of approval and agreement sounded.

Adriana could hear them and fought to open her eyes. So exhausted. So tired. Spent. She had no strength left. She was drained completely. Through quivering slits, she watched the people nodding their heads, turning to leave the room. Everyone left except one of the three blonde women, who stood at the foot of the bed watching her. Which one? She didn't care. She wanted to sleep. She wanted rest. Peace.

The slits closed and a deep blackness filled her mind.

EIGHT

Thursday, April 25, 1985

ADRIANA'S BODY told her it had happened. The
memory could have been that of a dream, of
something that had been imagined. But her body
ached. Her mouth held a bad taste. Every muscle
pained. It had happened.

She closed her eyes, swallowing the sob that
fought to emerge. How could they have done—
She stopped. She couldn't blame them—not completely. Their beliefs and practices were their
own business. The fact they had drugged her or
done something to her to make her participate
willingly was the thing that angered her. How
could they have done that?

She turned in bed, her head toward the open
window. The sound of birds chirping brought her
eyes open. At least they sounded normal. Sunlight filled the room, the same room where her
horror of the previous night had begun. But had

it been a horror? She recalled the agonizingly delicious feeling that had wrapped her body, consuming her energy in such a way that she had thought she would go mad with pleasure. She had enjoyed it.

The one aspect of the whole situation that kept her off balance was her own attitude. She had been drugged, raped, and had partaken in what she considered to be an unholy rite of some sort. And she didn't seem to mind. Any one of the three would have been repulsive to her in the past, but for some unfathomable reason she found herself at best indifferent to all thoughts concerning what had happened, the people she found herself associating with, and the idea that she was no longer a virgin. She tried to be angry but couldn't even muster an upset of weak proportion.

"Adriana?"

She jumped at the sound of a man's voice calling from the hall. "Y—yes?"

"If you're awake, we'd like to join you for a chat." It was Olda.

Why would they allow the door to stop them this morning? Last night it seemed anything—everything—was permissable. She wondered fleetingly who the "we" he referred to might include.

"Who's with you?"

"Dr. Lahpavi and Dr. Tyler."

Doctor? What had happened to the splended informality everyone had harped on when she had first arrived? Lahpavi? Did she even want to be in the same room with him? The man positively sent waves of revulsion through her. She had difficulty in placing a finger on the reason for such a reaction but knew that if they had been introduced under different circumstances, she would have reacted in the same way.

Morrison? And Olda? Did she want to see them much less speak with them? She felt she should be more upset with her piecemeal recollection of the previous night. But the same delicious sensation of wanton abandonment washed through her when she recalled her volcanic orgasm. They had raped her. But she had enjoyed it tremendously—more than her feelings of indignation could overcome. For a second, she tried concentrating her attention on the therapist and the owner of the island. Why couldn't she make a decision where they were concerned?

"Very well, come in." She sat up in bed, pulling the sheet up to cover her breasts. When she moved, an involuntary gasp broke the silence before the door opened. Her body felt as if it had been pummeled for hours.

The knob turned silently and Olda Revillion appeared in the doorway. Morrison followed him into the room, while Rizahghyny Lahpavi entered last, closing the door behind him.

"Have you slept well, my dear?" Olda asked, smiling enough to show his teeth.

"Can we cut the formalities, gentlemen?" she asked, wincing at the sharpness of her words.

"Formalities?" Olda asked. "We're merely interested in your well-being."

"You should have thought of that last night," she snapped.

"Adriana," Morrison said, "what happened last night was something that none of us, yourself included, could have changed for anything."

She stared past Olda, directly at Morrison. "What are you talking about? Why couldn't any of you have changed what happened last night? What *did* happen last night? I'd like an explanation."

Morrison turned to look first at the dark complected man before stepping next to Olda, at whom he stared for several seconds. "Why don't you begin, Olda, and tell her what happened last night. I'll tell her my part and then Rizahghyny can fill her in on the rest."

The old man nodded. "I think that will be best. You see, my dear, the Angel of Darkness has stretched his hand over you. You were chosen to be the altar in a most special rite. In fact you were selected by him specifically."

Her eyes widened. "Why me? For God's sake, why me?" she whispered hoarsely.

"Adriana, I will appreciate it if you do not defile my house with the name of your God," Olda said.

Adriana felt the color in her face drain. They were crazy. They had to be. But her thoughts quickly suppressed any desire to argue. "I'm sorry, Olda. I didn't mean to offend you." Why had she said that?

"Your selection was determined because of an incident that took place over thirty-three years ago. Your mother was in a convent and our master was about to take a member of that group as his own, for a specific purpose. She was to care for a child who was to be born in the East. A meddling priest managed to foul up the works and our Lord and Master had no alternative but to destroy the girl when his intentions became known. When your mother left that bunch and you were born, a new plan was devised."

Adriana dropped her eyes. She knew the story of which he spoke all too well. The feeling of guilt slammed at her. Her parents had been killed because she had told the story last Hallowe'en. "A—a new plan?" she asked quietly. "One involving my mother and me? My mother is dead. How could she be included in your plan?"

"Your mother played a small but important role. She died. That was imperative. We had to get Morrison and you together. It worked nicely."

"You—you killed my parents—so that—"

Morrison stepped forward, around Olda, to sit on the edge of the bed. He shot a defiant glare at the old man, turning his full attention to the chalky-white girl on the bed. "You're misunderstanding this, Adriana. We had nothing to do with the death of your parents."

"But—but—he—just said—"

"Let me tell you. When you were taken to my psychiatric clinic, I already knew you were going to arrive before anything had happened to your parents."

"How did you know?" She held a finger to her trembling lips, tears building in her eyes. What he said seemed impossible.

"Olda told me and he was told by—by—"

"Satan," Olda finished for him.

"By—by Satan?" Adriana asked, suddenly finding a bitter humor in what they said. Were these people for real? Or were they all crazy? Her laugh, short and acerbic, took the three men off guard. "You're all insane!"

"Most people are all too quick to call insane any mentality that deviates from their idea of conventionality," Olda said evenly. "There are many things on earth, in the heavens above, and within all minds never before dreamt of in your simple little philosophy, my dear Adriana."

"Paraphrasing Shakespeare isn't going to convince me that all of you don't belong anyplace but in a nut house," she said, backing further away from Morrison.

He smiled reaching out to touch her arm. "You must remember that the mind is my domain, Adriana. You will find some of the things we tell you difficult to accept, but given time you will understand everything."

She shook her head. "I don't think I have that much time or that you have anything that will convince me you're telling the truth."

"Unfortunately for you that is not the case.

You will begin believing within the week. Within a month, you will comprehend everything we have done here."

"I refuse to accept your—your religion."

"I didn't say you'd accept anything. You *will* understand and for your own sake, I hope you will believe—and accept. If you don't—" Morrison's voice trailed off.

"I suppose you'll kill me—like you did my parents."

"For the time being, let's just say I think you're intelligent enough to accept the most impossible thing when it is proven to you."

Adriana turned away. There wasn't anything they could do that would convince her that any of what had happened was meant for her or that they actually talked with Satan. "Why will I comprehend everything within a month? What is going to happen?"

Morrison smiled. "You asked me while we were waiting for the cruiser if it were possible for a pregnancy of one month to result in the birth of a normal child."

She puckered her mouth. She remembered asking the question, wondering at the time if he would think her a trifle off center. "I asked something like that. What about it?"

"You were merely recalling something I had told you many times during November and December of last year."

"You told me? You told me what?"

"I told you that you had been chosen for a great honor. That you would conceive and give birth to a child all within one month. I convinced you that it was possible and that it was a good thing for you to do. I also—"

She stared at Morrison, her eyes widening. ". . . Told me that I'd be happy if I did." He had told her all of the things—the bits of phrases, the words that had flirted with her memory since that first day in his office when she began speaking. He had—"Did you brainwash me, Morrison?" she asked, her voice steady.

He nodded. "You might say that. If I hadn't, the episode last night would have completely unhinged your mind. The drugs administered to you in the wine and food and the incense, aroused you until you thought of nothing else but your own sexual satisfaction. Isn't that right?"

A tiny smile involuntarily quivered on her full lips. She had enjoyed everything that had been done to her—she couldn't argue that. Drinking the blood had not been so pleasant but it hadn't disturbed her either. She recalled the tremendous outburst of pleasure when she climaxed with Olda's erection driving within her. The power of her orgasm had been something she had never before experienced. Still, it had been chemically induced, not the result of being aroused by someone she loved. She looked past Morrison at Olda, immediately conquering the shiver she felt. Forget him! Remember the pleasure she had had. Then, it wouldn't be so bad.

"Yes, I enjoyed it—very much," she said, the words barely audible. "What happens now?"

Lahpavi stepped forward. "Now, you must rest and eat the proper food so that the child within you will be able to grow and complete his full term of prenatal growth in one month."

"You're serious, aren't you? You actually believe I'll give birth to a baby by the end of May?"

"*Before* the end of May. More likely the twenty-fifth of May, one month from today." Lahpavi folded his hands, the fingers interlacing, and smiled, his lips peeling back to reveal yellow teeth.

"I'm sorry, I just don't believe it," she said. "The whole thing is preposterous! It simply isn't possible."

"I have powers," Olda said, drawing himself to his full height, "no man has ever dreamed could exist. My grandfather searched the world over for his books, his talismans, his knowledge. Now, all of it belongs to me. I have done things at which he failed. I have spoken with my Master and Lord. It is him we serve. Hail, Satan!"

The doctors responded in kind.

"That's horrible blasphemy," Adriana whispered. "Your minds are black and evil!"

"But they aren't, Adriana," Morrison said kindly. "Just because your ideas have been formed by concepts contradictory to ours doesn't make you automatically right and us wrong. The concept that the earth was flat was accepted for countless years. Everyone believed it except a few. Finally the few were proven right. The same is happening here. Tomorrow it could

225

be the entire world that learns of our concepts. But for now, it is you we are concerned with. We are not asking you to accept blindly everything we tell you. Make your decision after the birth of the child. Certainly, if you have a baby in one month, you will have to place credence in some of the tenets we hold, if not all. Don't you agree?"

"I think I'm losing my mind!" she said. "Why I want to go along with you is what I don't understand. I shouldn't—God knows." She quickly looked at Olda. "I'm sorry, Olda. Force of habit, I guess. Is the reason I find everything you've said not completely repulsive because of—of your brainwashing me, Morrison?"

"Why don't we call it indoctrination, my dear? Instructions, if you will, in the religion that will conquer the world."

Turning to Lahpavi, she said, "May I get up or am I to be bedridden during my pregnancy?" She purposely tinged each word with disbelieving sarcasm.

"By all means, get up," he said, moving back from the foot of the bed. "The more exercise you get, the better. This experience will drain you of much of your vitality. It will be most difficult but you are young and strong. I will make arrangements for your special diet. The more you adhere to it, the less likely the depletion of your own system."

"Why don't we leave Adriana alone so she can dress?" Morrison suggested, rising from where he had sat while they talked with the girl.

The other men moved toward the door while

Morrison turned to face Adriana. "I hope you don't hate me. I do value your friendship and would feel unhappy if you wound up not liking me anymore."

Adriana smiled, cocking her head to one side. "Let's say that while I'm on probation to approve your ideas and religion, you—all of you—can be on probation with *me*. Fair enough?"

Morrison bowed, turning to follow the others into the hall. When the door closed, the psychiatrist said, "That was easier than I thought it would be. Apparently my induced thought pattern worked better than any of us anticipated."

Lahpavi merely nodded, but Olda's face clouded. "We shall see. We shall see."

The three men made their way toward the staircase and the foyer.

When the door clicked shut, Adriana leaped from the bed. How could she get away from these lunatics? So far they had accepted her cooperation but that wouldn't last forever because she knew she couldn't continue fooling all of them. If she turned up not pregnant, which she felt positive would be the case, they might become violent. Within the next twenty-four to forty-eight hours, she had to devise a plan to escape this island of mad people. She dressed quickly, brushing her hair while she created plans of getting away.

By Sunday morning, Adriana had planned nothing. Without access to the outside world there were no routes of escape open to her. Without a boat, she would have to swim—and that was impossible. There apparently was no radio on the island to contact the mainland. Despite her sharpened vigilance in watching everyone and investigating behind every door in the house, she knew as much when she went to bed the previous night as she had when she and Morrison had first arrived on the island.

At least they were giving her tasty food. Lahpavi had said the diet would change sometime within the next week or so. She had eaten her fill of delightful concoctions she had never tasted before, and although she hated to admit it, she felt wonderful.

Golden sunlight streamed in through the heavy lace curtains creating tiny spotlights on the floor while birds chirped merrily in the trees outside. She stretched, immediately pulling her arms back. Her breasts hurt when she had thrown her arms out. Standing, she moved to the dresser, where she pulled her gown over her head. The pain began at the nipples, radiating outward in invisible spiderweb patterns. Why should her breasts ache? She had done nothing strenuous the last couple of days. Everyone had seen to it that she didn't overexert herself by bending or lifting anything. If she ever got off this island, she would embellish the story of being waited on by a movie star who most men lusted after in their minds if not physically.

Turning sideways, she examined her breasts. They seemed a little fuller, but perhaps they were growing and she had not noticed.

A churning, bubbling heave brought an acidic juice to her mouth. Throwing a hand over her mouth, she looked about, searching. When she saw the basin, she lifted the pitcher out, just before a stream of bile vomit splashed into the earthenware vessel.

When she finished, she stood trembling before the mirror. A frightened expression countered the look of panic filling her eyes, the arguments the three men had presented flooding her mind.

Part Four

GRAVIDITY OF HORROR

NINE

Sunday, May 5, 1985

ADRIANA STRETCHED on her bed. Would it happen again? She hoped not. Why she had been vomiting every morning during the past week puzzled her. Could she have stomach flu? Whenever she had suffered from it in the past, she had always thrown up. God, how she hated doing that. Whenever she had thrown up, her stomach's contractions always seemed powerful enough to wrench muscles out of place, to empty her body's cavity of all the mysterious organs and parts and expel them through her mouth. Then, when she finished, a drained sensation would hold her in its tight grasp for hours, managing to weaken her to the point of exhaustion.

But these bouts of sickness differed. She would throw up and then immediately feel fine. What she vomited hardly seemed worth the effort. Gastric juices but no solids, since she never ate before retiring. The taste of bile and the feeling of being ill had become her morning companions, barely warning her in the nick of time to reach the basin.

Morning sickness? Could she—? No, that wasn't possible. It was completely, irrevocably impossible. There was no way she could be pregnant. That particular thought had come the first time she had thrown up, a few days after Olda, Morrison, and Lahpavi had told her she would have a child. What little she knew of bearing children she had learned from her mother during an impromptu sex lesson when she had asked about her first menstrual period.

There had been sex education classes in high school but for all the seriousness of the subject, the teacher had lost control of the class early in the semester. Everyone who had enrolled for it looked forward to a lighthearted discussion of necking, petting, and "going all the way."

The one thing she knew for certain was that morning sickness usually didn't show up until the woman was at least three or four weeks pregnant. Olda had copulated with her only ten days before, and she had been vomiting for eight days. The time was too short to account for such symptoms.

Sitting up, she dropped her legs over the edge of the bed. That had been some introduction to the sex act. One she would never forget. She closed her eyes, reliving the fantastic sensations that had enveloped her. Never had she thought sex could induce such feelings of pleasure.

Stretching her arms behind and over her head brought a gasp of pain. She dropped them to her side, reaching up to tenderly rub her breasts. Why did they hurt? Ever since the previous Sunday she had experienced discomfort in her breasts.

The sudden movement of her arm set off a chain reaction in her body. First her stomach heaved, then the taste of bile rose to flood her mouth, and she leaped from the bed dashing to the basin on the dresser. The brown-green juices splashed in the bottom of the large dish, barely enough to half fill a coffee cup. Convinced she was finished, she dabbed at the corners of her mouth with a wash cloth and turned away from the bowl.

Moving to the window, she looked out over that part of the valley visible from her room. A cool morning breeze wafted the curtains aside, caressing her scantily clad body. Inhaling deeply, she stopped short. Now what was the matter with her? She couldn't suck her stomach in.

What had her mother said? Something about losing her waistline when she was three months pregnant? Hadn't she said something like that? But this was crazy. Until ten days before she had been a virgin. No one had ever entered her in any way. She couldn't be pregnant. Besides, her mother had said it hadn't happened with her until three months had passed.

Maybe she should have Doctor Lahpavi examine her. The obstetrician's dark countenance clouded her mind. No, that would be distasteful at best to her. She found even his looking at her in passing repulsive. There was no way she would allow him to touch her—professionally or any other way. She'd just wait until she got back to the mainland and have a complete physical. Maybe she should ask Morrison about the strange things that had been happening to her.

At first the soft knock at her door did not register and she jumped, startled when the heavy oak panel swung open. Rizahghyny Lahpavi stood framed in the doorway, a toothy grin highlighting his dark complexion.

"May I come in?" he asked, striding into the room.

"Do I have a choice, Doctor?" she asked, grabbing for her robe. Slipping into it, she knotted the draw string tightly around her middle in a defiant yet defensive gesture, as if attempting to hide her body and its peculiar behavior.

"How are you feeling, my dear Adriana?"

Surprised at the question, her hands froze on the completed knot. Had he been standing outside her room reading her mind? Could he do that? A mysterious air seemed to hang about the man whenever he entered a room, never really dissipating long enough for the real person to show through. For that reason, if no other, Adriana found his presence in a crowd or now, here with her alone, unsettling. What did he want? A report on the condition of her health. Wasn't that against the rules by which doctors played? They weren't allowed to solicit business or something like that. She was positive she had heard that from the doctor who had addressed the economics class on career day, her last year in high school.

"Why do you ask, Doctor?"

"We—that is, Olda, Dr. Tyler, and I—feel it is time for you to be examined. To see if you are truly pregnant with—er—Olda's child." He smiled, slightly bowing his head while he interlaced his fingers, thumbs straight up.

Olda's child? The thought repulsed her. She couldn't possibly be pregnant by him. He was too old. At least she hoped he was too old to father a child. My God! What if she were pregnant by the old—

"That isn't really possible, is it, Doctor?"

"We told you that the day after the rite."

"But—but I thought about what you said. A pregnancy runs nine months or as close to that as possible, doesn't it?"

"Normally, yes. But in your case, you were given a massive shot of proteins with suspended drugs and other inducements that will speed up the process by nine times. Consequently, you will give birth in one month. Have you been ill in the morning time?"

She looked away. How could she lie to him when he already knew the answers to his questions. She nodded.

"I think an examination is in order." His voice sounded oily.

He stepped toward her and she fell back until her legs touched the bed. She could go no farther.

When he stood opposite her no more than two

feet away, he said, "Have you noticed any changes in your breasts? An enlarging, perhaps?"

He knew. He was right. All of them were right about her being pregnant. She nodded again.

"Do you find it difficult to draw your stomach in?"

"Just this morning," she managed in a tiny, defeated voice.

"Fine. Fine. You're right on schedule. You see, the last ten days since you were inseminated have been equivalent to three months of normal pregnancy. Another five days and you will feel life moving within your body. Isn't that wonderful?"

She didn't answer. It was all true. She was going to have a baby—and in record time. But why her? They had said she had been chosen because of her mother's experience in the convent. But was that actually valid? Could there be some other reason? Some reason they didn't want to divulge to her? The question of how they knew what had happened to her mother buzzed in her mind, tantalizing her along with the other unanswered questions.

"If you will get on the bed, I will give you a pelvic examination, my dear," he said stepping back, away from her.

Slowly lowering herself to the bed, she watched him for some sign of direction. When he motioned for her to lie down, she panicked momentarily but then complied. What did she have to gain by fighting when she knew she couldn't win?

"Move down toward the lower end of the bed,

Adriana, and place your feet on the brass footboards. That's it," he said when she followed his instructions. "We'll have to make do since we do not have a regular examination table." He grasped her feet, moving them apart until they were separated wide enough for him to conduct his test.

Adriana stifled a tear when he pushed her nightgown up her thighs to bunch at her waist. Sucking in her breath, she held it and shut her eyes, quashing a sob.

Lahpavi produced a pair of examination gloves from his bag and pulled them on. Stepping closer, he reached out toward her vulva. Inserting a long, thin finger, he wiggled it about searching for the physical evidence that Adriana was indeed pregnant.

Why did it have to feel good when she felt so embarrassed? She wanted to say something that would confirm her own beliefs—that everything that was happening was merely her imagination working overtime.

She bit her tongue hard when she remembered who was standing next to the bed. Rizahghyny Lahpavi could not be considered a potential lover. Nor could Olda Revillion. Not ever again. Nor could Morrison Tyler to whom she had offered her body at one time. How could she ever consider him when he had taken full advantage of her mental breakdown. Who then? Who on the island could fill her need? Everhart Parrot? Hardly. He seemed manly enough but something about him paled when she thought of Bergen

Messenger. Bergen. It had to be Bergen. But where was he? Olda had said he had been called away, supposedly by business.

Wait a minute. How could he have been called if there was no phone or radio on the island? She had searched and found nothing. Had she understood Olda correctly? What had he said?

She stopped her mental meandering when Lahpavi withdrew his finger and said, "Very good, Adriana. You may get up. I'll need a sample of urine and blood to conduct a few simple tests." He reached for the small black bag again and withdrew a syringe. He swabbed her arm with an alcohol-soaked cotton ball and injected the needle, pulling back the plunger to fill the cylinder with her dark blood.

Why hadn't he just bitten her on the neck and sucked some out? She winced at the thought and the pain in her arm as he continued drawing blood.

He handed her another ball of cotton to hold on the puncture while he stoppered the vial of blood. When he turned back to her, he placed a bandage on the wound before handing her a small bottle for the urine sample.

"You may dress now, Adriana, and have breakfast. Beginning today, you will be on a diet different from the one you've been on this week." He smiled, closing his bag.

She remained silent as he left her room.

After dressing, Adriana tentatively walked down the stairs toward the foyer. The huge grandfather clock had just struck the quarter hour past ten. Everyone should have eaten their breakfast and be about their business of sitting with their hands held together, staring off into space. At least she hoped so. Right now she felt as if she couldn't face anyone staying at Revillion Manor.

Peeking into the dining room, she found one place setting on the table and Roseanne waddling into the room from the kitchen, carrying a tray.

"Good morning, Adriana," she said cheerfully. "That's what I call good timing."

Adriana stopped in the doorway. Everything seemed so maddeningly normal. A cheerful greeting from the maid. Breakfast for a late riser. Nothing on the surface appeared out of the ordinary.

"Good morning, Roseanne," she said, slipping into her chair.

"Dr. Lahpavi has changed your diet. You'll find that the food might not look familiar but it is more nourishing than anything you've ever eaten."

Adriana lifted the cover off the tray. Clouds of steam rose from what appeared to be rice swimming in gravy. But the smell was unlike anything she had ever experienced. She couldn't place it or even come close to comparing it to something she might have smelled in the past.

"What is it?" She looked up to find Roseanne gone.

Studying the bowl of food, she picked up a fork, picking at it. It certainly looked like rice. Lifting some to her nose, she still puzzled over the aroma. Familiar and yet completely

243

different. Would they give her something harmful? She looked about the room. Not if they wanted a perfect healthy baby. More than likely it would not harm her at this stage of her pregnancy. The one thing she felt she could count on right now, and at least for the next three weeks or so, would be complete safety here among the —the—what should she call them? Devil worshippers. If she were truly pregnant and they wanted her baby, they would never allow something adverse to happen to her. But what about afterward? Would she feel as safe then—once her function as a baby factory had been fulfilled?

Gingerly placing some of the food in her mouth, she rolled it about her tongue. Good. It tasted good. Very good. She took more, enjoying the palatable food—whatever it was.

When the dish was empty, she picked up the glass that had escaped her notice before. The clear, yellow liquid sparkled in the sunbeam, spotlighting her tray and dishes. Again, she sniffed it before putting it to her lips. No smell, no bouquet of any kind. Sipping it carefully, she swished it around her mouth. No taste that she could detect, although the ricelike dish's flavor remained, overwhelming any delicate scent the liquid might have possessed. She emptied the glass, returning it to the tray. Dabbing at her mouth with a napkin, she stood, spinning about when applause broke behind her.

Olda, Morrison, and the others surrounded Rizahghyny Lahpavi, who held out his arms to Adriana as he approached her.

She couldn't run. She wanted to but couldn't simply because there was no place for her to hide. Steeling herself for the embrace, she sighed deeply when he merely took her hands in his, holding her at arm's length.

"It's true, Adriana, my dear. You are truly pregnant. Within three weeks you shall give birth."

The others continued applauding for several minutes, smiles of satisfaction twisting their faces.

Adriana pulled herself free, moving toward Morrison.

He reached out, embracing her to kiss her on the cheek. "You have no idea how happy this makes all of us, Adriana," he whispered.

Pushing him away, she glared at him. "Why don't you tell me, Morrison. Just tell me how happy you are that I'm pregnant and by—by—" She could not continue, her throat constricting, tears welling in her eyes. The inexplicable reason for not rebelling at everything Olda had told her in the library suddenly cleared. That had been Morrison's doing with his goddamned brainwashing. How badly affected was she? Would she accept everything these people believed? Did she want to? How could two months of programmed indoctrination, as Morrison referred to it, undo eighteen years of training—training that she had been given lovingly by her parents? Right now, she had to think. To plan. To accept her present state. To wonder what would happen to her once the baby was born.

Bolting forward, she pushed her way through the group. "Let me alone. I'll be all right. But just

245

let me alone. I need time to think. To be by myself."

Ivy St. Clair reached out to stop her but was stayed by Olda. "Let her go," he said. "She can't go anyplace. Let her ponder this and she will accept it. She will, won't she, Morrison?"

"Of course, she will," Morrison said, watching Adriana run down the front steps.

Once outside, she slowed to a hurried walk, letting the fresh air and sunlight tranquilize her quivering nerves. These people were crazy. They had to be. Why else would they applaud when they found out the girl they had maneuvered into rape was pregnant and being attended to by a doctor who thought a pregnancy could be completed in thirty days? They had to be insane. Every one of them. Even Angelique Pantis, movie queen. Angelique Pantis, crazy devil worshipper seemed more approriate.

She walked with the sun at right angles to her shoulder, straight west. She had to be alone. To sort out her thoughts. There was no way she could think clearly with others trying to influence her.

Struggling up the hill, she paused when she reached the top. The Gulf lay at her feet, quietly massaging the beach with its gentle waves. So peaceful in front of her. So hectic and awful behind her. She started down the hill toward the white sand.

What could she do? Abort the baby? Possibly, if she had nerve enough to do so. But what would they do if she did? Would she be safe? Probably not. Besides, she had no idea as to how an abortion should be done, especially by the mother. That had to be ruled out. Escape? That was out of the question, too. She knew of no boat or other means of travel on the island. She could not call for help since there wasn't a telephone or radio—at least that she knew about. Olda had told her that Bergen had gone away on business. Had he been called or had he just gone. In either case, he had left the island. But how? Perhaps she should look again for a boat or telephone or radio or something. Just sitting around, waiting to give birth to a baby seemed self-defeating. What would they do to her if she tried looking around again, snooping for a phone or radio or boat? She had been lucky the first time. They wouldn't stand by, she knew that.

She shuddered when she considered her options. She had none except one. Give birth to the baby and wait to see what would happen beyond that point. No. There *was* one other alternative that had hidden in her mind. Lurking there, waiting to be recognized. To be invited to the fore. To be called upon as the solution to her plight. To succor her.

She lowered her head, gentle sobs releasing pent-up tears. Could she? What did she have to look forward to in the event she ever got off this island? She had no family. They had seen to that. At least they had seemed perfectly willing to accept responsibility for her parents' deaths. The rest of her relatives were nonexistent as far as she was concerned. But how? How could she kill herself? She had no weapon. No poison. No means at her disposal to end her life.

Raising her head, she looked out at the Gulf through writhing tears. She had nothing. No one. She had no reason to live.

Suddenly the tears dried. There was a way. Standing, she walked slowly toward the water. The cool waves washed over her feet.

Don't think.

One foot in front of the other.

Keep going.

How simple. How absolutely easy. What a convenient manner in which to solve her problems.

Don't look back.

The water swirled around her waist, reaching toward her breasts—breasts that would pain her no more. She and her unborn baby would lie together in the Gulf and watch fish swim by.

She laughed softly.

She kept walking, bobbing every once in a while when a wave lifted her off her feet. She refused to swim, to tread water, to hold her breath.

Water flowed into her open mouth, splashing in her nostrils. It would feel good. So comfortable. So safe. It would just be the two of them at the bottom. There she wouldn't mind having her baby with her.

From far off, she heard her name being called but ignored the voice.

"Adriana! Adriana!"

TEN

Monday, May 6, 1985

ADRIANA OPENED her eyes. Where was she? The off-white expanse that she could see appeared familiar but that didn't seem right. Why should something she saw after dying be familiar? Then she saw the rows of flowers extending down from the sea of whiteness. Wallpaper. Turning her head, she saw the dresser with the wash basin and pitcher. Her room. She was in her room. She hadn't died. She had failed.

Sitting up, she took note of the fact that she was dressed in the same nightgown they had given her after destroying hers. Why was she on top of the bedding instead of inside? What had happened? She recalled walking into the Gulf, the water rising as she moved farther and farther from the shore. Vague voices calling her name replayed in her memory. Someone had been calling her. Who? It had been a woman's voice.

The click of a key turning in her door brought her eyes to the knob, which slowly turned. The door swung open and one of the blondes entered.

"You're awake," she said, smiling.

Adriana turned away. She could feel tears running down her cheeks. If she couldn't kill herself when she had the chance, she had nothing more to look forward to than completing the pregnancy and waiting to see what her captors had in store for her once she had fulfilled their desire for her.

"Are you all right?" her visitor asked.

Adriana nodded.

"If you want to talk for a while, I'll be happy to sit with you. Charlene and Deirdre are busy and the others can wait for a while before I tell them that you're awake."

Adriana turned to face her. "What happened, Michele?"

"Deirdre and Charlene saw you standing on top of the hill. Once you started down toward the beach, they thought it best to follow and keep you in sight."

Adriana dropped her eyes.

"Why did you do it?"

"Wouldn't you have tried it if you had been in my place? Good God, I don't want to have a child. I'm not ready. Especially under these circumstances. I'm simply not ready to be saddled with a baby."

Michele reached out, patting Adriana's bare arm. "Would you be so concerned if you didn't have to care for the child?"

Adriana's brows knit. What did she mean? Not have to care for the baby? If she gave birth to it and it was hers, wouldn't she also have to be a mother to it as well? "I don't understand what you mean. You aren't talking about adoption, are you?"

"I'm not at liberty to say just now. Actually, Olda should be the one to tell you. When he feels you're ready, he'll tell you. All I can say right now is, cooperate. Have the child. Everything will work out in the long run." She stood, preparing to leave. "Is there anything you'd like? When they learn that you're awake, breakfast will be sent up to you."

Adriana shook her head.

"I'll be running along. I think Morrison will probably want to talk to you and help you understand more fully your responsibility where your pregnancy is concerned." She closed the door quietly, turning the key with a definitive, grating sound of finality.

Adriana got out of bed, crossing to the window. The sun shone brightly. She'd give anything if she could see a cloud. The thunderstorm the night she was taken to—where had they taken her? She wondered if the room where their unholy rite had taken place was behind the door with the carven face. She remembered hearing the thunder and seeing the lightning, but every day since then the cerulean blue, unbroken by even a white puff of a cloud, had become boring. She wanted something other than cheerful sunlight and singing birds outside her window. She wanted dark, ominous clouds, threatening thunder and lightning, and driving rain to match the situation in which she found herself. It would seem so much more appropriate and in keeping with the mood she felt she should maintain. The bright, cheery days were indifferent to her predicament.

Again the door was unlocked and Olda Revillion strode in, a smile creasing his face but failing to disguise his look of worry and upset. "I'm glad you're awake, young lady," he snapped, closing the door.

She moved defensively back toward the dresser which stood next to the window.

"Please, Adriana, I'm not going to hurt you. Why should I?"

"Why, indeed," she snapped. "Think of everything you've done to me since I arrived here and then ask yourself if you haven't hurt me already."

"Please," he said indicating the bed, "sit down and we'll talk. I'll answer whatever I can and perhaps you'll change your mind about certain things."

Adriana crossed to the bed. "I doubt it. But I don't have much else to do."

He sat down carefully on the chair next to the bed. When their knees touched, she moved farther toward the foot of the mattress.

"Ask whatever questions are uppermost in your mind, my dear."

"Why me?"

He chuckled.

"Don't laugh, damnit. I'm more than a bit confused and angry about this whole thing. I feel like a guinea pig. One month pregnancy. It's ludicrous."

"Not ludicrous but fact. You *are* pregnant. You *will* give birth to a child one month from the date of conception—or at least within a few hours of the month's time."

"But I don't want to have a baby. It might have been nice if you had consulted the mother-to-be but no, let's go ahead and have a ceremony and get the dumb girl pregnant. Why wasn't I asked?"

"Because you were given to us—to me—for that very purpose."

"By whom?"

"By my Master and Lord. Satan."

Adriana gasped. She had known what the answer would be. She had heard much the same the day after they had defiled her body. "You realize that none of that makes sense. Why would Satan direct me to have a child? I just don't under—"

"When your mother was in the convent, there was another young girl my master had planned to groom for a very specific purpose."

"I know the story," Adriana said.

"Not the whole story, I'm afraid. When the girl died, it was necessary to devise a new plan—"

"I know. I know. You've told me all this."

"You don't know what the first plan was. Nor do you know of the plan as it now exists and how it affects you."

Adriana frowned. He was right. She didn't know. Her mother had never mentioned anything about a plan. She wondered if Connie had ever known.

"The only reason I know about the plan is because Satan told me. I'm positive that the priest with whom Lucifer spoke never told anyone. The plan was simple. The girl was to be sent to a country in Africa where she would come in contact with the baby—a special baby—one she would care for under the guise of a good Christian woman doing the work of her Lord. However, the whole time she would have been in the power of Lucifer and Satan, grooming the child for the role of the Antichrist."

"The—the Antichrist?" Adriana asked, her face draining of color.

"Why do you find that difficult to accept? The Antichrist has been spoken of for centuries. Many men have been wrongly tabbed as the Antichrist—Nero, Attila, Hitler, but they were as children compared to the true Antichrist. He shall bring chaos and war and famine and death to this planet as no other person. Out—"

"How can you support something like that? What will you gain if the world is ruined?"

"As I was about to say, my dear, out of the ruin shall arise the most glorious and pleasurable time the earth has ever seen or witnessed. Debauchery will become the new virtue."

"It's wrong. It's evil," Adriana said softly. "I don't understand what any of this has to do with my situation now—" she stopped. Her hands flew to her mouth, eyes wide as the terror of knowledge took root in her brain. "I don't believe any of this. You're completely out of your mind if you believe it."

Olda smiled but said nothing.

"It has no purpose," she persisted. "Why change the world to something evil, backward, opposite to what it has been for ages?"

"Because the world *is* changing. It was made to reflect peace and tranquility, as your God wanted it for the benefit of his highest creature—man. But man has totally ruined the world out of greed. Wars—in the name of your God. People starving—in the name of your God. My Lord and Master is merely trying to set the record straight. Erradicate those who believe in your God and make way for those who believe in Satan and his tenets. You say there is no purpose. There is. A definite purpose. A well-structured plan.

"Lucifer told the priest at the convent that he and his demons know much—that they read the signs of the times, the wars, the sufferings, the starvation. He said: 'This is the last century.' Satan told me that this means the last century of existence on this planet as it has been known. Beyond the year 2000, the end will be at hand and the new reign of Satan and his followers will begin. He and he alone, through *HIS* son, will reign supreme."

Her eyes riveted to the old man, Adriana fought to tear them away. Despite the fact she knew Morrison had brainwashed her, and as a result could well understand her vacillation between acceptance and utter rejection of the philosophies Olda proclaimed, she had difficulty in understanding how anyone's intelligence could balance such evil.

"I—I think your ideas are totally insane. I'm not certain as to how I will ultimately receive them. But for now, they're insane as far as I'm concerned."

Olda smiled, a tiny laugh almost passing unheard. "In time, my dear, you will see everything in its proper perspective. You will profit handsomely because of your role. Do not run the risk of incurring my wrath or the wrath of my master." He moved catlike toward the door. "I will see to it that food and drink are sent here to your room. For now, until we can better trust your thought processes, I think it is in everyone's best interests if you are confined to your room."

Turning, he saw Adriana wipe a tear from the corner of her eye. "It will only be for a short time, I'm sure. Reflect on what I have mentioned. If you have any questions, tell whoever brings your meals that you want to see me. I will be most happy to visit and answer your queries at any time of the day or night."

He disappeared through the door, dramatically punctuating his departure with the turning of the key in the lock.

Adriana stared at the door for a long while. There had to be some way in which she could escape this island of madmen. Leaving the bed, she looked out the window. So peaceful. So quiet. So normal. How could anything be amiss on this beautiful island? Reaching out without looking, she grasped the nearby chair on which Olda had been sitting, to bring it to the window. It refused to move. She turned, placing both hands on the back and tugged. The chair didn't budge.

"What on earth—?" she mumbled and tried once more without success. Dropping to her knees she looked more closely at the legs. Small brackets tightly screwed to the floor and to the legs of the chair firmly secured it next to the bed. "Why—? Who—? For what—?" The unfinished questions hammered at her mind. Turning, she crawled to the commode, and examined its legs. Similar brackets held it in place. What were they frightened of? Her? How could she harm them? When she stood, the absence of the wash bowl and pitcher drew her attention. What was going on?

Then she understood. They had removed from her room anything that could potentially serve as a weapon. Functional items such as the chair, which might be lifted and smashed across someone's unsuspecting skull when he or she entered to care for the room's occupant, had been screwed to the floor. She checked the dresser. It too had been fastened to the oak boards, although she could see no reason for it. What else had they done while she had been sleeping or drugged or whatever had been wrong with her since she had tried to kill herself? The closet had been emptied. Her suitcase—gone. Even the clothes hangers—gone.

Now what would she do? Make a rope of the

bed linen and climb down to the ground below her window? She ran lightly to the open casement and peered out. The ground appeared closer than it actually was. The first floor's ceilings were at least twelve feet high and the front portico stood another twelve to fifteen feet off the ground, which meant that the second floor, where she stood, was at least twenty-four to twenty-seven feet off the ground. Too far to jump. But maybe she could make a rope out of the sheets on her bed.

Throwing the coverlet back, she found the bed stripped. The sheets and light blanket, which had been there, were gone. The drawers of the dresser yielded nothing except her cosmetics and her mother's crucifix. Picking it up, she kissed the figure on the feet and suddenly dropped it as if the simple wooden and metal cross had turned white hot. She quickly retrieved it, placing it in her cosmetic bag.

Nothing. There was simply nothing in the room that might serve her purpose of escaping. A light zephyr lifted the curtains as it entered the room, seeking refuge, only to disappear.

Lying back on the bed, Adriana studied the ceiling. Now what would she do?

Tuesday, May 7, 1985

Her head felt heavy, sluggish. What had they given her? Along with a large meal, which one of the girls had brought without saying a word, she had been given two capsules. Morrison had stopped by when she finished eating and told her to take the pills. They were for her condition and would help her experience little if any pain or trouble during delivery. Reluctantly taking them with water, she watched him over the rim of the glass. He seemed so sincere, so interested in her well-being. Was Morrison Tyler, psychiatrist, a devil worshipper who could play both sides of the net? In his daily practice, he dealt with neuroses, mental problems, and troubled people who needed understanding—situations that called for logic as well as empathy and sympathy. She wondered if he ever displayed the dark side of his being to those he helped. Did he ever try to cultivate converts among his patient clientele?

"What are you thinking about, Adriana?" he asked, turning his head slightly.

She studied the three quarter view of his handsome profile. She could not discount that aspect of Morrison. He looked distinguished with the flaglike waves of white at his temples contrasting with the rest of his graying brown hair; his well-defined nose and cheeks complemented his friendly eyes and mouth. Anyone seeing him on the street would take him for exactly what he appeared to be—a doctor (a lawyer, maybe, a banker, perhaps)—but never a devil worshipper.

"If I told you, you'd either tell everyone else or try to make something awful out of it because of your being a doctor." She returned the glass to the nightstand.

"I hope you understand that I was compelled

to do with you what I did. I—"

"Compelled? What compelled you? Who or what forced you to take full advantage of my mental state?" She managed to glare at him, although she found it difficult to maintain an air of anger toward him.

"If and when you join us, you will understand more about—well, everything. You see, as an individual, one does not count for anything unless it is as a member of the whole. When I was told you would become a patient of mine and what I was to do, I simply had no choice. I *had* to do it."

"Aren't you your own person? Can't you think for yourself? My God, don't you realize that you're probably an accessory to murder?"

He smiled broadly. "You, young lady, have watched too much television. You sound like an actress portraying an attorney, standing in front of an actor playing the accused. Someone would first have to determine that your parents met with foul play, then they would have to connect their deaths to our group. Since there is no known association between your late mother and father and any member of this organization, I suggest that anyone attempting to tell the authorities would come off sounding a bit on the disturbed side."

She frowned. He was right and she knew it. If they were truly responsible for her parents' deaths and had managed it without anyone being there or linked with them in any way, who would believe a teenage college drop-out who had suffered a mental breakdown? At best, she could probably look forward to being confined for lengthy observation. And what would that accomplish? Nothing that she could think of at the moment.

After discovering everything in the room fastened to the floor and her belongings, other than her cosmetics and crucifix, gone, she had lain on the bed pondering her dilemna. She wondered about the cross, concluding they had overlooked it or didn't fear it. Her only option at the present was to cooperate with them and wait for someone to slip up someplace. Perhaps they'd miss something more important the next time. Eventually they would lower their guard if they thought she was actually going to become one of them. Then she could take advantage of whatever the situation offered. If it were escape, she'd succeed. If it meant waiting to be taken back to the mainland, she'd wait. But somehow, she would get away.

"I hope you understand my point of view, Morrison," she said, carefully enunciating each word. The pills were beginning to take more effect.

"Of course I do. We all do. If we didn't, there's no telling what might have been done by now. After all, much depends on your successful pregnancy and delivery. In fact, everything does. My understanding of your grappling with this new philosophy is the difference between your being here in this room cared for night and day by dedicated people and being locked up in a room in the basement where it is dark and damp."

She tried desperately to hang on to each word he spoke but second by second, each became slurred into the next until Morrison Tyler, healer of minds, sounded as though he were speaking some foreign language.

Her eyelids grew heavy and she found difficulty in keeping them open. Smiling crookedly at him, she opened her mouth to speak but nothing intelligible came out. She waved one hand at him in frustration and he nodded.

"I understand," he said, rising to move toward the door. "Your medication is taking its toll on you. Sleep, my child. Tomorrow, you and I will talk more if you wish." He opened the door, turning to look about the room before leaving. Satisfied that Adriana would be safe for the night, he stepped into the hall, closing the door behind him. He locked it and walked toward the head of the wide staircase.

Adriana watched him walk through the door from beneath her half-closed lids. She felt so wonderfully warm and content. Snuggling into the pillow, she forced herself to think one final thought before slipping into sleep. Tomorrow, when they brought her medication, she would take only one pill. One of the two she had been taking since her evening meal last night had to be a tranquilizer or something very much like one. She found herself completely liquid in her thoughts, movements, and understanding. If someone came in right now and suggested she leap out of the window, she wouldn't even hesitate for a second to think of an argument why she shouldn't. She'd just jump. She had to find out which pill was robbing her of her mental strength and motor functions. Then she would be able to act the part of one who has been drugged and not take the pill any longer. She felt too vulnerable when she couldn't control her thoughts, even though most of the time they were erratic at best.

Closing her eyes, she drifted for a moment before plunging into a deep sleep.

Wednesday, May 8, 1985

The day had been as uneventful as the previous one. She had done nothing but lie on the bed, sit in her chair, walk a circular route about her room and look out the window. Meals became the high points of her day. She looked forward to seeing who would be bringing her tray of food and what would be on it. Would they stay and talk with her, and if they did, what would they talk about?

Dr. Lahpavi had stopped by in the morning and again in the afternoon to check her blood pressure. He studied her with an intensity that frightened her. His black eyes stabbed unmercifully into hers, seeking the deepness and bottom foundations of her being.

She had concentrated, as best she could, on anything but his eyes. When she pictured the beach on which she had tried to kill herself by drowning, he backed away, staring at her. What had he seen in her eyes that made him retreat like that?

"What—what is it, Doctor?" she asked.

"Nothing. You're doing well—very fine. I will check your blood pressure twice per day from now on."

"Why? Why do you have to do it so often? Is that normal?"

He smiled but said nothing. Closing his bag, he spun on his heel and left the room, the key turning in the lock the last sound she heard until her next visitor would herald their subsequent arrival by unlocking the door.

She didn't mind seeing him leave. She still found it difficult to look at him without visibly reacting.

After Roseanne left with her evening meal dishes, she studied the capsules lying in her hand, one a slightly darker shade of pink than the other. They were close, but side by side, she could distinguish them. Which to take? What difference? Tomorrow she would take the other if she didn't find her answer today.

Opening her jar of hand cream, she buried the darker of the two in the white balm. When she returned the container to the drawer, she poured water in a glass and downed the other pill.

Fifteen minutes later, her head was swimming and she staggered to the bed. She had taken the tranquilizer. Her last thought was to take the darker pill the next day. Then she sank into the morass of sleep.

Roseanne peered at Adriana through her thick glasses. "Why did you do that?" she asked.

"Do what?"

"Everytime I've seen you take your medication, you always took both capsules at the same time. This time you took them one after the other. Why?"

"How many times have you seen me take them?" Adriana asked boldly.

"Only Monday night. But Dr. Tyler said you took both of them Tuesday night."

"Did he say I took them together? Who saw me take them last night? Aren't you getting a little overzealous, Roseanne?"

She picked up the tray and lumbered toward the door. "I was told to watch you carefully whenever I came in here. I'm just doing my part, that's all."

"Thank you, Roseanne," Adriana said, trying to give an air of finality to her voice.

The heavyset woman left, her departure emphasized by the key turning in the lock.

Adriana spit out the capsule she had held under her tongue. It had softened but had not broken. Opening her jar of hand cream, she buried it. The next time she applied any to her hands, the skin would really relax. A smile crossed her face. She had won a small battle but would at least be able to retain her mental facility because of her victory.

A quarter of an hour later, she felt her eyes getting heavy. What was happening? Had they changed medication? Both capsules looked the same as the others. There was no reason for them to change—at least none predicated on something she might have done. Perhaps both were capable of affecting her. Tomorrow night, she would take neither and feign sleep if necessary. Tomorrow night, she would begin laying plans to get out of her room if it were humanly possible. Tomorrow night, she would plan a way of getting out. Tomorrow night—

ELEVEN

Friday, May 10, 1985

ADRIANA WATCHED the door close and waited for the sound of the key turning in the lock. The receding steps of Roseanne told her that she was alone. Spitting the capsules into her hand, she jumped from the bed and hid them with the others in the cosmetic jar. Whenever she had been alone during the day she had exercised, clearing her head and freshening her body from the effects of the drugs she had been given the last four days. She felt alert, confident that her plan for escaping her locked room would work.

It had occurred to her the day before that whoever visited her room, whether it was to bring food and water or one of the two doctors checking her physical or mental health, always left the key in the door after it had been locked. She would have to wait possibly three or four hours before implementing her plan. The others would have to be retired for the night.

Stationing herself at the door, she waited patiently for the sounds of people coming up to their rooms. After what seemed days instead of hours, she heard muffled voices at the top of the staircase. She could barely make out the "good nights" being said but knew she would have to wait at least another hour beyond the last sounds.

Slowly the minutes crawled by without notice. The last noise she had heard seemed to have happened only seconds before but she knew an hour had definitely passed. The clock downstairs had chimed the quarter hour three times since it last tolled the hour. It was late.

She had planned carefully. All she had to do was slip the throw rug by her bed under the door and knock the key out of the lock so that it would fall on the rug. Then she could retrieve the key by pulling the braided rug back into the room. Although she hadn't tried it by fitting the rug through the space, she felt reasonably certain that it would fit. She guessed the bottom of her mother's crucifix would fit into the keyhole.

Armed with her cross and rug, she moved toward the door. When she tried pushing the knotted rag rug beneath the door, she choked back a sob of frustration. It wouldn't fit. Mumbling under her breath, she replaced the rug and sat on the edge of her bed. Now what would she do? There were no bedclothes, her own things she had brought with her were gone, and the only piece of fabric in the room other than the lace curtains was her nightgown. Of course.

She pulled it over her head. The thin material would fit without a problem. All she'd have to do was slip it back over her head once she held the key in her hand.

She practiced sliding the gown on the well-polished floor to make certain it would not bunch up. Confident she could push the thin material into the hall far enough to catch the key, she grabbed the crucifix and returned to the door. When she hunched down next to the keyhole, she eyed the base of the cross. Suddenly it seemed as big as a telephone pole. Would it fit? She tried and stood, disgusted with her plan. So near to escape and yet her plan might just as well have involved walking on the moon for all the practicality of her untried scheme.

Throwing her nightdress on the bed, she lay down. Even though she hadn't taken the drugs, she felt sleepy. The residue left in her system, no doubt. Her breasts ached from the exercising she had done that day to rid her body of those effects. Standing, she moved to the mirror. They *were* bigger. There was no way she could deny that. Both were considerably more full than they had been the week before. She still wanted to deny the fact she might be pregnant but she could not deny the change in her body—the enlarging of her breasts, her morning sickness of a few days before, and her inability to pull her middle in. The only thing she had to do was get away from these people.

She returned to the bed and lay down, her head at the foot end. Her eyes traversed the ceiling, coming to rest at the top of the curtains. Strange symbols had been included with the fine lace work and she wondered what their meaning might be. They seemed esoteric—the inverted five pointed stars surrounded with double circles, the pointed "u's" that resembled horns or thumbs pointed upward. Of course. That had to be the meaning of the strange position the people held their hands in whenever they weren't occupied doing something else. Horns? But of what? The devil? Why not?

Then something arrested her attention. She scrambled to her feet, bouncing lightly on the mattress. Stretching her hand up, she came within scant inches of the pointed needle gracing the decorative ball at the end of the curtain rod. She stepped up, onto the top of the brass headboard, leaning against the wall to maintain her precarious balance. When the ball wouldn't turn, she lifted the rod, curtains and all, from its position and returned to the bed.

She studied them for a moment before giving a hard turn to the ball. It slipped about its thread easily. Unscrewing it, she found the sharp point also screwed out and quickly freed it. She replaced the ball at the end of the rod before returning it, the curtains hanging below, to its position above the window.

Hurrying to the door, she slid her gown under it and poked the needlelike point into the keyhole. Slowly jabbing at the rounded end of the key, she could feel it move little by little toward the other side. Then it was gone and she heard it hit the floor. Pressing her body against the floor, she peered into the darkened hallway. She couldn't see if she had been lucky. Had the key fallen on her gown? Standing, she went to the dresser and lifted the lamp. The flame would be too high and away from the crack at the bottom of the door to be of any use. Pulling open the drawer containing her cosmetic bag, she concealed the crucifix once more and withdrew a small mirror.

She returned to the door where she set the lamp down and began moving the mirror about, her cheek and nose hard against the floor. A faint glint showed the key lying no more than three or four inches away on the other side. Fighting to control her elation, she laid the mirror down and began pulling the nightgown into the room. She heard the key nudge against the door and held her breath. It wasn't coming in. She choked back the urge to vent her rage. Her hopes were dashed. The key had merely fallen off when the gown passed under it. Lying down on the floor, she could see the key just on the other side, not more than two inches away. Leaping to her feet, she grabbed the point she had used to dislodge the key from its resting place and threw herself back down. She thrust it beneath the door and began wiggling it back and forth until the prized bit of metal slid into the room.

She grasped it, holding it up to the light. Success. Before slipping into her gown, she placed the lamp on the dresser. Should she return the spike to its position at the end of the curtain rod? She had wasted enough time. Lifting the mattress, she hid it in the spring.

Quickly slipping the key into the lock without making any sound, she slowly turned it. The lock gave and the door swung in when she turned the knob. Stepping into the hallway, she closed it behind her.

Someone coughed. Someone nearby in the corridor. She froze, barely breathing.

It seemed like an endless second in the scheme of creation as she waited for whoever had coughed to speak. But nothing happened. Turning her head, her hand still clutching the door knob, she peered down the hall. There, seated in a straight back chair, head bowed onto his chest, Jefferson St. Clair slept away his turn at guard duty. If he checked upon awakening and found the key gone, he might sound the alarm. She opened the door, slipping her hand inside to withdraw the key. Locking it, she smiled. If the key were left in the door, they might not even think to check until breakfast time.

Tiptoeing away in the opposite direction from the sleeping man and the staircase, she held her breath until she had moved thirty to forty feet down the gloomy hallway. At least there were a few lamps left burning during the night. She would have to find the back stairway. It seemed impossible there wouldn't be one in a house this size.

She wondered what they would think when they entered her room to find her gone and every-thing in its place including the key on the outside of the door. Reveling in her feeling of self-satisfaction, the first she had enjoyed since shortly after her arrival on the island, she continued quietly down the hallway, away from the sleeping Jefferson St. Clair. Downstairs, the clock tolled the hour of three.

Olda studied Morrison Tyler who sat opposite him across the wide expanse of his desk. The single lamp flickered peculiar shadows on the men's faces.

"You can be thankful she's behaving herself but that's only because of the drugs we've been giving her," the old man said.

"I find it absolutely amazing that she has been able to resist the amount of indoctrination she received. Perhaps there's more work to be done on it before we use it again," Morrison said, his voice apologetic but firm. He hadn't wavered at any time during Olda's perusal of his records on Adriana or subsequent questions or chastisements. He felt he was winning. But winning what? An argument with Olda. It was nothing.

"I'm afraid we'd have our hands full if she were not being sedated each day," Olda said, scanning the few remaining sheets of paper.

"How long will we continue with it?"

He shrugged. "Perhaps right up until the time the baby is to be born. Perhaps she'll begin seeing things our way once she is absolutely convinced she is pregnant, then we might be able to stop."

"Is Lahpavi positive she won't suffer any consequences because of the drugs?" Morrison did not hold much admiration for the obstetrician and made no pretense of liking the man.

"He seems certain enough. It's a shame you couldn't have done better yourself," Olda said, displaying a mirthless smile. "You have only one person to thank for whatever degree of success you enjoy. And you have repaid it with an amatuerish job when asked to partake in what will prove to be the most important task relegated to man since—"

Morrison held up his hand. "Remember, Olda, we're dealing with a lot of unknowns. Lahpavi has been lucky—so far. When Adriana goes into labor and gives birth, then and only then will we know how successful that idiot has been. It seems to me that—"

"Don't be insulting, Morrison. We should consider ourselves thankful that Rizahgyhny was chosen by our Master. With the formula given him, despite your slipshod job of preparing Adriana, we might see this project through to a satisfactory conclusion yet. But if we had had to rely solely on your efforts, it would have been a fluke from the onset."

Morrison bristled, his eyes glaring. "Remember we are to share equally in the rewards from the Master."

"Yes, that is true—no thanks to you."

The clock sounded three times intoning the hour of Satan, and both men interlaced their fingers projecting their thumbs upright. "Be with us, Master," they intoned as the notes died away.

Olda stood. "It's time we retired. I'm satisfied you did your best after going over your notes. Unfortunately it wasn't the results we wanted, but then who's to say that perhaps anyone else under the same circumstances might not have met with exactly the same results?"

Morrison stretched before getting to his feet. "I'm glad to hear you say that. At least you understand that we *are* treading on totally unfamiliar ground. Perhaps we should have contacted an expert from China as I suggested."

Olda smiled wanly. "How can you get a Chinese Communist who doesn't believe in God, nor Satan either, to teach us the techniques necessary to prepare the womb of a woman for the Son of Evil?"

"I still think it might have been worth a try," Morrison said, taking the lead to leave the room when Olda gestured.

"I'll look in on Adriana before retiring," the old man said, following the psychiatrist up the broad staircase.

Adriana had tried every door she saw, opening each one as quietly as possible for fear of coming upon someone sleeping. But each room had been empty. Apparently she was the sole occupant of this end of the house. It disturbed her that she had been unable to find a second staircase that would undoubtedly lead to the kitchen and freedom from this madhouse. The thought of having to retrace her steps and try to get by Jefferson hovered in her mind. She wasn't completely sure she could get past him and out the front door without someone seeing or hearing her.

When she reached the end of the hall, she stopped. There was nothing here but the corridor draped in black extending to her left. Was there anything down there that might help her get out? She tried to recall if there had been any doors other than the one with the strange carving. At the time she hadn't been looking for a back stairway, only the way down to the foyer. Perhaps there was another door or doors, hidden beneath the black draperies.

Two dim lamps burned feebly, barely lighting the narrow passage. Tiptoeing, if for no reason other than the fact she was constantly reminded of the night they had carried her down here, she made her way toward the end of the hall. As she moved, she groped along the curtains on both sides, searching for a door, a window. Nothing.

When she stood at the end, she drew in her breath and reached out poking through the drapes. A film of sweat broke out on her forehead when her hand touched the carving. The door swung a bit. It was open.

Looking behind her, she stood, undecided as to what she should do when she heard voices. Someone was coming. First there were two. Then three. Someone must have found Jefferson St. Clair sleeping on the job. If she were to go back she would surely be discovered. What could she do? Go through the door that led to wherever it was they had raped her that night? She had no choice.

Carefully stepping through the folds of heavy material, she pushed the door. It swung open farther and she entered. The voices, despite being muffled through the curtains, grew louder, more angry as heated words were exchanged. Easing the door shut, she groped for the door knob to stop it from making a noise but it closed with a click that seemed too loud. She had to find the knob and reopen it so she could leave once the hall was clear. Her fingers flew over the hard smooth finish. She could not find the door knob. There was no latch on the inside.

Olda stared at the sleeping man. "Jefferson," he said loudly, "wake up. In the name of Satan if you want to sleep, go to bed and get someone who can stay awake to watch over our precious young girl."

Jefferson St. Clair opened his eyes, completely disoriented. "Huh? Who's there?" he mumbled, his voice thick with sleep.

"That's all we need. Indifference like this and the whole thing will collapse," Morrison said, derision hanging from each word. He was happy to be able to lay blame on someone else for inadequacies after Olda's earlier reprimand.

"I—I'm sorry, Olda," St. Clair stammered, embarrassed at having been caught sleeping.

"It's useless to ask you if you've heard anything.

I'll check myself. I was going to anyway," the old man said, hurrying toward Adriana's room.

Morrison followed. She might awaken at the sound of voices in the hall and someone coming into her room. If she panicked, he would have to be there.

Olda stopped at the door and listened closely. No noise. He smiled and turned the key. Swinging the door open quietly, he entered, gasping loudly. The bed was empty. The room was empty. "How can this be? Where can she have gone?"

Morrison stepped around him, entering the vacant room. Dropping to his knees, he peered under the bed. He stood and crossed to the closet door, opening it with a sweep, expecting to find the girl cowering in the small room. The smell of moth balls washed over him. "This is impossible," he said under his breath. "Where could she have gone?"

"Wherever she's run to, we've got to find her," Olda said, stepping back into the hallway. "Jefferson. Get the others up. Now. She's gone. Thanks to you."

"But—"

"Don't argue with me or make excuses," Olda roared. "The mistake has been made. There is no defending yourself. Get going."

The heavyset man lumbered down the hall toward the opposite end where the other members lay sleeping. He rapped on each door he came to, shouting, "Get up. Get up. Adriana is gone. Adriana is gone. Get up."

Adriana forced the painful lump from her throat, fighting the tears she felt rising. *Why? Why?* she repeatedly asked herself. She wanted to pound on the door. Break it down if she could, but that was not possible. What could she do? Turning, she blindly thrust her hands out in front of her. What kind of place was she in? To her left, she found more drapery and solid wall beneath it. When she turned around, the wall opposite the door revealed the same. Only to her left, with the door to her back, was she unable to find anything. Carefully reaching out with her toes, she felt for the edge of the floor on which she stood. She lowered one foot slowly, hoping to find a step. When she stood on the first riser, she clung to the drapery on her left. Step by slow step, she descended the black stairs.

Nearing the bottom, she detected a lighter, half dark seeping into the stairwell. She had to be careful. What if someone was down there waiting for her?

When she stood at the bottom, she looked about. One candle flame danced uncertainly on its wick, incapable of lighting much more than the immediate area around it. She could see nothing but the light. Moving toward it, she was thankful that she had nothing on her feet as they padded noiselessly on the stone floor.

The candle stood behind a table. She stepped closer. It was the altar on which she had lain and been raped. Fighting to keep her thoughts on the present situation and not on the rite in which she had been forced to partake, she moved around to the candle. Testing its holder, she found it to be easily removed and, armed with light, retraced her steps to the front of the black marble table.

What could she do now? She had light but was locked in. There had to be another way out, at best, some way to open the door at the top of the steps. Holding the candle high, she turned in a circle and stopped, her free hand flying to her mouth.

"Good God!" she muttered, staring at the letters which spelled her name, incised into the black stone. "What can that mean? How long has it been here?" She whispered the words, more in awe of the fact that her name was there rather than how it could have been done.

A low moan and heavy breathing from the blackness surrounding her took her off guard, her own breath catching in her throat.

Olda looked at the sleepy-eyed people standing in the foyer, mentally counting them. "Not every one is here. Where is Everhart and—and—Angelique?"

The people looked from one to the other but said nothing.

Jefferson St. Clair stepped forward, his eyes the only ones not fogged with sleep. Olda had managed to awaken him completely. "I knocked at both their doors. But I didn't wait to see if they answered. Everyone responded almost immediately."

Olda turned to face his three helpers. "Check their rooms."

In minutes the two women who had dashed up the stairs to do Olda's bidding returned, shaking their heads. "Nothing," one reported.

Deirdre, who had remained at Morrison's side, stepped forward. "Perhaps they're in the black chapel. They like to go there and make visits to pray to Satan."

"I'll check," Olda said. "In the meantime, the rest of you fan out in groups of two or three. She must be found."

"If she isn't," Lahpavi said, "she'll miss her drugs and medicines when she should be eating in the morning. If that happens, everything can be lost. Hurry. Find her."

The people dispersed in small groups. Some went up the stairs to check the empty bedrooms while others hurried to look into the first floor rooms and wings.

Olda made his way up the stairs, turning to hurry to the chapel. Striding down the raven hall, his footsteps muffled by the thick carpeting, he approached the end. Reaching through he touched the door but withdrew his hand when it popped open. Stepping farther back next to the drapes, he waited.

Adriana could not move. The noise came again. This time it sounded like someone snoring. Her eyes darted from side to side, the cords in her neck standing out like ropes. Who could it be? The guttural rasping continued and she relaxed a bit. Whoever it was had not been awakened by her. But the question as to who might be in the room with her begged to be answered. She stepped foward, toward the breathing.

As she neared the far wall that supported the staircase, shapes began taking on form. First one, then a second. There were two people lying on what appeared to be a chaise lounge. She inched closer.

The first thing that she recognized were Angelique's breasts, rising and falling in even rhythm. Next to her Everhart Parrot's bareness took on a grayish yellow cast, when she stepped closer. The back of his head rested on the woman's naked stomach, his body between her outstretched legs.

What should she do now? Adriana turned away but spun about immediately.

Everhart's snoring suddenly stopped as he inhaled deeply and turned more on his side. Angelique threw an arm protectively over his head and he murmured in his sleep. Both began wiggling about while their hands groped for each other's genitals. Adriana held her breath.

What if they saw her? She would be taken back to her room and subjected to only God knew what. Or should she say Satan? It seemed to her that God had abandoned her. Maybe she should consider the alternative as offered by Olda and his clan or group or—what was a bunch of witches called—coven? Yes, coven.

The thought sickened her. She had to get away. Backing away, the lounge fell into darkness again but suddenly she realized that, even though she couldn't see them, her whereabouts were highly visible because of the flickering light she held. Her back bumped the altar and she turned. On either side four large black candles stood blind guard. Moving to one side, she grasped one, twisting it from its holder.

Gliding across the floor, she approached the couple, who were locked in a sexual embrace, Everhart on top, his hips pounding at Angelique's body. She raised her weapon high above her head in one hand before smashing it onto the back of the man's head. Without a sound, he rolled off his partner's convulsing body. Angelique continued writhing, masturbating when she realized Everhart's erection was no longer inside her.

Adriana raised the candle again, breaking it over the woman's head. Angelique lay still except for diminishing thrusts of her full hips.

She had to tie them up before either regained consciousness. But what could she use? Hurrying about the room, she found a place behind the altar where tied-back drapes framed more drapes. Tearing the ropelike material from its duty, she returned to the prostrate forms, carrying four lengths. She quickly bound Everhart's hands behind him before securing his feet. Doing the same with Angelique, she stood over them, breathing a sigh of relief. For the instant, she was safe.

What if she had killed them? Had she hit them hard enough? Turning away, she crossed the room, forcing a smile to her face. They certainly didn't care what happened to her. Why should she be concerned for them?

"If I have to kill every one of them in order to get out of here, I will," she vowed quietly.

Lighting all the candles she could find, she relaxed when the room took on a more golden hue. At least she could see the entire area. Slowly circumventing the chapel, she poked behind the drapes, looking for a window or door through which she could escape to the outside. When she neared her starting point, she stopped, tears of frustration rolling down her cheeks.

There was only one way out. The door through which she had entered stood at the top of the stairs, locked. Returning to the altar, she leaned against it. There had to be a way. The door upstairs had to open. Mentally, she ran her hand over it again, searching for a knob or button or something that would open it. She shook her head. There had been nothing other than smooth wood. How did the rest of them enter and leave if there were no way?

Had anything happened the night she had been brought here that escaped her now? She desperately searched the deepest recesses of her memory. Nothing—nothing that seemed out of place. Then, step by step, she went through the night again: she had been brought down the steps, placed on the altar, two candles had been forced into her paralyzed hands, and her arms, when they were outstretched, made her body into the form of a cross. Olda had read some blasphemous prayers while he conducted the unholy rite. They had killed a lamb and they had taken some of her blood and mixed it with that of the animal. Then they had all drunk some of it and Olda had raped her.

Her stomach heaved at the recollection of the blood she had swallowed. At the time, she had thought nothing of it but now the recollection nauseated her. She retched, her stomach trying to throw out its contents. She left the altar and ran to the wall behind it, clutching at the drapes. Lightheaded, she lost her balance and leaned against the wall—and fell into an alcove.

She caught herself before falling to the floor and the sudden discovery wiped out the memory of the blood-drinking. Her stomach quieted down. She had stopped short of the point where she had begun her search, completely missing the small room. Returning to the altar, she grabbed a candle and hurried back to the draped opening. She parted the curtains, stepping inside, the odor of damp earth, the same that permeated the house, washed over her. The untreated rock wall reflected the light of her candle and her shoulders slumped. There were only three solid walls. No openings of any kind. But on one wall a small panel of some sort, with several buttons or knobs, beckoned to her. She found them marked with single words: music, maid, trap door, door. Controls? Hesitantly reaching out, she touched the one marked door and pushed. Nothing happened. She shoved harder, pushing it until something clicked. When she removed her finger, the button popped back. Had she opened the door at the top of the stairs?

Pushing the drapes aside, she hurried across the room to the steps and ran up. When she reached the top, she found the door open a few inches. Breathing quickly, her relief suffocated by excitement, she opened it more, stepping through the draperies.

Olda, waiting at the side of the door to see who would come through, grabbed Adriana.

At the touch of his hand, she whirled about, her eyes wide, frightened, like those of a trapped animal. Her mouth opened to scream. Instead, she fainted.

He caught her, cradling her body in his arms and walked down the black hall toward her room.

TWELVE

Saturday, May 11, 1985

AT FIRST Adriana thought she had gone blind. All she could see was whiteness—nothing else. Then, as her eyes refocused, she made out the flowered wallpaper and knew she was back in her room. What had happened? She remembered walking up the stairs to the door without a knob and stepping into the black-draped hallway. Had—had someone grabbed her? Yes. She recalled Olda Revillion's gaunt face, mere inches from her own, grinning down on her. That was all. She must have fainted.

She tried to move but found she could not. Could she be paralyzed again? Her arms moved a bit but were held in check. Wiggling her feet, she found the same to be true of her legs. She was tied to the bed. She raised her head as far as she could and saw Michele sitting at her side.

"What—what's going on?" she stammered.

Michele stood at the sound of Adriana's voice, looking down at her. "You're awake. Good. Dr. Lahpavi will be glad to hear that. He was concerned that something might have happened to you, which in turn might affect the child."

"Will you release me? Please?" Adriana looked up, her eyes pleading.

"I would if it were up to me, dear Adriana. But Olda and the doctors seem to think you can't be trusted anymore. I'm afraid they've decided you must stay on the bed until the baby is born."

Adriana choked back a sob. That wasn't fair. She would go crazy if she couldn't get off the bed once in a while. What about her bodily functions? Wouldn't they have to take her to the outside toilet whenever it was necessary? Or would they make her lie in her own filth?

As if reading her mind, Michele said, "We have all the necessary bed pans and washing facilities right here in your room. For the next fourteen to sixteen days, you'll remain strapped to your bed. You should not have tried to escape. Escape's impossible, you know. What did you hope to achieve by getting out of here? Where would you have gone?"

Adriana shook her head. She remembered her feeling of triumph after managing to break out of her room—her sense of confusion as to what to do and where to go once she had won her small victory. She thought of trying to find the back stairway only to stumble into the black chapel. The black chapel. What had happened to Angelique and Everhart? Were they still lying down

294

there, bound, naked? She looked up at Michele and said, "Did anyone untie Angelique and Everhart? I'm afraid—"

"We found them shortly after Olda brought you here. Don't worry. They're fine. They had headaches but that was all," she said, then laughed throatily. "Honestly, the way that woman wants to fuck any man she meets is unreal. She's almost as bad as Charlene and Deirdre—and me."

Adriana stared at her. Could she be serious? Would a beautiful young woman such as Michele or the others be so blatant about their sex lives? She supposed it could be true but she found it almost impossible to believe. Then she thought of the warm greeting Deirdre had given Morrison when they arrived at the island. How long ago had that been? It seemed like it all had happened in another world at another time.

At least she hadn't killed them the way she had planned if no other avenue opened to her. Now she was tethered like some animal. She turned away, facing the wall.

"I'm going down to tell the doctors that you're awake, Adriana. I'll be back in a few minutes." Michele glided toward the door, closing it with a quiet click.

Adriana was alone. What would happen next? She blamed herself for being captured. If only she had completed the circuit of the room, she would have found the alcove with the controls in it several minutes earlier and perhaps she would have missed Olda at the door when— She turned her head to stare at the ceiling. The buttons. The controls. How did they work? All she had done was punch the one marked *door,* and the lock had freed itself. It had to have worked by electricity. If that were true, then there must be other things on the island operated by electricity. There were no lights. She hadn't seen a light bulb anyplace— only kerosene lamps. But surely they wouldn't have an energy supply merely to open one door, would they? Her mind raced, exploring the possibilities.

Suddenly Bergan erupted in her thoughts. Olda had said he left on business. But Bergen had been called away, hadn't he? She couldn't remember exactly what Olda had said. Surely they had to have a radio of some sort to stay in contact with the mainland. What would they do if someone became ill? There were two doctors, but that didn't account for the times when Lahpavi and Morrison weren't present. What if some real calamity took place? What would they do? They had to have a radio someplace. If she ever was allowed to roam free again, she'd have to change her method of searching. All she had done before was open doors and peek in, never once looking beyond the mere surface of what she might have seen. A radio could be hidden in a desk or on a shelf in a closet or in the cabinets in the kitchen.

Closing her eyes, she relaxed her body. If she had to stay on the bed— Something moved on her stomach. She felt it move as if someone had pressed a finger into her body. Lifting her head as far as she could, she stared. Nothing. There was nothing on her body. Her gown looked as if it hadn't been touched. She moved her feet to make certain she wasn't dreaming or hallucinating. But what had— It happened again, while she was looking. A cramp? Her head dropped back on the pillow and she shut her eyes. The baby? The baby! She didn't want a baby, especially Olda Revillion's child. Oh, God help—

The door swung open and Michele entered, followed by Morrison and Rizahghyny Lahpavi.

Sunday, May 12, 1985

Adriana was struggling futilely with her bonds when Roseanne entered, carrying a tray laden with food. Deirdre, who had been sitting next to the bed, stood, taking the salver from the maid.

"It's time to eat, Adriana," the tall blonde said.

"I'm not hungry. I just ate breakfast."

"More time has elapsed than you think, my dear," Deirdre said curtly as Roseanne adjusted her thick glasses, moving toward the door.

"Besides," Deirdre continued, "this meal marks the beginning of Dr. Lahpavi's special diet."

Adriana looked up at her, quizzically furrowing her forehead. "Special diet? I thought the food I was eating was the special diet."

"It was to a certain point. When he discovered the baby moving yesterday, he began preparing it —and now it's ready." She removed the towel covering the dishes with a flourish as if waiting for applause.

Adriana watched Deirdre stirring something in a bowl. When she brought a spoonful toward her mouth, Adriana recoiled. Whatever it was, appeared to be as black as coal. Streamers of steam lazily wound upward from it, and Adriana turned her head away in revulsion.

"You must eat this, Adriana. If you don't I'm not sure what Rizahghyny would do. At least try it."

The thought of the obstetrician coming back into her room changed Adriana's mind. She said, "It looks awful. What is it?"

"I have no idea. All I know is that Rizahghyny said it would be the key to completing the pregnancy in one month. You don't want to be confined to your bed for another eight months or so, do you?"

The idea staggered Adriana. She didn't want to be pregnant at all, but eight months more of this was preposterous. She opened her mouth, and the loaded spoon slipped inside. Strange, it seemed to have no aroma but when she closed her mouth, she discovered an almost bittersweet taste. How could it taste and not have a scent? The pasty substance felt not unlike the consistency of thick, lumpy oatmeal. She managed to swallow it, reluctantly accepting another, and another. For dinner, she had more of the same.

"I won't eat this," Adriana screamed. "It's awful. It smells like—like something filthy—like something died and wasn't buried. I won't eat it." She clamped her mouth shut and turned her head. Squeezing her eyes shut, she hoped Charlene would leave—just disappear and be gone when she reopened them.

She heard the door close and when she opened her eyes, Charlene was gone. It had worked. Or had it? She heard voices in the hall and the door burst open. Lahpavi rushed in, followed by Olda and Morrison.

"Now what seems to be the trouble, young lady?" Morrison asked, trying to affect a bedside manner.

Adriana glared at him. He was the reason she was in this situation. He was the reason she found herself suddenly pregnant. If she hadn't met him, she would never have come to this island. If her parents hadn't died— They had done that, too. Killed her parents.

Her mind fogged. Parents. Parent. She was going to be a parent. But she didn't want that. Her child? Hers and Olda's? The idea sickened her, making her shudder mentally. What a thought. Preposterous.

But if she really, truly were going to be a parent, how should she act? What should she do? Would it hurt? She remembered her mother telling her of the pain connected with labor. Could she stand the pain, the hurt, the strain of having a child, caring for it, loving it? If she had to see this through, and at the moment she could think of no alternative plan, she might as well intend on being good to her child as her parents had been to her.

"We cannot waste time," Lahpavi said, his voice more of a snarl than that of a doctor treating a patient. "She must eat all of this within an hour. How much time has been spent trying to get her to eat?"

Charlene stared back at him without flinching. "About fifteen minutes."

"We've no time to waste then. Help me force feed her," he ordered, moving to sit on the bed next to Adriana's shoulder. He directed Morrison to take a seat on the opposite side. "You," he barked at Charlene, "feed her when we open her mouth."

Charlene stepped closer to the bed, spoon in hand, ready to feed Adriana when they forced her mouth open.

Her jaws clenched tight, Adriana struggled as best she could but Morrison pinched her nose shut. She held what little breath she had retained after exhaling just before her nostrils were shut. She wouldn't breathe. She demanded her body stop ordering her to open her mouth—to take in a breathful of sweet, life-giving air. She wouldn't. Her eyes rolled in their sockets, watching the spoonful of dark brown mush poised in front of her mouth. Oh, God! She opened her mouth a bit to suck in air through her teeth. But the instant she did, Lahpavi painfully pressed her jaw at the hinge and her mouth opened more.

"Now," he snapped, and Charlene pushed the full spoon into her mouth. The scent was bad but the taste, even worse. Her stomach heaved, trying to expel the food before she swallowed it. Inhaling deeply, she tried to spit it out but Morrison slapped his hand over her mouth and nose, preventing her from breathing. The food in her mouth began digesting in saliva, thinning to a watery gruel. At least she had taken in a breath before her friend, the psychiatrist, made certain she would eventually have to swallow. She held the air in her lungs while it was stripped of its oxygen and loaded with carbon dioxide to exhaust into the air. Her head spun, the room began turning. Bright little black and white spots undulated in front of her eyes.

Please, God, let me die! Let me die right now. She prayed desperately, but her body, fighting for its survival, preferred to accept the vile concoction in her mouth in exchange for oxygen. It effortlessly slid down her throat and the hands left her face the instant she stopped struggling. Resigned to accept this new form of torture, she drew in as much air as she could, knowing the process would be repeated—again and again— until they got what they wanted—her baby. Did she even care? She had fought the idea long enough and barely wanted to accept it when she first felt the fetus move. How long ago had that been? It seemed like eons of time had passed, but when she concentrated, she knew it had only been on Friday. Could she survive another thirteen or fourteen days of this treatment? She hoped not.

When they finished feeding her the putrid mess, they stood around the bed, frowns on all three faces. Lahpavi balefully stared at her before raising his gaze to Morrison.

"This will not do at all, Morrison. Come. We'll have to devise some other means."

The two men swept out of the room. Charlene followed but returned after depositing the tray outside in the hall.

Adriana closed her eyes. She found it unbelievable that she hadn't vomited. But at least she had them running back to plan something else. She hoped and prayed it would be something more palatable than her last meal.

Tuesday, May 14, 1985

Although last evening's meal had been a repitition of the one at noon, Adriana discovered that the unsavory taste did not linger for more than a few minutes. Still, passing it beneath her nose and into her mouth did nothing toward her anticipating the next spoonful. Breakfast had been the same, but Deirdre, who had helped at that meal, smiled knowingly when she took the tray to the corridor—as if she knew this would be the last time they had difficulty in feeding her.

Adriana's suspicions were confirmed when Morrison, Lahpavi, Olda, and two of the girls entered shortly after the first meal. While Olda and Morrison held her arms to prevent her from

302

moving about within the limited range of her bonds, Lahpavi prepared an injection. After eliminating any remaining air from the syringe, he deftly drove the hypodermic needle home, pushing the clear liquid into her bloodstream.

Within minutes she felt a strange disconnected sensibility overcoming her body. She seemed to feel as though her arms and legs were no longer attached to her. Whenever she tried moving, the reaction to her brain's command took longer than it should have until several seconds would pass before a finger would wiggle or a foot change position. Although she found she could think clearly, she found herself unable to control her body in a normal way.

She looked at Deirdre who stared back with an intensity that frightened her. "What's happening to me?" she asked, startled by the strangeness of her voice. It sounded to her as though she had spoken into a metal drum.

"You're all right, Adriana," the woman said. "Dr. Lahpavi has given you a nerve retardant that slows your body's actions but not your mental capabilities. You'll be fine. You shouldn't have fought us so diligently. Now you'll be like this for the next couple of weeks—until the baby is born."

"That's not fair," she managed weakly.

"Oh, but it is. At least you'll be able to talk with whoever is sitting with you. What would you like to talk about?"

Adriana shook her head. "Nothing."

Adriana held the tiny form over her head. The baby cooed, gurgling its feelings for its mother. What had she birthed? A girl? A boy? Why didn't she know? She brought the child down to look closely at its little, round face. Tiny button nose. Snapping black eyes. Perfectly shaped pink rose-petal lips. Ears that were masterfully formed. The child's head, round with a thin blanket of fuzz, flopped about and she propped it up with her fingertips in back. The baby's face and head were picture pure—picture perfect. She felt so fortunate that her offspring was not malformed in any way. But she didn't know that for a fact, did she? Had she even checked the body? She couldn't recall.

Miraculously, a table appeared out of nowhere and she lay the infant on it. Then she discovered the babe wore nothing. It was naked and she looked at the crotch. A boy. She had given birth to a boy. She lifted the small manchild to her breasts, hugging her son, who whimpered his affection.

She suddenly felt exhausted, as though she couldn't hold the precious little body any longer. Surely if she didn't find a place to put him, she'd drop him, hurt him, mar his perfection. When she saw the door, she knew what she had to do. Hurrying toward it, she opened it, instantly smelling the friendly scent of moth balls. Of course. This was where she kept the baby. In her closet. Dropping him to the floor, she closed the door and sighed.

Adriana opened her eyes. How foolish. She was not ready to become a mother—regardless of what these idiots caring for her said. Besides, she still didn't believe she was or could be pregnant. The movement she felt in her stomach had to be something else. A baby? Ridiculous.

When she turned her head, she saw Ivy St. Clair sitting near the window, staring into space, her hands folded, thumbs upright. These people believed she was pregnant and would give birth to a baby who would grow up to be the Antichrist. None of them *seemed* mad, although Adriana thought that each one of them was a raving lunatic for holding such beliefs. What if they were right and she were wrong? Then, she *would* be pregnant. She *would* give birth to the Antichrist!

Tears welled in her eyes, trickling down her face. Perhaps she was the one who was mad . . .

Thursday, May 16, 1985

Other than the oil lamp's glow, lighting as much of the bedroom as it could, nothing other than shadows fell into Adriana's line of vision. She turned her head to see who sat with her. When she saw Roseanne, her head hanging down, the sleeping woman's guttural snores first became apparent to her. For some reason she enjoyed wakening during the dark hours when everyone else was sleeping—or at least when they were supposed to be sleeping. She enjoyed the peacefulness—not that the island, the valley, and the house itself ever emmanated anything but calm. The feeling she picked up was that of solitude. She felt totally alone. As if no one else on earth existed.

Ever since she had awakened to find herself bound to the bed, she had slept a lot. But because she did nothing to tire her muscles or joints, she found herself sleeping less at night. It amused her that the guards sitting in her room were invariably sound asleep whenever she woke up and she rather looked forward to those moments of aloneness. At first she had tried praying but quickly decided that since God had allowed her to be caught up in this predicament, He would not help her. Then she fantasized about Bergen. What was he really like? Could he be as warm and friendly as he had seemed that first night when they met? She shook her head. Probably he was just as crazy as everyone else she had met. But even that evening, with all its glamour, had not been fair—like so many other things that had happened to her. They had barely met and then he was gone. Gone as if she had imagined their meeting, his handsome features, his touch.

She closed her eyes. What had his voice sounded like? Replaying the scene in the drawing room, she contemplated the face she had conjured up in her imagination. The features were right, she was positive about that. The hair seemed styled correctly and the proper shade was well. But the voice . . . there had been something unique about his voice.

Roseanne snored loudly, forcing air through lips tightly clamped by the weight of her head resting against her chest. The sounds came in short, high-pitched squeaks.

Adriana turned her head toward the noise. It sounded like—like Bergen's voice. She chuckled quietly. Of course! His voice had seemed all wrong for the rest of him—his height, his well-proportioned physique, his handsome face. His voice had been too small for the rest of him.

She smiled in the darkened room. Now she had Bergen complete in her mind's eye, voice and all. Now that she had him, what could she do with him?

Recalling her own situation like the dreaded memory of her parents' deaths, she remembered the night Olda had raped her—fornicated with her—fucked her. She choked back a crying whimper. Another thing that had not been fair! But she had thought of Bergen when her body zigzagged toward orgasm, wishing that it were he instead of Olda.

Roseanne stirred in her sleep again.

Adriana turned her head, staring at the gloomy ceiling. Her eyelids drooped. Drowsiness was taking over once more. She wanted Bergen Messenger to lie down beside her. To make love to her.

She fought to hang onto that simple thought as her consciousness spiraled down into the morass of sleep . . .

It couldn't be. There, standing at the foot of her bed, completely naked, Bergen Messenger smiled down at her.

"Bergen? Is that you, Bergen?" she asked in a hoarse voice, whispering for fear of waking anyone.

He nodded.

"Come here. Come, lie next to me," she said, gesturing with her arm, unmindful of the fact it did not seem to be tethered for a change.

He stepped around the brass footboard, nearing her.

"You're so handsome, my darling," she said, holding both arms up to accept him to her breast.

Bending, he moved closer until she should have felt his breath on her cheek. His body felt hard, unyielding, firm in the way she felt his mind would be once it had made a decision.

"I love you, Adriana," he said quietly.

"And I love you, Bergen," she whispered, moving her hand toward his lower body. She wanted to touch his penis, his manhood. What would it feel like?

Her fingertips moved downward, past the bottom of his pectoral muscles, over the flat, hairy plane of his stomach to the navel. She stopped for a second, searching for it. She wanted to play there for a moment but could not find it. She would do that later. Now, she had to reach out for his erection, guide it to the place it belonged.

Her fingers continued on their probing

journey. The hair grew thicker, more dense and she found her prize. The tips of her fingers could feel the base of his penis as it throbbed upright, waiting for her. She tried to move closer but could not. What was wrong? Why couldn't she reach it? Stretching every muscle, every fiber, she vainly tried to grasp her prey but could not. Something was very wrong. She should have been able to reach anything she wanted. Perhaps if she opened her eyes, she could see what the problem was.

"Wait a moment, my darling," she whispered.

"I will, my sweet Adriana."

It would be best if she opened her eyes with her fingertips, she decided and brought her hands toward her face. Just as her fingers should have brushed her cheeks on the way to her eyes, her hands stopped abruptly. Now she couldn't touch her own face.

When the impact of realization struck her, she knew why she couldn't touch anything. Her hands were still tied and she was alone in her room with Roseanne. Her eyes opened wide and a whimper broke through her lips.

"What is it?" Roseanne asked, jerking her head to an upright position.

Friday, May 17, 1985

Adriana tugged at the bonds holding her wrists. God, how she wanted to move about a little. She felt as if her legs had atrophied from her body, simply disappeared from her hips. She willed her toes to wiggle, her feet to move, her legs to bend at the knee. Did anything happen? She couldn't tell. Her entire body felt numb—useless. If an arm or leg moved out of her line of vision, she had no way of knowing since she felt nothing.

Why didn't they let her walk around a bit? Wouldn't that be good for her and for her baby—for the child they were all eagerly anticipating? Perhaps she could drive a bargain with them. She'd cooperate and give birth to the baby without any resistance on her part. They in turn would let her move around some. That seemed fair. But not fair enough where she was concerned. She wanted more. Perhaps they could arrange for Bergan to be her boyfriend—her lover, her husband, the child's stepfather. She certainly didn't want Olda hanging around her and the baby. Even if he was the father. She should at least have the say in who she slept with once the child was born.

Closing her eyes, she smiled, picturing the image of the baby, her, and Bergen. *Jesus, Mary, Joseph, the Holy Family. Antichrist, Adriana, Bergen—the Unholy Family! She ran across the room in her vision, threw open the closet door, hurtling the child inside. Turning, she confronted Bergen. Effortlessly, she picked him up, flinging him after the baby. She slammed the door shut.*

"Oh, God," she muttered. "I'm going insane!"

"What did you say, Adriana?" Angelique asked, breaking out of her meditative trance.

Adriana looked down the length of her body. She could no longer see her feet. It was totally unbelievable. Her stomach rounded out, blocking her view. It just couldn't be but she found it impossible to argue against the evidence.

Everyone who came into her room seemed highly pleased with her progress and she found it difficult not to think of herself as a prize animal who was about to give birth to an offspring that would be top of the line. She seldom spoke to anyone, preferring to close her eyes and ignore her visitors whenever they entered to view her. View her? Wasn't that the expression people used when they visited a mortuary—"to view the body?" She involuntarily shuddered several seconds later. On rare occasions she found that aspect of her confinement amusing. When she thought of the idea of a mortuary, the revulsion was immediately there in her brain, and she had begun thinking about something else when her whole body gave a convulsive shake. Delayed reaction.

The only one of her visitors with whom she was willing to carry on a conversation was Michele. At least Adriana found her to be more friendly than the others.

Angelique would sit with her but never speak to her. But Adriana could understand her reason. The first time the actress had come in, she had told Adriana that she would decide if she were angry about being knocked unconscious in the black chapel after the baby was born. If the child were healthy and Adriana cooperative beyond that point, there would be no anger on her part. After all, such a blow to the head could have marked her beauty and affected her career in Hollywood and abroad.

Ivy St. Clair also didn't try to converse with her, only telling her that she didn't appreciate Adriana's getting her husband, who even refused to enter the room, into trouble by sneaking out when he was supposed to be guarding her.

It seemed as though all of them were angry or about to be angry at her for one reason or another. Morrison—because she hadn't responded more fully to the mental manipulations he had implemented during her breakdown, and Deirdre for the same reason, only on a once removed basis. Olda and Lahpavi—because she refused to cooperate with them, refused to accept their perverted philosophies and happily agreed to bear a child destined to become the Antichrist. Everhart Parrot didn't like her because of being knocked unconscious while making love to Angelique in the chapel. Roseanne and Charlene just seemed to function around her and did not attempt to engage in any kind of dialogue.

Which left Michele. Michele would smile and talk when she came into the room, fluffing Adriana's pillow and smoothing the sheets.

Adriana wondered, after running down the list of people who stayed at the manor and tended to

312

her needs, how Bergen Messenger would have reacted to her after everything they had done. Would Bergen be kind and understanding? Was Bergen a member like the rest? She decided that he was but entertained herself by daydreaming about him, making him unlike the others, transforming him into her lover. She planned a wedding for them, doing it over and over in her mind, changing the guest list, the site of the reception, the church, and the priest.

Priest? Would she ever be able to face one again after all she had been through? Would a priest, acting as Christ's representative on earth, ever grant her absolution for the sins she had committed here? She hadn't really done anything wrong as such. Yes, she had enjoyed the night Olda had had relations with her but she concluded that her behavior had been the result of something she had been given to heighten her senses, her reations, her baser instincts. She had delighted in the experiences through no fault of her own and had enjoyed them.

But it was the fantasy episodes with Bergen that brought her the most pleasure now. The only pleasure. She looked out of the corner of her eye. Michele merely sat next to her, mindful of her duty but not of her patient's being awake.

"Michele?" she asked slowly.

Michele turned to face her. "You're awake. That's good. Would you like to talk?"

Adriana ordered her head to nod but said, "Yes," when she realized the motion would come later. "Tell me about,"—her head nodded—

"Bergen. What's he like? Does he belong to—to the cult—or group or whatever it's called?"

Michele smiled. "Yes and no. In a small way, he's much like Deirdre, Charlene, and me. Only he works outside in the world. We stay here—helping Olda."

"Why? Why stay here?"

"It's—it's our home."

"But you're wasting your lives here. You—all three of you—could be stars like Angelique. Or models. Or—or—just about anything you decided."

Michele looked at Adriana in a kind manner. "We cannot," she said simply. "This is our home. Where we belong. With Olda."

Adriana had no idea what she meant and didn't want a long, detailed account of how they came to be here in the first place. Nor did she want to learn in the end that Bergen was as strange and weird as the others. She preferred to go on with her fantasies about him instead. "Tell me about Olda."

"I thought you knew everything about Olda."

"I guess I do—sort of—but Deirdre said something about him that didn't sound right."

"Such as?"

Adriana had thought about the discrepency for the last several days. Deirdre had said that the picture she had looked at in foyer the day before they took her to the black chapel had been taken a long time ago—a few days before Olda's parents had died. But it had been Olda who had said that they had been killed in a train accident

314

while on their way to visit the island and Olda's grandfather or something. She told Michele of the two different versions, granting that she may have misunderstood one or the other.

Michele studied her for several minutes before speaking. "Olda's parents weren't killed in a train accident."

After a moment passed, Adriana turned her head as far as she could. "I don't understand."

"Olda's grandfather sacrificed them—to our Lord and Master."

"Sacri— surely you don't mean that he killed—"

Michele nodded.

"But," Adriana said, her mind flashing through the facts as they had been presented to her, "Olda said he was taken to an orphanage after the wreck—that he had been shunted from one to another until his records were hopelessly confused."

"Some of that's true. There was a maid working here at the time of the sacrifices who dearly loved Olda. She took him and fled from the island during the sacrifice ceremony. After a while when she found out she couldn't properly take care of him, he was placed in an orphanage and moved around a lot. It wasn't until a few years after his grandfather's death that Olda was located and told of his inheritance."

"How do I know I can believe you? After all, Olda lied to me."

"Olda wasn't old enough at the time to know anything."

Adriana found herself shaking, reacting to the fate of Olda's parents. How could someone kill his own son and daughter-in-law to please Satan? These people were completely mad. She had to change the subject or run the risk of losing her mind as well. "What did you mean before when you said that Bergen was like you and the other two girls?"

Michele smiled demurely. "After the baby is born, I'll tell you. Perhaps, I'll—we'll show you."

Adriana eventually turned her head away, puzzled. What did she mean by that? Show her? What could they show her that would be so different—different from the others? What could she and Bergen have in common that was so uncommon?

Outside, a breeze ruffled the trees, fighting its way into the room through the lace curtains.

Sunday, May 19, 1985

Adriana hadn't seen Michele for two days and she wished the friendly blonde would come back. The others, like Ivy St. Clair, who merely sat near the window, staring out, did just what they had to do and no more. Only Michele offered to brush her hair and apply a little makeup. Adriana always felt better after she had done that and enjoyed the little ritual of seeing herself in the small mirror Michele would hold up for her.

When the door opened, Michele walked in and Adriana whimpered quietly in relief. At least she'd have someone with whom to speak today.

Ivy left and the first thing Michele did was get out the brush to straighten Adriana's hair. When she finished, she applied lipstick and held up the mirror for Adriana to see herself.

"My God," Adriana gasped at the ghostlike image staring at her. Eyes, dark circles beneath them, appeared sunken into her head, accenting the prominence of the bones above her caved-in cheeks. "My God, what's happening to me? Michele, tell me. What's wrong?"

"I don't know what you mean, Adriana. Why don't I get Dr. Lahpavi and he can visit with you," she said, striding toward the door.

"I don't want to see him." She continued protesting for several minutes but her words fell on the closed door.

She wanted to scream, to curse, to cry out in desperation. The face she had seen, just barely recognizable as Adriana Brevenger, had appeared more like a death's head than that of a living, breathing woman. She was dying. She had to be. There could be no other explanation. They had lied to her all along. Every one of them. They had tried to protect her from the truth.

No. They had *not* done that. They were serving their own selfish ends—theirs and Satan's. She suddenly believed everything they had said.

If only she could move—not much—just enough to find some way to kill herself. Kill herself and the child growing within her body. She could not allow any of this to happen. She could not give birth to a child they would raise as Christ's mortal enemy.

317

When the door opened, she turned away. What could she do?

Rizahghyny Lahpavi looked at her from several different angles. "I don't think there's anything to be concerned about, my dear. The baby is taking its toll on your body, absorbing more of the food you're taking in than you are. Your body is giving its all to your child."

"Will—will I stay this way once the baby's born?" she asked, fearful of what his answer might be.

"Once the child is born, you will recover fully. Don't worry about it. You have less than a week to go." He stood, moving toward the door and was gone.

Adriana looked at Michele for support.

"I told you there was nothing wrong," Michele said.

How could she believe that? If Michele thought she looked normal, what other lies had she been told?

Friday, May 24, 1985

It seemed to Adriana that she had lain on the bed for months. Her body ached from inactivity. How she longed to run, exercise, or just walk a little. Since she had seen herself last Sunday, she had kept her eyes closed trying to remember how she should look. When her eyes were shut, at least she couldn't see her protruding belly, which seemed gigantic to her.

318

Squinting at her companion, Ivy St. Clair, Adriana knew she must be getting close to the time of delivery. Although she had lost count of the days since they had strapped her to the bed, the size of her abdomen told her it wouldn't be—couldn't be—too much longer.

When Adriana grunted from the baby viciously kicking her, Ivy snapped her head in the direction of the bed. "What's wrong?" she asked sharply.

Adriana smiled. Score one for her and the baby. They had made Ivy speak to them. "The baby just kicked me a good one. I think he was kicking a field goal or something."

"Not funny," Ivy snapped, glaring at her.

Suddenly Adriana felt as though she were going to be folded in half, that her head and feet would meet someplace above the bed. Then the pain left. She turned to look at Ivy. The woman seemed oblivious to anything that might be out of the ordinary. Again the pang came, and Adriana wondered if it was actually happening now or had taken place several seconds before. It subsided and she relaxed again.

Several more minutes slipped by without anything happening. Then she felt as if she were being torn in half and cried out.

"What's the matter? What's the matter with you, anyhow?"

Adriana fought the restraining straps, trying to bring her knees up to relieve the awful pain she felt in her middle. "Oh—my—God—it—hurts!" she panted.

319

Ivy's eyes widened, her mouth flapping up and down giving motion to the double roll of fat hanging beneath her jaw. Finally, all parts worked and she jumped from the chair, screaming, "It's time. It's time! The baby's coming! Dr. Lahpavi! Dr. Lahpavi! Hurry! Hurry! Adriana's having her baby. Hurry!"

She ran to the door, throwing it open and charged down the hall, shouting her news for all the people in Revillion Manor to hear.

The Antichrist was about to be born.

Part Five

HAIL TO
THE MOTHER

THIRTEEN

Saturday, May 25, 1985—2 A.M.

RIZAHGHYNY LAHPAVI sat close to Adriana's bed. Her eyes opened and closed periodically, seeing but not comprehending her surroundings. Ever since Ivy St. Clair had alerted the entire household, Lahpavi, Morrison Tyler, Deirdre, and Charlene had been ready to assist at the birth of the child. The first thing Lahpavi had done, after examining her cervix to find it dilating, was give her a sedative. She was not yet ready to deliver and he wanted her to relax as much as possible before the ordeal began.

The doctor called Charlene to his side and said, "Have Everhart prepared. We want a record of this momentous occasion."

She glided from the room, closing the door behind her without a sound.

Adriana moaned, turning her head. The drugs which had been slowing her motor responses had dissipated and her reactions were normal. At first the obstetrician had voiced concern that she might be worthless in helping the baby along if her reaction remained several seconds behind her mental commands. If that had proven to be the case, he would have performed a caesarian to make certain the child was not placed in any jeopardy. When Morrison, concerned about Adriana's welfare, asked if that process were necessary, Lahpavi merely shrugged and said, "The baby is of importance—not the mother. If she lives—fine. She will be rewarded. If she doesn't—it really doesn't matter, does it?"

Morrison turned away, a frown creasing his face. Walking to the window he looked out into the night. "Why didn't you coach her in natural childbirth, Rizahghyny?"

"Because when she proved to be difficult, I had no choice but to administer the drug that made her controllable. It became next to impossible to instruct her when her actions and reactions were slowed by several seconds from the instant of the brain's command."

Morrison pivoted and stared at the dark man. "How far along is she? How much longer before something happens?"

Lahpavi smiled, his teeth gleaming against his olive complexion. "She is dilating quite well. Her contractions are about eight minutes apart. As soon as they come at four-minute intervals, I will give her an injection and the baby will be born within a short time. Patience, my dear Morrison. You must be patient. You have fathered children.

326

Certainly you remember the waiting room at the hospital, the pacing, the smoking, the paging through magazines. Patience, patience." He grinned, but said nothing more, then turned, placing a hand on her bulging abdomen and checking his watch. Five minutes had passed since the last contraction. Adriana's face twisted as her muscles squeezed mightily.

The door opened and Charlene entered with Everhart Parrot dressed in white like the rest present, carrying his photography equipment.

Four minutes later, Adriana experienced another contraction, and the obstetrician prepared his injection.

Adriana watched the masked Lahpavi, who held a huge hypodermic needle in his gloved hand, approach her out of the fog. How could there be fog in her room? Her eyes felt sandy—gritty. Disembodied hands gently turned her over on one side and she looked up into the face of an angel—no, it was one of the three girls she knew. Was it Michele? She couldn't be positive since they resembled each other so closely. She tried speaking but only a garbled sound spilled from her mouth. Forget it.

She felt a shock of pain in one buttock and winced.

Then her abdomen contracted, pulling her body together even more. "Oh—my—god!" she managed. The pressure intensified downward, toward her pelvis, toward her vulva. The baby moved strongly, exerting itself down, down,

down until she thought the strain would tear her body apart. Then it stopped and she breathed easier without effort. Was that it? Or would there be more?

Several minutes later, she felt it beginning again, only this time the pain lessened as the shot took effect. Off in the distance she could hear someone speaking—so slowly. How could they talk that way?

"How—is—she—doing—Riz—haw—ja—knee?"

"Fine—the—shot—is—doing—its—job—Mor—ri—son."

Her mind swirled, black clouds rolling about her, washing over her body, her face, and head, penetrating her mouth and nostrils, her eyes and ears, filling her head and mind and brain with a stygian night through which she could see nothing, feel nothing.

The slow voices continued penetrating the blackness. "Good. That's—very—good—Ad—ri—ana."

Wasn't that her name? Adriana? The voice came again, but this time it seemed different, sounded like someone she knew once. A woman's voice.

"Adriana. Get up! You'll be late for school."

She fought to open her eyes. Her mother was calling her. Where could she be? Certainly not here on this island of crazy people. Why couldn't she open her eyes? Something had been done to her that would make everything she wanted to do take forever to happen. Desperately trying to mouth words, she burbled in her throat but nothing intelligible came out.

"Adriana! Are you up?"

"Yes, mother, I'm up."

"You stayed out too late last night, didn't you?"

"I was home by eleven. Truly I was, mother. Don't be angry."

"I'm not angry with you, dear. I just don't want you to be late for school this morning. My, your senior year in high school and then—"

The voice drifted off into the vapor of nothingness and a sharp stab of pain lanced through her, attempting to tear her in half. Why did it have to hurt so much? What had she done that justified such torture? Who—what fiend was doing this to her?

The blackness cleared for a second and she saw a blindingly white light. And nothing else. What was that? She squinted, trying to make out the source of brightness and could see dark blobs moving about the edges of the spot.

Too long . . . She stared too long, and yellow and red shadows crowded out of the sunlike light. She closed her eyes for the relief it would give her. Instantly the onyx of before enfolded her again.

Thoughts like bolts of lightning zigzagged past her mental eyes, startling her with their suddenness. *Catch one.* She tried to seize one of the fleeting glimpses of her past, but failed—until one came directly at her and she wanted to duck out of its way. It exploded before her eyes. She stared in awe at the campus of Claremont

College. It looked just as it had the day she arrived—how long ago?—with her parents. It would be her first time away from home for any duration. She turned. Both her mother and father stood nearby, admiring the wooded hills among which the buildings of the school nestled.

"It's beautiful," her mother said, a smile curving her lips.

"You'll be happy here, darling," her father said, turning away.

She knew he was fighting tears. They had been very close, but not as close as she had been to her mother. She also knew her mother wouldn't shed a tear until they were in the car and on their way home.

"Mom—"

The pain came again and off in the distance she could hear the slow-motion voice say, "P-o-o-osh—p-o-o-o-osh—Ad—ri—ana."

A flash of light penetrated her closed eyes for a brief millisecond.

She pushed. She tried to push the torture right out of her body. Why did she hurt? Never before in her life had she felt anything so distressful, so excruciating. Why?

The command to push sounded slowly once more and she forced downward with all her might, but nothing happened. Her head spun from the exertion.

The pitch black clouds swiftly closed in, completely engulfing her. When she lifted the lids of her mental eyes, Ramsey Flint's face suddenly filled her vision. The girl smiled

330

wickedly and said, *"Tell me a story, Adriana. Please? Please tell me a story?"*

"I—I don't know any."

"Tell me about your mother and the time she was in the convent and what happened to her there," Ramsey said, teasing, taunting with her eyes.

"No—nothing happened. I don't know anything."

"P-o-o-o-o-o-o-sh—Ad—ri-ana!   P-o-o-o-o-sh! No—o-o-o-o-o-w!"

Another brilliant spot of white light pierced her darkness.

She tried to obey the command. She forced herself to shove against the weight she suddenly found in her midsection. Hunching her body over in her mind, she exerted another terrific move and then—the pain was gone again.

The ebony night closed in only to disappear the instant she opened her eyes. She was in a room— a strange room—one she had never seen before. Who was that coming toward her? A tall man. Handsome. Silver patches at his temples, which disagreed with the rest of his hair, distinguished him from the others, she was certain. Of course there were no others here with whom she could compare. However, she liked the man but felt she shouldn't say anything to him. After all he was a stranger. They had not been properly introduced. He smiled at her but she did nothing.

"Adriana," he said, *"over the next while I'm going to tell you about something that is going to happen to you. You see, you've been chosen for a*

great honor. This honor will make you very happy. Not everyone was considered and after everything was taken into account, it was decided that you should be the one honored in this way. You, Adriana, are the chosen one. The chosen one will be most happy because of this honor and this honor is good, Adriana. It is so very good—for you —for me—for the whole world. It will take only one month for you to become the most envied person on the face of the earth. Only one month."

What was he talking about? One month? It is so very good? Chosen one? For what? What had she been chosen for? If she would be so happy, why didn't he take the honor for himself? All she wanted was to be left alone.

Suddenly the handsome man changed. He looked so old, his face so wrinkled, in fact he didn't even look like the same man. He wasn't. The prominent nose, the shallow cheeks, the white hair. She had seen him someplace before. But where? The old man got to his knees, crawling toward her, drool running down his chin, dripping unto her bare skin. She shuddered. He lay down on her body and she felt something pushing inside her. In and out. In, out. In. Out.

The slow voice broke through. "D-o-o-o-o-i-i-i i-t n-o-o-o-o-w-w-w, Ad—ri—an—na! Po-o-o-o-o-sh! Th—at's i-i-i-i-t! F-i-i-n-n-e!"

A series of flashes popped again and again.

She pushed and shoved and forced the weight inside her to move, to move again, to move some

332

more. She could feel it moving, sliding—Oh, God —the pain—the terrible pain.

Then the pain was gone. Simply gone and she heard something far off in the distance. A wail. A cry in her night. She drove her eyes open to see who or what was making that sound. The bright light was gone. A dark man held a tiny form—a baby.

"It's a boy," he said simply as the clock struck the hour of three.

The door opened slowly, Olda Revillion hesitantly entering the room. His quizzical expression rested on each of the people for a brief second before stopping at Rizahghyny Lahpavi.

Lahpavi looked up and said, "It's a boy, Olda. A boy. Just as the Master said. Aren't you proud and happy?"

Olda stepped closer, peering at the naked bit of humanity. His face crinkled in a smile. "I'm overwhelmed. Not that I didn't believe it could be done. Not that any of us doubted. We know the power of the Master too well than to question anything he says."

Morrison, the two women, and Lahpavi nodded gravely. Everyone on the island had Satan to thank for his or her success. Anything they had asked for had been granted—as long as they obeyed blindly any directives given them.

Lahpavi called the two blondes, handing one the newborn infant. "Clean him up as you were instructed," he said curtly, staring at the woman

333

who accepted the tiny body.

"Will you want one more picture of the mother and child?" Everhart asked.

"Yes," Olda said, stepping forward. "In fact perhaps two. One now before he is cleaned, and one after."

"Do it," Lahpavi snapped.

Charlene tenderly placed the boy in the crook of Adriana's arm and stepped back. The light flashed and the camera whirred. Stepping back, Everhart made room for Charlene to retrieve the child. Adriana had not moved in her exhausted stupor.

Lahpavi turned to Olda. "What time can the helicopter be here?"

Olda shrugged. "I'll radio immediately and tell them to get here as soon as possible."

Lahpavi checked his watch. "Tell them to be here as soon after dawn as possible. I'll need that much time to prepare food for the infant."

Olda studied Lahpavi for a moment. "You're absolutely positive that everything is fine with the baby? Normal?"

"I would not lie about something as magnificent as this project has become. The child is as healthy or healthier than any I've seen who have taken nine months to form."

Morrison, who had hung back when it developed that his services as assistant to Lahpavi would not be needed, stepped forward, confronting the obstetrician. "Is it wise to move the baby so soon after birth? Isn't there the possibility that something might happen to him?"

"What could happen, my dear Morrison? He will be in the best possible hands—mine. Whether I stay here or go, the child will be with me and that is all that matters at this stage of his life. Charlene will be with me in the event I need assistance. By tomorrow noon, he will be in the most excellent of nurseries."

Morrison turned to the bed, looking at Adriana who had not moved since the birth of her son. "Is she all right?" he asked.

"I suppose. It doesn't really matter, does it? She is in your care. If she survives and wishes to join us, she will be afforded the highest treatment and accord because of her station in life as the mother of the Antichrist. If she chooses not to join us, it is her—how do you say?—funeral?" He laughed and left the room.

Shortly thereafter, Charlene and Deirdre returned with the baby completely cleaned and wrapped in a blanket. They returned the child to Adriana's arms, who stirred this time when they positioned her to hold her son. Everhart stepped forward, taking several pictures and then left, rushing to his dark room.

The sun bobbed out of the water on the eastern horizon to the accompaniment of whirling blades. The helicopter lowered gently to the lawn in front of the mansion. As the rotor slowed, the front door opened and a small entourage exited to hurry across the porch. Lahpavi carried a small bundle while Charlene held a large suitcase in each hand. Olda, Deirdre, and Michele were followed by Morrison, Everhart, Angelique, who wore dark glasses lest the pilot recognize her, and the St. Clairs.

When they neared the helicopter, its door popped open and Lahpavi was helped inside. He moved slowly, careful not to disturb the sleeping child. After Charlene boarded, the door closed and the blades began moving faster.

Those remaining stepped back, safely away from the rotor and formed a straight line, their hands interlaced, thumbs pointed upward.

"Satan be praised," Olda intoned loudly over the roar of the engine.

"Hail, Satan! So be it," the others enjoined.

The chartered helicopter rose majestically into the azure sky, hovering for a moment as if unable to decide which way to go, and then spinning about, chopped its way through the morning air toward the mainland.

Upstairs, Adriana slept soundly.

Fourteen

Sunday, May 26, 1985

THE ROOM seemed different. The wallpaper's flowers had changed to a pastoral scene with trees, and bushes bordering portions of a stone wall. The greenery held her gaze until she blinked. Where was she?

Sitting up on the bed, Adriana quickly took in her surroundings. It was a different room, not the one in which she had been confined for the last—how long?—it seemed like an eternity. What had happened? She didn't remember much and when she concentrated, her thoughts, her recollections spun about, forming a psychedelic pinwheel, which flipped out bits and pieces of memory, taunting her but never staying long enough to be clearly recognized or remembered.

What had happened? She recalled voices of some sort—voices that sounded peculiar, not quite right for some reason. If she remembered

339

correctly, they kept repeating the same idea over and over. What had that been?

For the first time since she had sat up, she noticed that straps no longer confined her. What a relief to be able to move. One hand tentatively made its way to her face, gingerly feeling it as if it were a stranger. The sensation of touch tingled at her fingertips and on her cheek. How strange.

Her mouth felt dry and when she reached for the glass and pitcher sitting on the nightstand, she hesitated. She felt weak—afraid to even attempt lifting the partially filled container and small glass. Still she needed a drink to ease the parched feeling in her throat. Slidling closer to the stand, she reached out with both hands, shakily picking up the pitcher. Carefully pouring half a glass, she returned it to the table and reached for her drink. Although the water was room temperature, it felt cool, refreshing, invigorating when it coursed down her scratchy throat.

She wiggled forward until her feet touched the floor. It too felt strange. Would she even be able to walk? She stood, clutching the edge of the bed. Her head swam and the room careened about for several minutes before slowing to a stop. She stood unsteadily, waiting for strength to flow into her legs. The muscles reacted lethargically for a while until they began assuming their normal role. Finally she felt strong enough to stand by herself without the aid of the bed. For just a second, the room gyrated and then stopped. Adriana stood by herself, examining her surroundings.

Looking through the window reaffirmed in her mind that she was in a different room, since everything outside was completely unfamiliar. She must be on the other side of the house. Nothing seemed the same as she looked out. The furniture too was darker in color, and of a style quite unlike that which had been in her room. The bed was of wood and not brass. Definitely, she was someplace else in the house, but why? She took several steps toward the window, every move a painful exertion.

When she reached the casement, she leaned against it resting. How long would she be like this, barely able to walk? Did confinement to bed for a length of time make one feel weak, not unlike a newborn infant?

Infant! That word registered, banging into her consciousness. What did she have to do with an infant?

Phrases, words, faces spiraled to the surface of her mind, intermixing over and over into a soup of confusion. Her mother's face flitted by her mind's eye for a brief second before being replaced by a girl's face, which seemed familiar. Who was it? She was someone from Adriana's past—at school—college—a million miles away and a thousand years ago.

Ramsey Flint.

"The placenta is broken—dilating—eight minutes—the baby will be born—" What did all

that mean?

Dreamlike, she remembered her pregnancy and the reason for being confined on her bed. Her hands flew to her middle and she pulled them back, looking down at the trim waist below. At least that part had been a dream—something she didn't seem to mind at the moment. What if she had been pregnant? Lahpavi's statements along with Olda Revillion's smashed into the fore of her memory.

"One month. A one month pregnancy." She would give birth to a child—the Antichrist—one month after having been impregnated by Olda. She shuddered, and could see him crawling onto her once more. She was blushing when she glanced up, catching her reflection in the mirror. She looked awful. Dark shadows hung below her eyes, complementing her doughy complexion and sunken cheeks. Turning away, she covered her face with both hands, stifling an involuntary sob.

The meaning of the bits of phrases made sense for the first time. She could remember being told that she had been the chosen one and all the other fragments of senseless ideas. For the first time, she realized that if she actually had been pregnant and given birth, the message behind the odd memories would have held high significance. But it had all been a dream—a horrible nightmare. One from which she had finally awakened.

Where were her clothes? Stumbling toward the dresser, she gripped the edge waiting for her equilibrium to return. When it did, she opened a drawer and smiled. Her cosmetics bag. Another revealed her underthings. Surprisingly, she felt clean. How long ago had she bathed? No span of time formed. She could not recall the last instance. Raising an arm, she sniffed. Absolutely clean—the fragrance of a delicately scented soap clinging to her skin. When had that happened?

Selecting bikini panties and a bra, she pulled her gown over her head. When it floated to the bed where she threw it, she looked at it more closely. It wasn't hers. The closet revealed all her clothing and she dressed quickly in a skirt and blouse. After pulling on a pair of deck shoes, she brushed her hair for a few seconds. Lipstick drew attention away from the circles and depressed cheeks. Satisfied, she moved slowly toward the door.

For all she knew, she had dreamed the other room and this was the only one in which she had ever slept since arriving at the island. She would have to talk with Morrison about her dream. It seemed it had been a masterpiece of mental gymnastics—an aberration that might defy understanding.

Momentarily confused when she stood in the hall, Adriana hesitated for a second until she heard distant voices from her left and moved in that direction. At the end of the hallway, she turned entering the large corridor where the paintings hung. In familiar surroundings, she soon found the wide staircase and descended toward the voices.

The clock struck the hour of ten as she stepped

into the dining room doorway. "Good morning, everyone," she said as cheerfully as possible.

The heads of everyone present turned to face her. Applause broke out and everyone began greeting her.

"Good morning."

"Praise be given to the mother."

"Hail to the mother."

"Glory to *his* mother."

"She is with us."

Adriana stared, puzzled at the strange reception.

"Come, join us," Morrison said, standing to hold a chair for her at the head of the table opposite Olda Revillion.

She moved slowly toward the proferred chair and sat down. Her eyes drifted from one person to the next until she had made a full circuit of the table. Each beamed happily, eagerly leaning forward toward her as if they expected her to say something profound.

"How are you feeling, Adriana?" Morrison asked.

"A little disconnected but fine otherwise. Why?"

"We—all of us—have been concerned. I'm so very proud of you and for you, Adriana," Morrison said, reaching out to touch her hand.

"Pr—proud? I don't understand."

"The child. Surely you remember?" Ivy St. Clair said, her face assuming a serious expression.

"The child?" Adriana stared at her. What was she talking about?

"Your baby. Our child," Olda said simply from the far end of the table.

"My baby? Our child? How did you people find out about my dream?" She stared at the group. Had she already told Morrison about it? Would he have told them? She looked to the psychiatrist for an explanation.

Morrison motioned for the others to be quiet. Turning to face Adriana, he said, "You had your baby yesterday, my dear. If you don't remember it as reality, it's probably because of the medication you were taking. But all of that is behind you now."

Her eyes opened widely. "You're insane. I haven't given birth to any baby. That's completely impossible. There's no way."

Morrison smiled kindly. "It *did* happen, Adriana. Just as you were told it would. Rizahghyny did a masterful job once Olda impregnated you."

Adriana's eyes made the circuit of faces once more. Lahpavi was not among them. And one of the blond women was missing as well. But which one at first seemed impossible to tell. Deirdre sat next to Morrison and the other one was next to Olda at the opposite end. Her smile told Adriana that it must be Michele. That would mean Charlene was not here. Could she be with Lahpavi? But where were they?

"I—I don't understand, Morrison. Take it slow

and tell me everything that has happened. I remember strange things but I attributed them to a bad dream. Are you telling me it wasn't. That I actually gave birth to a baby?"

Morrison nodded.

"I don't believe it," Adriana snapped, turning her head away.

"Tell her, Morrison, for all our sakes," Olda said.

"I will if she looks at me. Please, Adriana?"

She reluctantly faced the psychiatrist again. Could he be serious? Had she given birth? When she saw the serious expression holding his handsome features, she steeled herself for the explanation he was about to give.

"You were chosen by Satan to bear his offspring," he began. "His plan for the Antichrist was thwarted by a priest years ago at the convent where your mother was studying and preparing for her life as a nun. The girl there who was to care for the child until he reached adulthood was allowed to die, and Satan had to wait for thirty-three years before he could do anything about renewing his efforts."

"Why thirty-three years?" she asked.

Morrison looked to Olda, who said, "He told me the reason was because it is a form of punishment meted out by God for his having tempted Jesus in the desert. The term of time represents the life span of Jesus on earth."

Adriana, not sure she understood, turned back to Morrison when Olda did not say anything further. "But this doesn't tell me what I really want to know. How could I have given birth to a baby if I was made pregnant by—by—him," she head motioned toward the old man, "so short a time ago."

"The pregnancy lasted only one month," Morrison said.

"But that's not possible," she protested.

"Normally, of course not," Morrison said. "But this was anything but a normal pregnancy. I was given instructions by Olda, as given him by Satan, to prepare you for the honor. You asked me about a one month pregnancy right before we arrived here. Remember?"

She nodded slowly.

"In the same way, Rizahghyny was given secrets to prepare special foods for you and medications that would allow the fetus to achieve full term growth in one month. It obviously worked."

Adriana shook her head.

"Honor to Adriana, mother of the child," the people seated at the table said, rising to their feet. They bowed from their waists, chanting the phrase over and over.

They were crazy. They had to be. Normal people could not believe in such strange, wild things. She stared from one bobbing face to another, each beaming an exuberant acceptance.

Olda spread his arms, calling for quiet. "I can see by Adriana's expression that she is still doubtful, which is to be understood when the circumstances are considered. However, let us prove to her that the Antichrist was born—that

347

she is the mother of he who will bring about the new age."

The others clapped, resuming their chairs. Olda nodded to Everhart Parrot who remained standing. He moved along the table toward Adriana, a brown manila envelope dangling from one hand. When he stood at her side, he opened it and withdrew a stack of photographs.

"Here," he said simply. "Proof. Even you must believe this."

Tearing her eyes from his, Adriana dropped her gaze to the table and gasped. The top photo showed her on a bed, belly protruding as she remembered—not from a dream but from reality —her legs spread, cocked at the knees. Lahpavi stood at one side, one of the blondes on the other, Morrison Tyler behind the obstetrician. Her own face, although drawn and gaunt, appeared peaceful. She looked at the next. Her mouth open, Adriana could almost hear the scream crying from her lips, frozen in a grimace on the picture. The others had moved, Lahpavi bending over her, the blonde hunched next to her head, Morrison leaning over the other man, looking at her groin area, expectation imprinted on each visible face.

She turned away when she looked at the next photo. The baby's head and upper body protruded from her. She quickly turned it over and looked at the next. Her body was back to normal and nestled in the bend of her arm lay a beautiful naked baby—a boy baby. Her eyes rested on the image of her face—so at ease—so peaceful. She looked ravishing, despite the tired, worn-out pallor that seemed of secondary import when she studied the overall beauty of mother and child—her child—her baby.

Raising her head, she found the others staring at her.

"Now, do you believe, Adriana?" Morrison asked quietly.

"Where's the baby now?" she asked, hoping wildly that she might still be dreaming.

"Rizahghyny Lahpavi has taken the child. You will not be allowed to see him until he has reached adulthood. None of us will. But when we do, the new age will be dawning and we—all of us —will be highly rewarded for our efforts here. You, most especially you, Adriana, will be revered by all of *his* followers when the Antichrist comes."

"Hail to the mother!" the others cried over and over.

Tears filling her eyes, Adriana bowed her head and wept.

At least they had not confined her to her room or placed any restrictions on her movements around the island. But then, where could she have gone? The thought of merely walking into the Gulf crossed her mind for a fleeting second but was rejected when she concluded that would solve nothing. True, her own worries would be ended but she felt there had to be more to her life than the function of birthing the Antichrist.

Walking across the floor of the valley, Adriana shook her head. She still found it difficult to believe. They had assured her that no more than one month had passed since the conception and here she was as thin as she had ever been since her freshman year in high school.

The only aspect she felt good about was the fact they had believed her when she told them she wanted time to think over the things they had told her. The one thing she needed now was time to think—time to be by herself, unencumbered with the others forcing their strange creed on her. There had to be a way out of this—there simply had to be. Right now, she was hard pressed to see any solution other than killing herself, and she felt that was not the answer. Dead, she could do nothing to fight this unholy coterie. But did she actually want to fight it? Oppose it?

She ran the fifty yards separating her from the trees. She wanted to be cut off from the mansion as much as possible. Even now, she felt their eyes on her back. Out of their sight, she could concentrate better. The brush and trees swallowed her and in seconds the house was blotted from view.

Slowing to a walk, she questioned the thought of wanting to retaliate. Why did she question it at all? That made no sense. Everything Olda and Morrison and the rest stood for and believed in was the complete and total opposite of everything she had ever learned. Her vacillation over the right and the wrong—the rejection and the acceptance of worshipping the devil, Satan—ate at her like a cancer. Why did she hesitate on making a decision one way or the other?

Possibly the *instruction* or *indoctrination*, as Morrison referred to it or *brainwashing* as she preferred to think of it, had not taken complete root. That could be it. Some of the time she accepted without question the bizarre things they believed, and on other occasions rejected them with a passion that almost made her ill. But did she? Did she really accept them? It seemed to her to be more a state of neutrality—as if a friend of hers might change religions or marry someone totally unexpected. It would not be the end of Adriana Brevenger. It was something to accept about someone but involved no change in herself because of it. On the other hand, there was the thought that her rejection might not be strong enough—that it was a behavior she modified in retrospect to salve any guilt she might have experienced for not reacting more strongly.

Puffing up the hill, she reached the top. A tree trunk blocked her path and she elected to rest on it. Any definition of her feelings escaped her. She didn't know if she hated Morrison and what he had initially done to her in preparing her for this whole episode or merely accepted in a passive way. Did she loathe Olda for his physical attack on her or reflect on it as a pleasant memory? How did she feel about the others who believed they were in league with Satan?

Angelique Pantis. Did that woman retain her youth and beauty because she had given her soul to Satan?

Everhart Parrot? What about him? He was a

351

highly successful photographer, who had won several worldwide prizes. He was wealthy. Had he sold out to the devil?

The others—the St. Clairs, the three blondes, Lahpavi, Morrison? Morrison had a monied clientele. She had deduced that from his office and the few names she had heard him banter about nonchalantly.

Olda? A former priest? Maybe. Perhaps that story had been concocted to impress her since her own mother had been a Sister of The Bearer of The Divine Word. How could his grandfather have killed his own son and daughter-in-law— Olda's parents? Actually sacrificed them to Satan for some unknown reason?

What about Lahpavi? She decided she felt good about his having left the island, if indeed he had. He was one man who sent shivers throughout her body just by looking at him. There was something decidedly evil about him, just as there seemed to be about the others now.

The St. Clairs both sported large diamonds on both hands. Had they sold out to Satan for a few baubles or were the stones emblems of their untold wealth, gained through a deal with the netherworld?

That left the three blondes and the maid, Roseanne. How did they fit into Satan's plans? More lackeys to do his bidding? Roseanne, she could understand. She was not the most attractive person Adriana had ever seen. Thick glasses, overweight, hair slightly unkempt, but the woman managed to maintain a cheerful attitude for those around her. What did she know that the others didn't? Why should she be so happy, looking so ugly around such attractive women as Deirdre, Charlene, and Michele? What had Roseanne gained by selling her soul to Satan?

The three blondes, she reasoned, must have made a similar deal as had Angelique Pantis. But Angelique was world famous for her beauty and sexual escapades. Why had the three elected to seal themselves off from the rest of the world on a tiny speck in the Gulf of Mexico?

Adriana lay back on the trunk. The walk had exhausted her, and she found her mind suddenly wandering because of her pondering over the others on the island. She closed her eyes for a moment. It felt good. Perhaps a little nap. She allowed them to stay closed and soon fell asleep.

She awoke with a start. Where was she? A cool breeze rippled through the undergrowth before sweeping down into the valley. Then she remembered. Sitting up, she stretched. The nap had done its job. She felt relaxed and better equipped physically and mentally to cope with her situation.

She stood and heard the noise. Turning, half expecting to see someone approaching, she saw the sun, a huge ball of fire balanced on the horizon, ready to die a watery death for another day.

She heard the noise again—a moan. She looked about without moving from her spot by the fallen tree. It sounded like—like two people—groaning —making love or—or something.

Pinpointing the source, she tiptoed toward a clump of bushes and peered through. She could make out Morrison Tyler's face clearly as he lay on the ground, writhing, fevered passion twisting his face. She could not make out who was with him, although she assumed it had to be Deirdre. Crouching, her eyes locked with another set of eyes and she screamed.

Birds flitting back and forth overhead, gathering their night supply of insects, squawked loudly at the interruption, fluttering off in hasty retreat.

Adriana, held by the burning gaze, stood, screaming as loud as she could. Then she fainted, crumbling to the ground.

FIFTEEN

Sunday Evening, May 26, 1985

THE VOICES seeped through the cotton of her un-
consciousness, barely audible but each word
strangely distinguishable. Who was speaking?
Both sounded like women. But which women?
Who were they? What were they saying? Adriana
forcused her attention on the tiny voices.

"I don't care what you have to say, you were
careless."

"I simply couldn't help it. My barriers were
down—Morrison was so good—so horny. I'm
sorry. I couldn't help it."

"You are absolutely positive she saw you?"

"Yes."

"In your natural state?"

"In my natural state."

"You fool. It was premature. I don't know what
will happen from this point on, Deirdre."

Deirdre? One of them was Deirdre but what

357

were they talking about? That voice sounded upset—angry.

"You said you told her she would be shown, Michele."

Michele was the other person talking. Adriana could not grasp what they were implying. Why didn't they come right out and say it. Both women seemed to be agitated about something. She wondered if they might be troubled because of something she had done.

"Yes, I said that. But you know as well as I do that the conditions must be right or we'd run the risk of her losing her mind."

Deirdre snorted derisively. "Well, she knows now."

Michele didn't respond.

"Look at her," Deirdre said, "sound asleep as if nothing happened. We've nothing to worry about, I tell you. She's all right."

"Perhaps," Michele said softly, "we could convince her that she was suffering from hallu-cinations—imaginative figments of her tired mind. It might work—"

"Hah, I doubt it. She's too intelligent and has been told too much to believe any more lies. It'll be interesting when she awakens."

"I guess you're right. We'll have to play it by ear. But I still maintain that it was careless of you to let yourself be seen, Deirdre."

Adriana stirred when the conversation died. Turning her back to the source of the voices, she tentatively opened her eyes, squinting at the wall. Trees and bushes hugged a stone wall,

358

fading into nothing only to have the scene repeated above, below, and to either side. She knew the picture. It was the wallpaper of the room she had awakened in before going downstairs.

What had happened? She had talked with everyone in the dining room and then went for a walk. She must have fallen asleep and when she awoke—How did she get back here? What had taken place after she had awakened?

Focusing her mental eyes back to the hill where she had awakened, she stopped, listening intently. There had been a sound—yes. A moan—no, more like an animal growling or—or—something like that.

Then those horrible smouldering eyes had held hers and again she felt a primeval scream building in her chest. She clamped her eyes shut, forcing the mental image from her consciousness but was too late to control the piercing loud cry that erupted from her lips. Rolling on the bed, the shriek built in volume until she felt her throat roughen under the intense effort.

"Oh, my God!" She sat bolt upright and saw the two women.

"There, there, Adriana, you've had a terrible nightmare," Michele said, sitting on the edge of the bed, her arms around Adriana's shoulders.

"No—no—not a dream—real—I saw it—awful —hideous. Oh, my God, help me someone— please help me!" She struggled, trying to break the restraining hold Michele held on her upper body. Just as she was about to free herself,

Deirdre stepped forward, helping to subdue her.

"Listen to me, Adriana," Michele said firmly, "calm down. This won't help anything. What did you see? Tell me. Then maybe the memory will go away."

Adriana stared at her, eyes wide, mouth agape. Beautiful Michele, so kind, so understanding. Maybe she could tell what had stared at her through the bushes.

"Yes, tell us, dear Adriana," Deirdre said. "Tell us exactly what you saw."

Adriana turned to face the second girl holding her by the legs. Deirdre seemed to be as interested in her welfare and well-being as did Michele. At least she wasn't acting aloof as she had every time Morrison had been around.

Adriana opened her mouth, trying to speak but nothing would come out.

"Can you tell us, Adriana?" Michele asked.

Adriana managed to shake her head, unable to tear her eyes from Deirdre who stared back. Just like the ones she had seen through the bushes. But it hadn't been Deirdre she had seen. It had been something awful, something ugly and—she screamed again at the mental picture. It dissolved and she turned away from Deirdre.

Grasping Adriana's chin, Michele brought the terrified face around to hers. "Take it very slowly, Adriana. What did you see?"

Adriana took several deep breaths before whispering hoarsely, "Morrison—on ground. He—he —he was being—attacked by—by—" She shook her head vigorously.

"Go on," Michele said, head motioning for Deirdre to leave. "*Get the others,*" she said, mouthing the words. "Tell me, Adriana. It will help if you tell me."

"Oh, God, it was awful," she moaned. "I've never seen anything so terrible looking, so horribly ugly before in my life."

A tiny smile played on Michele's full lips. "Go on."

"It—whatever it was—was leaping on Morrison."

"How did Morrison look?"

"I—I—don't remember. I—I think he might have been unconscious."

"Or deliriously—"

The door opened and Morrison followed Deirdre into the room. Olda closed the door behind him, then stepped close to the bed.

"How is she?" Morrison asked.

"Confused but none the worse for wear and tear," Michele said, smiling up at the psychiatrist.

Adriana caught the grin. How could she take what had happened so lightly? Didn't Michele believe that she had seen a monster or animal of some sort? Michele was making fun of her—that was it. Michele was not the friend she had thought the girl might be. Adriana struggled to free herself of Michele's grip and leaned toward Morrison when she could.

"What seems to be the problem, Adriana?" he asked, taking Michele's place on the edge of the bed.

Adriana fell toward him, shoving her face into his shoulder. "You're all right? You're all right?" she asked, relief at seeing him washing over her, cleansing her of the awful fear she had felt.

"Of course I'm all right. Why wouldn't I be? Tell me, Adriana, what do you think you saw up on the hill?"

His words hung gravely in the air frightening her. *What she thought she saw?* What did he think she was—one of his patients who needed counseling? True, she had been that, but he had discharged her, cured. He was precisely right. She shut her eyes, holding back tears. Had she imagined the whole thing? Had she seen nothing but hallucinatory images that didn't really exist? Perhaps it was some reaction to her experience of being bound to the bed for so long. But *had* that happened? Or had she created in her mind that episodic experience as well—the straps, the guards sitting with her constantly, her belly swelling up, having a baby? Had she fantasized the whole thing? Was she losing her mind after all?

"You don't believe me, do you?" she said flatly, seemingly defeated.

Morrison good naturedly squeezed her shoulder and said, "I believe you think you saw something. After all you have been under a strain the last couple of weeks. I'm sure your imagination is trying to make up for the time lost while you were confined in bed. It's probably nothing more than a reaction to some normal, everyday occurrence."

Rhetoric! That was what Morrison was giving her. The fact he admitted she had spent time in bed told her she had not imagined that part. If that were real, the thing she saw on the hill had to be real, too. But what was she to do if they merely patronized her and fed her more drugs?

"Perhaps," Michele said, stepping forward, around Olda who crowded next to Morrison, "some of the medication Dr. Lahpavi left might be in order."

"I think you're right, Michele," Morrison said. "Would you get it, please?"

She left the room and no one spoke until she returned several minutes later carrying a small bottle of capsules and a glass of water.

"This is nothing more than a tranquilizer, Adriana," Morrison said. "It will not put you to sleep or immobilize you. You'll merely relax and be able to talk with us."

He held out a capsule nestling in the overturned bottle cap. Adriana took it, examining it before accepting the glass from Michele. Placing the capsule in her mouth she took a long drink, swallowing the medication. After several minutes, she turned to Morrison. "Is Dr. Lahpavi really gone?" she asked, handing the glass back.

Morrison nodded.

"He—he took my baby?" Her voice cracked and she wondered about it. Did she really care if the infant was gone? Why would she feel an emotion over its absence?

He nodded again.

"I—I didn't even get to see it. It was a boy, wasn't it?"

Again, Morrison nodded. "Don't worry about the baby, my dear. Charlene is with Rizahghyny and the child will be cared for better than any baby in history—now that we have him."

Adriana blinked back a tear. Why did she suddenly miss the baby? A baby she didn't really want? Could her motherhood instinct have been aroused so that she wanted the child to be at her side? "How—how big was—was he?" she ventured.

Morrison smiled at her interest. "A little over five pounds. Not too big."

"I don't know if that's big or small," she said softly.

"Considering you were pregnant only for a month, it's truly remarkable that he was that big."

"Where did Dr. Lahpavi take him?" She looked up at Morrison, her eyes large, wet with unshed tears but trusting now that the tranquilizer had taken effect.

Morrison looked at Olda, who shook his head. "I believe someplace in western Europe. Italy. He's perfectly safe. Believe me."

"I—I want him—if he truly exists," she managed thickly. "If he is mine, I want him."

Morrison patted her shoulder but said nothing. Olda motioned for him to follow into the hallway. The psychiatrist stood, Michele taking his place next to Adriana's head.

Soundlessly closing the door, Morrison faced

the owner of Revillion Manor. "What is it, Olda?"

"I think she is ready to join us. What do you think?"

Morrison shrugged. "Perhaps."

"I know it was a close call up on the hill but that is our ace in the hole if she refuses."

"I know. I know."

"If she still hesitates now," the old man said, "Michele and Deirdre could surely convince her, don't you think?"

Morrison pursed his lips. "I guess so. Let's try by telling her of them first—prepare her for the shock if it's necessary to show her—to prepare for the repetition of what she saw on the hill."

"Very well," Olda agreed and stepped toward the door. Morrison followed him back into the room.

"Hello, Olda, Morrison," Adriana said languidly, each word a struggle to utter.

"My dear Adriana," Olda began, "it is time you learned a little more about Revillion Island and Manor. What our group's function is and about the two lovely creatures caring for you right now."

Both Michele and Deirdre jerked their heads toward him. "You're going to tell her?" the former asked, her voice almost snarling the words.

Olda nodded. "This house," he began, "was built in 1880 for the sole purpose of worshipping Satan. It was built by my grandfather and as I've been told, you already know about his sacrifice to our Lord and Master. How he offered the lives of my parents for Satan's glorification."

Adriana stared at him. A question. She had a question for him and waved her hand to attract his attention. "Why—why didn't he do the same to you, Olda?"

"Because, dear child, my governess was not as devout in her worship as my grandfather and those surrounding him. She loved me and feared for my safety and somehow managed to get me off the island. How I was placed in an orphanage and all was true. The fact that she escaped with my grandfather's hope for the future, namely me, prompted him never to have a boat kept on the island.

"At any rate, we—my grandfather before me and I—have been preparing the way for the Antichrist since that time."

Adriana grinned wickedly. "It's certainly taken you long enough."

No one reacted to her statement.

"Don't be smart, Adriana," Olda chastised. "Satan knew and we have known it would not be easy. Since he could only try every thirty-three years, this is only our third attempt—and we have been successful. The first time ended in failure, when the woman Satan possessed recovered with the help of three priests. The second time you know about—in the convent. Even though our Lord and Master cannot be with us now, success is his and because of that—ours as well. We have our Antichrist and he will rise to power more quickly than anyone can imagine."

366

"Praised be Satan," the two girls and Morrison chorused.

"My three helpers—Deirdre and Michele here, and Charlene, who is caring for your child—have been here on the island since 1885."

Adriana gasped, staring first at Olda, who had paused for dramatic effect, and then at the two girls, who simply looked back at her. "I—I don't believe that. That's completely impossible," she mumbled settling back on her bed. She felt so relaxed, so comfortable that even Olda's lies had not fazed her. On this island for a hundred years? Did he actually think she would believe that?

Olda looked at Morrison who checked his watch. "The drug has taken its effect by now. More than enough time has passed. She'll not overreact."

"Good," Olda said, rubbing his hands together. "I want to say that—"

"Just a minute, Olda," Adriana said, struggling to sit up. She felt calm, although she knew she should feel angry. Had they given her something other than what Morrison had said the pill was— the one she had taken earlier? "What did you give me, Morrison? Tell me!" She wanted to yell and scream but could not work up the necessary anger.

"Don't be concerned, Adriana. I gave you nothing but a tranquilizer. You're relaxed now and can't even become angry with me because you think I've duped you again. Believe me, I haven't. We want you to join us and be stationed

367

in our group as no other person alive has ever known. *You*, my dear Adriana, are the mother of the Antichrist. The whole world will fall at your feet for having given birth to our leader—the world's leader. What we are about to show you could mentally unhinge your mind if you saw it without some preparation. You saw or almost saw it on the hill."

"Wait," Adriana interrupted, blinking her eyes in an attempt to focus on Morrison. "I don't understand. What are you talking about?"

"It's better to show you, my dear," he said, nodding to Michele and Deirdre.

The two of them stepped to the side of the bed, staring down at Adriana. Both smiled while slipping out of their clothes. They stood naked, their breasts jutting upward, prominently calling attention to their upper bodies, which curved inward to tiny waists. Their middles flared into perfect hips, which in turn tapered downward, blending into shapely legs. They were beautiful. Adriana could not help but admit that much. But what did an impromptu striptease have to do with proving something to her?

Suddenly, their breasts grew large, heavy, sagging, lengthening until the nipples hung well below their navels. The small-waisted bodies began puffing up into rounded ball-like shapes without lines other than those of a sphere. The hips disappeared altogether and the well-formed legs thinned and thinned until spindly; vinelike extremities, fanning out at the bottom into flat, duck feet, supported the fat bodies.

Adriana gasped, unable to comprehend what was happening to the girls. They weren't beautiful. They were ugly creatures of—of—she couldn't put a name to what she saw. They were absurd-looking—not beautiful.

When a smile twisted Adriana's lips, both creatures dropped their arms in front of their bloated bodies trying to hide them. But their arms that had been so well formed were now as skinny as their legs and failed miserably in concealing their farcical nakedness. The dainty, manicured hands had grown into flat, pancake paws with long curving nails. Open, draining sores and warts popped to the surface of the skin as it turned a mottled color of purple and black.

Adriana closed her eyes.

"Open your eyes, woman," the two things standing in front of her growled in unison. "Open your eyes and look on our faces."

Adriana had not felt her pulse increase when the transmogrification began and decided she would suffer no consequences if she did look. She slowly opened her eyes. The green countenances turned downward to her—mouths dripping saliva from pendulous lips that hung loosely, exposing broken teeth and a blood-red tongue. The nose plastered against the face snorted as each breath was taken in and exhaled. Long hairs of varying shades of red mixed with graying black sprouted from their heads, arms, and legs.

But the eyes stopped Adriana. She had seen them before. Eyes at least three inches across and slightly askew in the heads stared at her malevolently.

"Now, human slut," they chorused, "you have seen us as we really are. You believe now what we say is true, don't you!"

Sitting up, Adriana wiggled toward the headboard, horror twisting her face. This couldn't be happening, but it was. Two hideous, ghastly creatures stood there, threatening her while Olda and Morrison stood by, breathing with no more difficulty than if they had walked up a flight of steps.

She turned her head away. "I—I believe. Go away. I don't—I can't look at you anymore."

"Thank you, girls," Olda said softly.

After several minutes passed, Adriana turned back and opened her eyes. Michele and Deirdre stood at the foot of the bed, dressed, wide smiles showing even white teeth once more. "Thank you for believing, Adriana," Deirdre said.

Adriana looked up at Morrison. That—that thing had kissed him on the mouth when they had arrived. That thing had been copulating with Morrison on the hillside. But how could he bring himself to perform such actions if he knew what Deirdre actually was? "Don't you care?" she asked him.

"My dear Adriana," he said. "I know exactly what is in your mind. Making love to a succubus is something most—practically all men—never experience. A succubus can elicit such feelings from a man, such emotional highs that the rapture is impossible to describe. I have been madly in love with Deirdre ever since she first came to me in the night, here on the island years ago. In fact coming here eventually cost me my marriage, but the idea of growing old with an old woman and watching my children become old held nothing for me when compared to one night of Deirdre's love." He nodded to the blonde who blushed before returning the gesture.

"Now that you believe, the only thing you must do is elect to join us, my dear Adriana," Olda said, bowing from the waist. "We will leave you. You may take the night to think about it. You are royalty. You are cherished. You are beloved. You —are the mother of the Antichrist. Come, join us."

He walked toward the door and stopped after he had opened it, holding it for the others. Michele and Deirdre, her arm linked through Morrison's, departed. Olda followed.

Adriana lay on the bed, staring at the ceiling.

Monday, May 27, 1985—1 A.M.

Sleep had come easily to Adriana's befogged brain. The tranquilizer eventually wore off, but not until she had been deeply asleep for several hours. Dreams had evaded her and she slept without incident until the clock downstairs tolled the hour of one.

She heard a strange noise, but failed to recognize it. Then the sound came again, a soft knocking on her door. Opening her eyes, she looked about the gloomy room, barely lighted by a subdued lamp. What had awakened her?

The knock came again.

Someone was at her door. But who? And what time was it? It seemed as though it should be the middle of the night. How long had she been sleeping? Hours had passed since Olda, Morrison, and the two girls—the memory of their bodies and faces changing froze in her mind. What had Morrison called them—succubus? Yes, that was it. Succubus. What was the plural? Succubuses? Succubi? She shuddered when she thought of their breasts sagging, their bloated, infected bodies, ugly coarse hair growing at all angles. Were they demons or devils or what?

The knock sounded louder.

The door. She had forgotten. "Who is it?" she managed.

The muffled words seeped into the room.

"Who?" she called again, louder than before.

The same choked voice again. Not choked— just not very clear through the closed door.

She jumped from the bed. After slipping into her robe, she moved to the door. Placing her ear against it, she asked once more, "Who is it?"

She listened intently. When the words were spoken again, her face brightened, her mouth splitting into a grin. She stepped back, opening the door.

SIXTEEN

Monday, May 27, 1985—1 A.M.

THE GLOW of the oil lamp in the hall opposite the door to her room radiated from behind Bergen Messenger's head, giving the illusion of an aura. Adriana stared. It couldn't be. It just simply couldn't be Bergen. She felt her jaw drop and forced her eyes to blink.

Bergen smiled and said, "May I come in? I know it's late but—"

Snapping out of her momentary confusion, Adriana said quickly, "I'm sorry. Of course, come in. Where have you been?"

Bergen strode into the room, displaying confidence in every step, every movement. When he stood in the center of the bedchamber, he turned and laughed softly. Adriana still held the door open, staring at him. "You may close the door now, Adriana. I'm in."

"Huh? What? Of course," she mumbled and swung the door closed.

"It's certainly good to be back here."

She studied him. He hadn't changed—at least she didn't think he had. If anything, he seemed more handsome than she had imagined him to be over the past weeks. Had it actually been weeks since she had seen him? She felt her pulse throbbing and wondered if she might not need another tranquilizer. That was foolish. She didn't want any more medication of any kind. Not ever again. Her eyes felt dry from looking at him so intently without winking her lids. Massaging them with a forefinger and thumb, she chuckled. "Where have you been, Bergen?"

"Are you all right?" he asked, apparently preferring to ignore her question for the second time.

She looked away. Why would he ask if she were all right unless he knew that she might not be? Did she look that bad? Moving around him, she went to the dresser and peered into the mirror. The dark circles under her eyes had been gradually diminishing since she had awakened the previous morning until in the wan light of her room her natural beauty seemed to be enhanced rather than lessened by them. "Why—why do you ask?"

He shrugged. "I thought I detected a tad of hysteria in your voice just then. Are you all right?" The last words held a demand to be answered.

"I think I am—now that you're here." Why had

she said that? What could his presence here possibly have to do with her feeling safe and secure? Granted, she had fantasized about him while she had drifted in and out of consciousness while strapped to the bed, but that hardly constituted his being catagorized as a knight in shining armor. If nothing else, her thoughts had been more than a bit on the erotic side whenever Bergen had penetrated the clouds in her mind.

"Now that I'm here?" he echoed. "Has something happened to make you feel uneasy, Adriana?"

A tingle sped down her body when he said her name. "Uneasy is hardly the word for it, Bergen."

"All right," he said good naturedly, "let me try another word. I had no idea you'd be in the mood for word games so late at night. Does—ah—upset fit the way you feel?"

"Don't wisecrack, Bergen," she snapped. "I'm very upset at what has taken place here in the last month."

"You should be happy. This island—"

"Happy? How could I possibly be happy? I've been drugged and raped and forced to give birth to a baby I didn't—"

"Whoa! Wait a minute. You're going too fast. Why should any of that upset you? Certainly the end result is worth any pain or discomfort you might have felt."

She glared at him. Was he serious? He acted as if he knew about everything that had taken place. "You know?" she managed when the indirect revelation took firm hold in her mind.

He nodded. "Olda told me. I've been called back to—"

"To what? Finish the job?" She sensed anger rising within her, welcoming it after having been so lethargic from the various drugs they had been giving her. The furious indignation wrapped itself about her, squeezing. She relished the sensation.

Holding up his hands, palms outward, he said, "Just a minute, Adriana. There's no sense in getting all worked up for nothing. I'm to talk with you and do my level best to convince you to join us. That's all."

The rage slowly subsided within her, only to be replaced with a sad acknowledgement. Bergen Messenger was one of them, too. One of them? One of the blondes had said something about Bergen being like them. She trembled at the memory of Michele and Deirdre changing into monsters. Had she dreamed that? Looking up at him, she said, "You, too, Bergen?"

"Hey, don't make it sound so final—so irrevocable. Nobody twisted my arm. No one is going to twist yours."

"Of course not," she said sarcastically. "They didn't even try twisting my arms or legs. They raped me and drugged me and played with my mind until I'm so confused I don't know what to believe or do. Everything that I've been told here is so contrary to the world outside that—"

"Is it so contrary, Adriana?" His voice, mellifluous in its quiet timbre, washed over her, soothing her, relaxing her.

378

"What do you mean?"

"There is so much in the world that cannot be explained by simple right and wrong. There are people who have everything they desire and have obtained their worldly goods through questionable means. In other words, why do you think right is right and wrong is wrong? Especially when the results of unjustifiable means are so attractive most of the time."

She hesitated. He was actually giving her a chance to argue her points. Before she could speak, he added to his statement.

"Why couldn't right be wrong and wrong be right? Good be evil and evil be good? Just because most, if not all of the world's religions are based on the principles contained in your ten commandments, acceptance doesn't necessarily make them correct, does it? Cults usually make the mistake of breaking from organized religions only to write their rules parallel to those they left behind. They simply use different wording to set down the same rules. Science and new discoveries have eroded much of religion's traditional beliefs, and people are unhappy. They need to belong, to believe. That's why cults are so popular today. There are thousands of them, but they won't last long because they duplicate in time the very thing the people were unhappy with in the first place. And, my dear Adriana, that is precisely why Satan, through your son, will rule the earth in the not too distant future."

He was coming at her too fast with too much. If he'd only slow down, she could voice her points one at a time but he wasn't about to give her that chance. Bits and pieces of what he said stuck in her mind. People leaving organized religion, joining cults or other "new" religions based on scientific principles—she had read about them. But Bergen seemed so well schooled, so confident in what he said. But why wouldn't he be capable? It was his job to wear her down, erode her resistance until she was left without protection. How could she possibly argue with him?

When she didn't speak, he smiled and said, "There are people who—"

"Stop!" she screamed. "Give me a chance to say something—anything. You're bombarding me with all these arguments that don't make sense and I need time to think."

Bergen smiled. "Forgive me. I guess I was getting a little overzealous. What did you want to say?"

Her mind went blank. She stepped away from the dresser, moving to the bed where she sat on its edge. What had she been taught all those years in Catholic grade school and high school? Why couldn't she remember one bit of Catholic teaching, one iota of religious training, anything that would counteract the inane arguments he was uttering?

"While you're thinking," he went on, "I'll finish what I started to say. There are people who think of Satan as a joke or myth. The bad guy, so to speak, who will tempt the followers of God and Jesus Christ into doing bad things—no-no's.

Sins! Both big ones and little. They've been told that he's a man dressed in red who has a tail and horns and carries a pitchfork around with him to stab at those who are weak. Others believe he is an impersonal power, a negative force that comes from within those who do not lead a *good* life."

"Isn't that true?" she asked weakly.

He laughed. "Let me tell you who and what Satan really is. He is an intelligent powerful being who rules the world of darkness and is master of the earthly plane. Some say he is evil. If evil is accepted as a way of life leading to salvation, then evil becomes good as in the other concept. Do you understand?"

"You're saying it's all a point of view?" She moved farther on the bed when he took a step toward her.

"I suppose one might say that. All I know is that I've been taught and shown. Satan is alive and well, working diligently toward ruling the earth. He's working very hard in contemporary society—right this instant."

"But Olda said he was powerless except every thirty-three years. How can—"

"Powerless to do the great things your God has prevented him from doing. But he is still strong enough to wreak havoc among those weak in their beliefs—those who do not fully believe in God *or* in Satan. He woos and wins those souls easily, and they number in the millions. He controls everything not taught by your God or Jesus."

"You say, 'my God.' If you want me to join you, why persist in saying He is my God? I'll draw strength from that." She smiled coquettishly at him, believing she had scored a good point. At the same time, she wondered if she could win Bergen to her way of thinking.

"Are you saying you're ready to forsake your beliefs and join us to be glorified as the mother of the Antichrist?"

Adriana shook her head angrily. "I didn't mean that. I was merely asking a question."

"Then he is your God until you deny him and accept Satan as your Master and Lord."

"I don't know what to do," she murmured.

Bergen stepped closer to the bed, sitting next to her. Cupping her chin in his hand, he turned her face to him. He kissed her lightly on the forehead, tracing a route with his lips toward her mouth. She didn't resist, turning instead to confront him more fully, to allow his perusal of her face to be complete.

Tiny shocks of electricity warmed her as the lips touched new areas on her cheeks, her chin, her nose, her eyes, her lips. A sensation of weightlessness prevaded her, and she did not resist as he lowered her to the bed.

"Morrison told me I cannot have relations with you," he whispered hoarsely.

Had he read her mind? Already deciding not to contest any overtures at lovemaking on his part, she forced herself to sit up. "Why would he tell you such a thing? Am I to be so revered that my humanity is to be denied?"

"Because of the stitches that were necessary following the birth of—of your son."

She dropped her eyes. "Oh."

"Once you're pronounced fit, you will be able to do anything you want—regardless of the consequences. Such is the kingdom of Satan!"

Adriana gulped. She had actually wanted to cry out, "*Hail Satan!*" but caught herself. Could she deny Bergen's effect on her—that she felt like melting wax both in her mind and in her body now that he had returned? Where was her strength of purpose? Had she been abandoned by her own convictions? Why wasn't she angry anymore? Why was she no longer enraged at the treatment afforded her since arriving on the island? Did she feel so strongly for Bergen that her reaction to him outweighed her own sense of dignity?

His mouth closed on hers, his tongue penetrating deeply, probing, caressing the inside. Reacting instinctively, she threw her arms around his neck, pulling him closer until he lay on top of her. She wanted him. She wanted him desperately. She wanted him to penetrate her, to send his penis thrusting in and out of her body.

When he withdrew his tongue, she sent hers in quick pursuit, jabbing it into his mouth, exploring, feeling the delicious taste of Bergen Messenger. It slithered over his teeth, between them and his cheeks and lips, through them, into the cavity of his mouth, touching, fondling the softness she found there. She wished it were longer so she could send it down his throat, to reach every square centimeter of his insides.

He rested on one elbow, his mouth still locked on hers, while he brought his free hand to her breasts, first gently kneading, then squeezing with more authority. She arched her back, raising her front, offering her breasts to him. It wasn't enough. They weren't close enough. She pushed him back, tearing at her robe and gown. The thin material ripped away exposing her small firm mounds of flesh, their nipples standing erect.

"Now, take them," she ordered huskily.

He returned his hand to her breasts, his mouth to hers, and they rolled back and forth on the bed. Side by side they lay, her head in the bend of his arm, his other hand snaking down her body, pinching, stroking the velvety silk of her skin. One finger traced circles on her belly, drawing inward, closer and closer, the circles constricting in size, homing in on her navel. Again she raised her body to meet the delight the digit promised. It hesitated for a moment at the lip of the birth cup, vibrating, teasing, taunting her before plunging into the shallow depression.

A cry escaped her lips. She moaned. Ecstasy. The sensation burning in her hips roared intensely. She felt on fire. Their mouths still clung together, their tongues acquainted intimately. The finger at her midsection rammed gently, roughly, carefully, carelessly until tears of sheer joy, pure pleasure overran her closed eyes. Then the tip of his index finger moved out and away and down, down, down toward the hair that seemed more like live nerve endings. Each one reacted as it passed through, searching, prodding gently until it found her clitoris. Barely touching it, he slowly moved his forefinger from side to side.

Her insides reacted violently, the fire raged, consuming her, flushing her electrified skin from within until she tingled madly, each hair follicle trembling in anticipation.

The hand stopped. The mouth left hers.

"Don't. Don't stop," she managed breathlessly. "Keep doing it. I need you. I want you."

He said nothing but lowered his head to her breasts. The tongue—the tongue she claimed as her private property—slipped from between the lips—those delicious lips—touching her skin. Again she moaned. The wet spongy surface swept over her fibrillating skin toward the nipples. He closed on one, sucking gently, pulling, releasing, pulling again. Finished, the smooth lips freed it, tenderly hovering a hair away from her, to move to the other. Clamping onto it, he rolled it between his teeth, nuzzling it, biting it. The tongue continued on its erotic journey, touching, testing, sampling her florid skin.

How could she stand any more? The thought of Olda's small penis poking at her suddenly crossed her mind. Laughable at best, but he had entered her, had fucked her, had impregnated her. She wanted Bergen to do the same. *Now. Right now. This instant.* She forced her eyes open and said, "Please, Bergen. Please. Do it."

He stopped, raising his head. "I can't. You know that. I've been told what I can do and what I can't. Morrison was most emphatic on the subject of copulating with you."

"Why don't you say *fucking*, Bergen? Fuck me! Fuck me, now. Do it, goddamnit! You're driving me crazy. Fuck me!"

"No," he said simply and continued licking her lower abdomen.

Tears of frustration replaced those of pleasure. "Why *not?*" she screamed. "I want you to fuck me."

Without raising his head, he merely said, "There's danger of infection—because of the stitches and proximity in time to the birth."

"Bullshit!" she snapped, pushing him away. Her hand flew to her crotch, one finger reaching for the neglected clitoris. Roughly manipulating it, she groaned, moaning intensely.

"Let me," he offered.

"Only if you'll fuck me."

He sat up. "I can't. I won't disobey."

She continued, the waves of fierce release washing over her as she wiggled her finger. Her breaths came in desperate heaves as the concentrated fury of her orgasm rose. The supporting walls within her caved in, collapsing. Violent contractions jerking her body doubled her over on one side.

Slowly, mercifully, she spiraled down until her hand fell from the lips of her vagina. Exhausted, spent, weakened from the unshackling of her sexuality, she rolled on her back.

Bergen leaned down. "Are you all right?"

She nodded her head, the motion feeble. "Yeah. Wow! I didn't think anything could be so great and not even be consummated." She looked at him. "What's the matter?"

"I—I'm sorry. I just couldn't disobey my orders."

"Your orders?" she whispered. "You mean, you were sent in here to seduce me?" Her eyes, despite her spent physical state, widened as if she were about to scream.

"Don't misunderstand, Adriana. I was told how you talked about me and what you'd like to do with me while you were drugged. I'm only human. I found it flattering. When Olda called me back to the island, I was told you had for the most part accepted our ways and would, with a little encouragement, probably join."

Adriana looked away. Only human? She hoped that were the case. She recalled the dreams she had had about Bergen but did not remember talking in her sleep. But then that was normal. "Is this big takeover that the—the Antichrist—my—my son is supposed to lead—is it supposed to be Armageddon?" She stared up at Bergen, waiting for his answer. At least he seemed to be honest in what he said. He was open about why he believed and what he expected.

He smiled blandly. "No. No, it's not Armageddon. That's to be a big battle. Your son will pull together all of the fringe elements that are contrary to what has been accepted as *right* and *good* over the centuries and simply take over.

You'd be amazed at how few people believe the way they have been taught religion. Your son's victory will be so massive, so overwhelming that it will seem pitifully simple."

"And I'm to be revered as his mother?" she asked.

He nodded.

She reached out to touch him. "I'm sorry we couldn't—you know—go all the way."

He laughed. "You were begging me to fuck you a few minutes ago. Why so proper all of a sudden?"

Dropping her eyes, she blushed.

"The heat of the moment?" he asked, a tiny laugh hiding in the words.

She nodded.

"If you join, in a short time you and I can do whatever we want. Does that sound appealing to you, Adriana?"

In way of answer, she leaned forward, offering him her lips. "Anything?" she murmured without taking her mouth from his.

"Anything," he mumbled, drawing her to him. After several moments had passed, he pushed her away. "Why don't you get dressed? The others are meeting in the chapel and are waiting word of your decision. We can join them down there."

Adriana studied his eyes for a moment. Clear, penetrating and opened widely to expose the insides of his mind. She found nothing there to dissuade her. Wiggling off the bed, she said, "It'll only take a moment."

"Here," he said, handing her the robe she had

torn off, "this is good. We'll only be there a few minutes."

She took the garment, slipping into it and pulled the tie about her waist before going to the dresser. A few strokes of her hair brush and she looked at her image more closely. The coppery-colored hair hung almost to her shoulders in a planned, wild way. Opening the top drawer, she fished about in the bag for her lipstick and applied a dab of color to her still flushed mouth. When she dropped the tube back in, she stopped. Her mother's crucifix lay on its side in her open cosmetic bag. A quick glimpse in the mirror showed Bergen straightening his clothes, tucking his shirt into his pants, head bent. How had they overlooked the cross? Did they even know of its existence?

Her hand flashed out, grabbing the cross and jammed it into her robe pocket. Closing the drawer, she turned and said, "I'm ready, Bergen."

"You know, Adriana," he said, looking up to find her smiling broadly at him, "I think I'm falling in love with you. I've never met anyone quite like you and, to be truthful, I've been thinking about you the whole time I was away."

She lowered her head a bit. "Some day you'll have to tell me what was so important that it kept you away for a month."

"If we ever find enough time to just talk," he said laughing.

Bergen led the way to the door, holding it open for her. Stepping into the hall, she stopped and waited for him. He took her arm and started down the hall. "Everyone is going to be so happy that you've decided to become one of us."

She nodded, taking notice of the kerosene lamps glowing along the corridor, barely lighting the black maw as they moved along. At the draped hallway they turned and hurried along its length. When they reached the end, Bergen pushed aside the curtains.

This time Adriana did not gasp at the sight of the carven head but merely stepped back to allow Bergen to open the door. She noted the key protruding from the lock.

Reaching out, he swung it wide and said, "After you, Adriana."

She stepped forward but stopped, peering into the ebony blackness ahead of her. At the bottom of the stairs, she could barely discern a lighter shade of black-gray that showed the landing where the steps turned at a right angle to enter the chapel. "I—I'm afraid of falling, Bergen. Will you go first and take my hand?"

"Of course, darling," he said softly, stepping around her. He moved down two steps before stopping. Turning, he held out his hand.

Without a word, Adriana raised her foot, kicking Bergen in the face. Soundlessly, he fell backward, down the steps, hitting hard half way to the landing with a bone-breaking crunch.

She didn't wait to see what effect her kick had had but jumped quickly back into the black hallway. Slamming the door behind her, she turned the key and dropped the curtains in place.

How dare they think she would join them after the atrocities they had subjected her to since her arrival? When she reached the first lamp, she tore it from its mooring and threw it against the draped end. The flame died but the reservoir broke, splashing the oil onto the curtains. At the next one, she blew out the flame, opened the lid and emptied the contents over the black material. Repeating the same ritual at each light, she finally had one left at the end of the corridor. Discarding the glass lampshade, she turned up the wick, the flame soaring a foot into the air. Heaving back, she threw the lamp down the hall, igniting the kerosene-soaked drapes.

Spinning about, she fled down the hall. Wherever she found a lamp, she started a fire. Hesitating at her room for a split second, she continued on her way, igniting rugs, decorations —anything that would burn.

Downstairs the clock struck three times, as she stood at the top of the steps. She'd have to hurry. She wasn't positive if there was another way out of the chapel. She hadn't found one, but that didn't preclude the fact that there could be a secret passage she had not discovered the night she had accidentally locked herself in. The roar of flames devouring the century-old mansion filtered toward her as she raced down the steps two and three at a time. She smashed lamps downstairs and started fires wherever there were draperies and furniture that would burn fast.

Returning to the main foyer, she looked up at

the flames dancing, writhing, eating at the aged wood and furnishings. They dashed along the carpet, gnawing at threads, up the walls devouring the ornate wallpaper; they lapped slowly at the woodwork, making certain that everything was tasted and would be consumed.

"Our Father, who art in heaven," Adriana screamed at the top of her voice, "hallowed by Thy Name. Thy kingdom come. Thy will be done on earth as it is in heaven. ON EARTH AS IT IS IN HEAVEN, YOU HEATHENS, YOU DEVIL WORSHIPPERS! Do you hear me? You're all dead. I've killed all of you for the love of my God." She turned, dashing into the night, hysterically laughing at the incongruity of her reasoning.

"They're coming," Olda chortled, as the door above opened.

"He's done it!" Morrison said softly. "Bergen has won her over completely. Otherwise she wouldn't be coming down with him."

They heard a strange muffled noise above. Their upturned faces and those of the others pressing in about them at the foot of the steps froze, blood draining from them. The sound of bumping, plummeted down the stairwell, taking on the form of Bergen Messenger as he smashed head first into the wall at the landing above them. The concussion split open his forehead, grayish ooze slicking the skin on either side of his skull. His upper body lolled toward the people at the bottom of the steps, head downward, eyes staring blankly at them.

Before they could move, they heard the door click shut upstairs. Then the key turned, grating in the lock.

"She's locked the door," Morrison said. "Unlock it, quick, Olda."

"The latch doesn't work from down here if the key is turned. I'm afraid we're trapped," the old man cried, his voice cracking as he continued staring at the corpse.

The message of doom slowly sunk into their collective brains. They could not get out. As one, they turned to the blondes who crouched in one corner whimpering, expressions like trapped animals contorting their faces.

"Deirdre, Michele, come here," Olda ordered after staring at them for several minutes.

Both shook their heads.

While the others looked on, Angelique Pantis said, "Can't they save us? Can't those two do something to get us out of here?"

Morrison stepped forward. "Do something, Deirdre. Please? If you love me, you'll do something."

Deirdre looked up, tears streaming down her face. "I—we can't. A move against Satan renders us helpless. We—we'll have to leave. Go back to our Lord and Master. He awaits us. We are his."

Morrison's eyes bugged in his head. "Leave? No! No-o-o-o. You can't go. Leave me? What will I do? I need you. I want you. I love you."

Deirdre shook her head. "You don't love me. You love my cunt. My sexuality. I don't love you —I don't even like you—or any man. I only like men's cocks."

Morrison wailed when she finished speaking. The others looked on dispassionately. What would happen now? If the two blondes left and Adriana could somehow escape from the island, what would happen? Would Adriana report them to the authorities? Would they all wind up in jail for kidnapping, rape, and whatever other charges could be levied against them?

"What—what's that noise?" Ivy St. Clair asked, holding up her hands for quiet even though no one was speaking.

"I don't hear anything," her husband said.

"Neither do I," Everhart said after listening for several seconds.

"I hear something," Ivy insisted. "I know I do. It sounds like—like—" She lumbered up the stairs, stepping carefully around Bergen's body and hurried up to the locked door. Pressing her ear against the wood she listened intently. She turned, half running down to the others waiting at the foot of the steps.

Morrison looked at her horror-struck face, and wildly pleading eyes. "What is it? What's wrong, Ivy?"

"She's—she's started a-a-a-fire. The house is burning."

"What?" Olda screamed.

"No. No. No." Jefferson chorused with Everhart and Angelique.

394

Roseanne stood dumbly by, watching the others rave and rant.

Unnoticed by the others who stared or ran about wildly, the two blondes stood, leaning against the black drapes, their bodies shifting in appearance, bloating, swelling to rounded proportions. Their arms and legs thinned to matchstick thickness. Their lips drew back, thickening to pendulous globs of fat, until they hung down exposing broken teeth. Eyes bulged, almost popping from their heads.

Crackling and popping drew the attention of everyone to the high ceiling, where the heat of the fire had already worked its way through. The second floor served as the ceiling of the chapel, and flames peeked through irregularities in the subflooring as the rugs and finished surface burned. In seconds, the beams would ignite, tongues of fire eating through them until the whole second floor would shower down on those below.

Angelique tore her eyes from the ceiling to pound on Morrison. "Can't they do something?" she screamed, turning to point at the things that had been Deirdre and Michele. The actress's scream grew until the shrill whistle of it drowned out the other cries of anguish and the sounds of the fire.

None of those present, except Olda and Morrison, had ever seen the girls in their proper state. Angelique hissed madly, tearing handfuls of hair from her head, clawing at her face, the sight too much for her. The St. Clairs lay on their backs, rolling about, babbling incoherently. Everhart Parrot, rooted to the spot on which he stood, could not tear his eyes from the demons.

Roseanne, breaking from her trance, moved closer to Olda and Morrison. "What are we to do now?"

Olda looked down at her, a sadness, a look of defeat in his eyes. "We are about to die, dear Roseanne."

Morrison stared at him, shaking his head. "No. No. I've got too much to live for. I can't die. I'll break down the door."

Olda grabbed him by the collar of his shirt, pulling him backward off the first step. "That door is eight inches thick and weighs over four hundred pounds. Do you seriously think you can break it down? Be patient. If we are to live, our Lord and Master will provide a means of escape. If we are to die, we have served our purpose. Remember, the Antichrist lives."

Morrison nodded slowly, sinking to his knees to await the inevitable.

The room brightened as the beams overhead caught fire. The burning crackle of hundred-year-old wood grew loudly, almost insulting in its merry snapping and popping. In minutes the beams weakened, and the second floor dropped into the black chapel in a coruscating firefall of burning death.

Adriana ran blindly away from the burning mansion. Where could she go? Where could she be safe? Safe from the lunatics she left behind.

Would they get out and chase her? Recapture her? Kill her?

When she reached the trees, she stopped to catch her breath. Turning, she gaped at the conflagration. Leaping flames played fifty feet above the structure as it burned. Smoke billowed up, only to disappear in the gloom. A smile creased her full lips. They could not get out of there. That was impossible. She was safe.

"Safe," she said aloud, rolling the word around her mouth. It felt good. It felt good to say it. It felt good to feel it, experience it, know for certain it was real. She felt as safe as she ever had in her life.

She turned, making her way up the hill. She walked slowly. Why did she feel so torn apart? Guilt? Hardly. Not after what they had put her through. They deserved whatever happened to them in the hell she had created for them. They wanted Satan as their lord, Satan as their master, Satan as their leader. Well she had given them a good sample of hell here on earth. A half smile cracked her mouth. Humor? She was able to make a joke about that which she had just done.

She blessed herself with the sign of the cross, before withdrawing her mother's crucifix. Pressing it to her lips, she prayed, "Dear God in heaven. Forgive me for the murders I have committed. I had no choice. I could not deny you at the last minute. I love *you* and worship *you*. Save me now from this mess I've gotten myself into."

For some inexplicable reason, her prayer did

not satisfy her. She stopped, looking down into the valley. The crucifix almost slipped from her hands. The fire continued unabated. Except for one small wing to the side of the house, every window belched fire and smoke. Closing her eyes, she turned to continue walking to the top of the hill.

"Why?" she said aloud. "Why don't I know which way to turn? My God waits for me on one side and Satan on the other. Why can't I decide?"

Morrison Tyler suddenly filled her mind. He was to blame for her vacillations. Her mind was completely mixed and confused. She both hated him and loved him—for having exposed her to Satan, for her having given birth to the Antichrist, for her having met Bergen Messenger.

Bergen! Bergen was what she wanted. Not God! Not Satan! Not a child! Not any group of lunatics. But Bergen—Bergen Messenger. She wanted him more than anything. More than her own safety, more than her own life. She loved him, needed him, wanted him.

One hand flew to her mouth as the full realization struck home that Bergen was caught in the fire below. As if it had a will of its own, the other hand began beating at her head. *She had killed the one thing she had loved in the last*—how long had her parents been dead? No matter. Her love for Bergen would have grown into a monument of lust, a pillar of sordidness that would have satisfied the most jaded of minds. *And she had killed him!* Pulling at her robe, she tore it off, throwing it to the ground. The crucifix felt white hot and she dropped it.

She stood on a small promontory, staring into the flames below her. "Bergen!" she screamed. "Bergen! Come back! I love you! I love you! Come back to me, my darling! Forgive me! I didn't know what I was doing when I hurt you. I want you—*you*. Not God! Not Satan! Only you!"

Suddenly she stopped, her eyes widening until they could have fallen from her head. There—in the flames—she could see Bergen Messenger's face, undulating, writhing, changing from happiness to utter sorrow to lustfulness to desire—as the flames sought to consume him once more.

"Oh-h-h-h-h, Bergen," she moaned. "What have I done? We could have been so happy together. Together—together—together—" She repeated the last word over and over while the flames leaped higher and higher below in the valley, vomiting filthy smoke and soot into the air.

Adriana sank to her knees, her hands folded in supplication to the master of the burning building below. "Satan!" she cried. "Help me!"

The loud crack of thunder from the cloudless sky overhead, passed unnoticed by her. Instead, she riveted her eyes on the dancing, cavorting flames in the valley.

Her lips pressed against the knuckles of her thumbs, tears waited patiently for a blink to send them crashing down her cheeks. She wept uncontrollably after a while, failing to notice the smoke and ash drifting toward her in the predawn air. The black haze settled over the island, touching the trees, the grass, the earth.

Still Adriana did not move.

Floating about, the ash and corruption of the fire settled in toward the point where she knelt. When it touched her, she felt the solidity of its obscene lust and repulsive impurity. A tiny speck touched her shoulder, then another and another. Tears, their saltiness of regret nestling in the corners of her mouth, flowed steadily, uncontrollably down her cheeks. The ash continued sailing in the air, drawn to her like filings to a magnet, touching her skin, her face, her head, her flaming red hair. The weight of the fire residue pressed in on her, and when she could feel it, she could no longer move, taking only an occasional breath with the greatest of difficulty.

The fire died as the sun rose afresh out of the eastern horizon—rose to fill the valley with bright light. And the birds were silent. And the sheep were gone. Most of the mansion had been consumed and other than the small wing, all that remained were a few upright beams, standing guard over the charred ruins.

On a point jutting from the hillside, a statue of a young woman, nude, kneeling in prayer, her hands humbly folded, their knuckles touching her perfect lips, stared out over the desolate valley. Furrows, etched deeply in her cheeks by bitter tears, marred the otherwise beautiful face while sightless eyes stared at the grave of her lover.

A crucifix, face down, lay on the ground at the statue's knees, the inscription on its back partially covered with ashes.